WHEN SHE VANISHED

A MAK AND WILTON THRILLER
BOOK 2

ADDISON MICHAEL

PAGES & PIE
Publishing • Marketing Writing • Distribution

2024 Pages & Pie Publishing

Copyright © 2024 by Addison Michael

ISBN: 979-8-9862920-8-3

Library of Congress Catalogue-in-Publication Data

Michael, Addison

When she vanished: a mak and wilton thriller/Addison Michael

Cover Design by Art by Karri

Editing by Tiffany Avery and Jayne Shaw

While set in real places, this novel is a work of fiction. All characters, events, and police agencies portrayed are products of the author's imagination. Any resemblance to established practices or similarity that may depict actual people, either alive or deceased, are entirely fictional and purely coincidental.

www.addisonmichael.com

*For my Grandma H. who introduced me to Mary Higgins Clark books,
which changed what I read forever*

PROLOGUE
LACY

Lacy Donovan jogged up the steps to her tiny one-bedroom, one-bath bungalow, careful to avoid the rotting side that led up to her door. She juggled her keys, a bag of groceries, and her phone, which was tucked between her ear and the crook of her neck. As the darkness set in, she walked inside, suppressing a shudder from the February chill.

"I'm fine, mom, really," Lacy said for the fifth time during the call. *I know I'm only nineteen,* Lacy answered her mom in her head, feeling exasperated. *And yes, I am on my own for the first time.*

Lacy could acknowledge her mom's point. Lacy *was* cute, little, and had the body of a slim yoga instructor. Lacy was aware she turned heads when she *flipped her long, blond ponytail over her shoulder*. But what *really sealed the deal*, according to her mom, was Lacy's *big, innocent blue eyes*.

Not so innocent anymore, mom, Lacy thought as she finally popped her front door open. Lacy had been on too many dates by now to say that. She was living her own life in a different state. She even refused to tell her mom where she lived.

When Lacy first tried to move out, she'd quickly discovered

rent was out of control. Then Lacy found this place, and it had been a steal. Until she saw it in person, of course. The pictures on the rental site showed a cute little home at the back of a fifty-acre property where one other home—the home of the landlord—sat a good half a mile away.

The reality of the tiny home was peeling paint outside that looked like it had once been seafoam green. The place was smaller than she'd thought it would be. The front stairs were rotting and a little slanted. There were obvious shingles missing from the roof. The windows had been painted shut, which limited the air flow through the place.

But the wooden door was solid, so that was a plus. Not to mention, it had all the amenities inside that she needed. It had a living room, a kitchen, a bedroom, and a bathroom. The structure was sound, and the doors locked. But the house was not fit for entertaining. Nor did she think that she'd be able to convince anyone to come visit her any time soon on account of where the home was located.

The fact that her tiny home was secluded in the country at the back of someone's property should have made her feel safer —less findable. But it didn't. Truth be told, where she lived creeped her out most nights. But there was no way she was going back home now. She'd made her choice and she would live with it.

Lacy listened to her mom prattle on about how much they missed her. Lacy caught the hints of manipulation that her mom dropped into conversation. She wanted Lacy to come back home. Her mom thought she was so subtle. But she wasn't.

Lacy was so intent on her mom's words that her brain missed important details upon entering her home. She didn't register that something was wrong the minute she walked through the door. She dropped the groceries on the kitchen table and started taking off her shoes. The first odd thing she noticed was a picture that hung crooked on the wall. Then she saw the couch cushions were pulled sideways and some were thrown to the floor. Drawers were dumped out and tables were overturned. Messy piles of Lacy's belongings lay on the floor underneath the drawers.

"Mom, I'm gonna have to call you back," Lacy said as she hung up on her mother mid-sentence. "Why would someone come all the way back here just to rob me?" Lacy speculated aloud to herself.

Lacy backed out of the still-open front door, her hand positioned on her cell to call 911, until she bumped directly into something solid and dropped her phone. She froze in place when she realized she'd bumped into a large human resembling a wall. A big, hulking giant of a man stood behind her, breathing loudly through his nose. She could smell his hot breath on the back of her neck as he loomed over her.

Before she had time to process the situation and run, the man grabbed her from behind, his arms in a tight bearhug, circling around her upper body and rendering her motionless. Lacy twisted slightly and saw that the man had tanned, leathery skin with a thick, light pink, weathered scar that ran from the corner of his mouth down his chin.

This is so much more terrifying than it is on TV, she thought. But this wasn't happening on TV. This was happening in real time, right here and now. She'd do well to use her brain to focus on escape. That couldn't happen because Lacy couldn't move. Her body had frozen up.

All thoughts slammed to a halt, freezing her with immobilizing fear. Then Lacy felt her feet lift off the ground. His arms were so tight, she couldn't breathe. She felt herself being carried backwards and down the steps, away from her tiny home. Then she realized that her feet were dangling. She began to kick and flail her legs about, connecting with his shins several times.

"Shit!" her captor growled. He lost his grip and dropped Lacy.

Lacy gasped as she felt herself fall. Her tailbone instantly ached with a burst of pain as her bottom connected with the ground. She could see the black Brooks tennis shoes the man wore.

Before Lacy could get a shoe on the earth to spring up and run, the man threw a fist at the back of her head. She felt a throbbing zing radiate down her skull to her neck. She saw stars, then darkness, but only for a minute. Or was it longer?

When she gained consciousness, Lacy realized she was upside down. Her body was moving but not by her own volition. She opened her eyes and lifted her chin. She could see the red, clay dirt moving quickly underneath her. Her arms dangled a few feet from the ground, and she tried to move them or flail them to fight. Then she saw the rope tied around her wrists. Perhaps in denial, Lacy attempted to move her fists, but they were bound tightly. She must have been out longer than she thought.

Kick! her brain shouted at her. *Get free!* Lacy tried to move her feet but could not.

She heard a laugh so low it almost sounded like a growl and reminded Lacy of pure evil. That's when she figured it out. Her captor had thrown her over his shoulder. He tightened his grip on her. In that moment, Lacy lost all hope of getting free.

She shifted her focus from escape to surveying her surroundings. Trying to ignore the way the blood ran to her brain and made her feel dizzy and the way her head throbbed, Lacy made an attempt to figure out where she was going. There was nothing around but woods bordering the property. Was that the smell of impending rain? What had she been thinking to move so far out of civilization and isolate herself like this?

Where was he taking her? Lacy couldn't see her bungalow anymore, but she knew it must be somewhere behind her. The only other home on the property was the hulking mansion that sat out front about half a mile to the north of her. Was he taking her to the mansion?

Her question was answered when her body abruptly stopped moving. He shifted her weight until he held her like a baby in his arms. Then he let her fall on her bottom roughly enough that she was sure she would have a bruise tomorrow. She saw the man open a hidden hatch in the ground that was indistinguishable from the rest of the property—all red clay with minimal grass around until it opened up like a storm cellar.

Lacy blinked a few times to clear her eyes. She had a hard time comprehending what she was seeing. The man had opened a trick door that had looked like solid ground minutes before. When he pulled on a latch, it had become a door to some underground hole. She couldn't even see how he'd opened it. There was nothing around to indicate where this place was.

"Don't get any ideas. I'm going to untie your feet." The man carefully unbound the rope from her ankles. Her muscles tensed when he bent down and shoved her toward the ledge, his large hands digging into her back and hips until she was sitting on the edge of a giant hole in the ground. Her feet dangled over the pit.

"Down," he ordered. He sounded out of breath, the only indication that carrying her body had been hard for him.

He grabbed her still-bound wrists, picking her body up with one powerful movement, and swung her to the hole. Her arms were in a point over her head, her legs dangling freely, suspended over darkness. Lacy gasped as she looked down. She could not see the bottom.

He released his grasp and let Lacy fall. Less than a second later, she hit the ground and landed in a heap. She'd fallen a good five feet from where she'd been hanging. Unable to catch herself because her hands were tied, a sharp, instant pain registered where she landed on her left hip. She cried out in surprise and agony upon impact. She heard, rather than saw, the door above her fall shut with a muffled thud.

Everything had seemed to be moving in slow motion, but now she realized it had all happened fast. Like lightning speed. One minute she was on the phone with her mom walking into her house, the next minute, Lacy was trapped underground.

She began to cry.

A hand touched her shoulder. Lacy screamed, whirled her head around, and dug her feet in the ground, awkwardly scooting herself backward.

A young woman sat down on the floor next to her and stared at her. Lacy noticed the woman was her age with a sunken appearance, gaunt cheekbones, eyes that looked too big for her head, and thinning hair.

"It'll be okay," the skeleton woman said. It seemed like the effort to get out that hoarse croak took all her energy. The woman put her hands on Lacy's and began to untie the knots at Lacy's wrists.

"Where am I?" Lacy asked. She looked around and gasped. It was dark, but there was some sliver of light coming in from somewhere above her. It must have been a full moon because it cast a circular light on the ground in front of Lacy's feet. Three more sets of eyes peered at her. There were other women, all in various stages of starvation and dehydration. Lacy's breath caught in her throat. She felt afraid. She wasn't sure if she was more scared of the women or the possibility that she might be looking into a future mirror.

Lacy could see that these women were dying. She wondered if they knew how bad a state they were in. They must have been here for a very long time and were perhaps delusional. One of those women had just assured Lacy it was going to be okay.

But it wasn't going to be okay unless she could find her way out. She could only guess what her mother would say to her now.

I told you, Lacy. It's not safe for pretty girls like you to live alone.

Lacy had ignored her mother. She had decided she knew better than the woman who had raised her. She'd moved to a place in the middle of nowhere with no forwarding address just to spite her mother.

Now Lacy would pay the steep consequences.

1

WILTON

Stephen held the Glock 19 in front of him with both hands. He adjusted his grip, his left hand under his right hand, holding his gun firmly. His finger rested against the barrel of the gun, not on the trigger. Not yet. Stephen was trained to keep his finger off the trigger until he was ready to shoot.

Know your target and what's beyond it.

In this instance, Stephen's target was the outline of a person on a piece of paper hanging fifty yards away in the outdoor shooting range. Beyond it was a big, open field with green, rolling hills for miles. He took a deep breath in and smiled. He loved the smell of gunpowder that lingered in the air.

Stephen shifted his focus back to his paper victim. His stance was perfect, if he did say so himself. He stood wide and staggered with his weight shifted slightly forward, his footing solid. There was a slight bend in his elbows.

He lined up the site on his gun, then squeezed the trigger and shot off five rounds. The pop of his gun sounded hollow and far away in his noise-cancelling headphones. He hit the bullseye every single time, demolishing the place right in the center where the heart would have been.

Stephen looked over to see his partner finishing her rounds.

Mak looked up in frustration and peeked from around her booth and over at Stephen's target.

Stephen grinned, feeling like a little boy proud of his accomplishment.

"Show off," Mak said, gritting her teeth.

Stephen moved over to invade her shooting space. He eyed her target critically with a lifted eyebrow.

"What? I was close," Mak defended herself, her voice pitching upward.

"Close enough to have my back in a gunfight?" Stephen challenged.

"It's not fair," Mak whined. "This left-eye dominance thing sucks!"

Stephen nodded. "I have an ex-girlfriend who has the same problem, which gave her a hard time hitting the target, too. You either need to train your right eye to be stronger—"

"How?" Mak interrupted impatiently.

Stephen closed his left eye and mimed picking up a book to read.

"Ugh! One, I don't have time to read. Two, I can't sit still long enough," Mak sputtered.

"You wanted my help," Stephen shrugged.

"Right, but I wanted a quick fix. I don't have time to train my eyes—"

"Eye," Stephen corrected her. "And my running skills aren't exactly improving overnight, either."

They had several foot chases during their first case, proving Mak could easily outrun Stephen. While it was true Mak was slim and athletic, Stephen had been surprised by the powerhouse of speed she possessed. Mak always had to wait on him to catch up. In the meantime, Mak had already apprehended the perp before Stephen even got there. At some point, Stephen realized he needed to improve his stamina and speed.

That's why they created a running regimen after their last case. The plan meant meeting up with Mak before the sun came out to run several miles a day four days a week. They'd created this habit months ago. Just when Stephen started to feel comfortable, Mak leveled up the intensity by increasing her pace or adding another mile.

Before he'd met Mak, Stephen had prided himself on his cardio. Now, with his calf and quad muscles screaming at him from their latest sprint at the end of their hour-long run that morning, he'd never felt more out of shape.

"Improving yourself is not supposed to be easy. If it were—"

"Everyone would do it," Mak interrupted.

"I was going to say I'd be a superhero," Stephen grinned. He wasn't going to say that at all. He just secretly wished she would learn her lesson about interrupting all the time. Though, he did think her habit might be getting a tiny bit better. That, or maybe Stephen was just getting used to it.

Mak racked her gun and dropped the magazine.

"You done for the day?" Stephen asked in surprise.

"We've been here for two hours. Let's give it a break," Mak decided.

"It's been one hour and twenty-five minutes. But I'm going to let you call it because we only ran for an hour this morning," Stephen quipped and made a face as he walked over to put his gun away.

"Oh, did you want me to go easy on you?" Mak called to be heard over the wind that seemed to blow in small microbursts. Her ear coverings were a basic, low-quality grade she had rented from the shop.

Stephen smirked at her. His expensive headphones dulled the loud gun shots but made Mak's words clear enough that she didn't have to yell. "You, go easy on me? That's laughable!"

Mak rolled her eyes as she zipped up her US Marshal jacket.

The sun was shining today, but there was a slight chill in the not-quite-spring air.

"How's Alyah?" Mak asked when they were on their way out to the parking lot.

Stephen took a deep breath in and blew it back out. "There's really nothing to tell. She's in DC, and I'm here. I call her, leave long voicemails, and she responds by text days later. Another one..."

"Bites the dust," Mak finished.

Stephen's mind wandered as he thought about Alyah, the beautiful petite brunette with a sharp temper when on the wrong side of her and a warm heart when on the right. Which he had managed do, and he'd thought about little else ever since.

District Attorney, Alyah Smith, had taken a piece of Stephen's heart with her when she transferred to Washington, DC, to further her career. Stephen had a theory that Alyah was running away from the feelings she had for him. He knew this had to be true, because he had the same feelings. But they hadn't given him the nickname *Love 'Em and Leave 'Em Wilton* at the office for no reason. He had a reputation for moving through relationships too quickly. Burning out of them was more like it.

Mak got into the driver's seat of the Range Rover with the impressive *US Marshal* stencil across the door. Stephen grudgingly got into the passenger side.

"You could let me drive sometimes you know. Partnership means working together," Stephen grumbled.

"Do you know how to drive?" Mak asked with wide, innocent brown eyes. She ripped her rubber band out of her shoulder-length auburn hair, smoothed back the pieces that the wind had blown, and pulled it back into a neater ponytail. Mak was pretty in an unassuming way, but she didn't know it. Nor did she seem to care.

Stephen laughed but found Mak regarding him seriously in her position of authority behind the wheel. "Of course, I know how to drive. I drive to the station every day."

"But do you *really* know how to drive?" she asked. "Like with speed and precision?"

"Yes," Stephen answered in his best dumb jock voice. "Stephen can drive."

Mak snorted and let out an exasperated sigh. "But have you ever raced?"

Stephen's eyes bulged. "Like illegal street racing?"

"Yes."

"No. Have you?"

"Yes."

"I don't believe you." Stephen's skepticism was evident by the way he raised his eyebrows.

"I could take you to a street race tonight." Mak glanced at Stephen, then back at the road, her eyes serious.

"You're kidding me," Stephen gawked at her.

"I'm not. My dad is a pro street racer."

"Huh. Let me guess, you raced to get daddy's attention growing up?" Stephen smirked.

"No, Stephen, I'm a daddy's girl. I didn't *try for* his attention, I always had it," Mak's voice sounded icy and defensive now. "I raced because I wanted to, and I loved it. The adrenaline rush—it's like nothing you've ever known before."

"I'll take your word for it," Stephen said wryly.

"Oh, Stephen. Just once I'd like to see what would happen if you lost control."

"Sorry to disappoint. It'll never happen," Stephen promised.

"Never say never," Mak said.

"That's something you think would be fun to see? Me losing control?" Stephen felt confused.

"Not necessarily. It happens to the best of us. It's just not the end of the world when it does," Mak shrugged.

"Sounds terrible. I think I'll sit that one out," Stephen shot back.

"Might not have a choice. You need an outlet, a way to stay healthy, or it's inevitable. You just..." She mimicked the sound of an explosion and mimed it with the hand not on the steering wheel.

Stephen's phone buzzed before he could answer. He pulled it out of his pocket as Mak drove into the parking lot of the building with the words *US Marshals* in bold lettering across the top.

Stephen wondered if the awe of being a US Marshal would ever wear off. He hoped not. He felt like he had the job of his dreams. But he knew his dream job was going to get tough again real soon because Deputy Director Rob Sikes had just texted him and Mak.

They had a new case.

2

LACY

Light from the outside world above them lit the dark hole in the earth whether it was day or night. Except, Lacy surmised, on nights when there was no moon. That hadn't happened yet, so she didn't know. But she assumed those nights would be extremely dark. She shuddered just imagining it. So far, the moon had shone brightly through the hole.

It had taken Lacy a few hours to understand why there was a hole letting in light in the first place. Someone had created it to make this prison functional. A steady supply of water funneled in and split to run down two different paths. One streamed down the earth wall into a bucket that formed a small supply of drinking water. The water carried in was eroding silt. By the time it reached the bucket, the water was murky, but Lacy supposed it was better than no water at all.

The other stream provided a bathroom of sorts. There was a bucket with a rope attached. The rope looped over a contraption at the top of the earth wall that Lacy couldn't see. The remaining cord dangled down to the floor on the other side. Lacy watched one of the girls weakly pull the rope until the bucket lifted. The bucket would hit a place in the earth ceiling and tilt, unloading excrement into a different hole where the ceiling jutted unevenly. The second water path streamed in that hole. This efficiently dumped the waste down a hole where water could wash it out of their prison. Lacy didn't ask what happened if the bucket tilted the wrong way. She didn't have to. The answer was too disgusting to consider.

While it would be useless as a means of escape, Lacy had to appreciate the ingenuity of this mastermind kidnapper. She'd always been a glass-half-full kind of person and she felt grateful for water and a way to relieve herself.

Then there were the other women. Three pairs of eyes peered at Lacy, looking lifeless, hopeless, and full of despair. It was unnerving the way they stared openly without saying a word. The girls all looked the same with almost identical physical attributes. They had blond hair that had thinned so much, Lacy could see their scalps. Their bodies were all thin—too thin —and she could see the outline of their ribs under their shirts. Giant eyes, some green, some blue, stared at Lacy. Each of them laid or leaned weakly against the dirt wall.

Lacy turned and put a hand out and rubbed the wall, which was made of the same solid red clay that they stood on and looked up at. They seemed to be in some hollowed out square under the earth.

They must not be too far from her bungalow because the man had carried her here. Lacy shuddered. These women had been here, under the earth while she had been living her life in the bungalow at the edge of this property. What was wrong with her? Did she really have no gut feelings about danger? Or did she have them but ignored them?

"How long have you been here?" Lacy asked them.

The girl sitting across from Lacy had dirty blond hair that looked greasy. She pointed to the wall. There were tally marks there. By quick glance, Lacy could count forty days.

Then there was the smell. The stench of body odor and an unemptied bathroom bucket was overwhelming. But there was something else. She could smell wet earth. The smell of the ground after it rained. That didn't smell bad to Lacy. More than once, Lacy had turned her nose to the wall and sniffed.

Tears sprang to Lacy's eyes as she accepted her new truth. There was no way out of here. There was nothing here in this eight by six foot hole in the ground except the three other girls staring at her with zero expression, no energy, and a lack of will to live.

"I'm gonna get us out of here," Lacy broke the silence with determination to not end up like they were. She took a deep breath in and screamed as loud as she could. "Hey!"

Lacy continued to scream for what felt like hours.

Miraculously, the earth ceiling opened up. She saw a large rope swing down.

The girls around her started whimpering and shrank away.

Lacy reached up and grabbed it with both of her hands. She felt herself lifting. Her heart soared with hope.

That's when sudden pain exploded in her head. She lost her grip and all control of her body at that moment. She fell painfully back to the earth and fought unconsciousness. She heard someone crying. Was it her?

"Shut your mouth. The next time, I'll do worse than punch you," the gruff voice said angrily from above.

The trap door on the underground earth cell shut with painful finality.

Lacy couldn't move, the pain was so great. She hadn't gotten over the ache in her hip from when she'd fallen before. Now, she lay face down, defeated and crying into the clay floor.

She felt, rather than saw, the circle tighten around her. The three women had crawled closer and were lightly touching various parts of her body. Patting her, comforting her, and showing their understanding for Lacy's pain.

Lacy welcomed the motherly hands. She calmed. Her body went still. Then she passed out.

3

WILTON

Stephen and Mak sat in the conference room staring at the big screen showing the picture of a large man who, despite his height and broad shoulders, distributed his weight well. His silver hair was on the long side with a slight wave to it. He looked like he'd been good-looking in his younger days.

"Anthony Gerritt," Sikes began his brief. "One of our most elusive criminals over the past ten years. He is currently wanted for questioning over the disappearance of a woman he has been dating."

A real charmer with the ladies, Stephen assumed as he peered hard at the photo. "Elusive in what way?"

"He's been in and out of trouble throughout the years," Sikes explained. "A lot of accusations but never enough evidence for anything to stick in court."

The man on the screen wore a nice grey Italian suit and slick dress shoes. A pair of Ray Bans covered his eyes. The photographer had captured him getting out of a black Porsche SUV. The high-end vehicle looked out of place in such a quaint city. There was a tiny, small-town diner in the background of the photo.

Gerritt's face covered most of the name on the outside of the building.

"Hey, is that a scar on his chin?" Stephen asked.

Sikes zoomed in on the photo to study the man. "There is, indeed."

Mak tilted her head to the side. "Huh, I don't remember him having a scar."

"You know who this is?" Stephen asked Mak.

Mak nodded. She opened her mouth to respond but Sikes caught her eye. She promptly shut her mouth.

Sikes cleared his throat and gave her a look. "For the rookie in the room, Anthony Gerritt is a well-known drug trafficker and, rumor has it, sex trafficker—though no one has ever found evidence of that."

"My question is *why now*? Where has he been all this time?" Mak asked.

"I was getting to that," Sikes gave Mak a warning glance.

"Sorry," Mak said, looking humble.

"The APB crossed my desk about three months ago. The woman who went missing was a carbon copy of the last woman Gerritt dated who also *disappeared* during their relationship. He's wanted for questioning, but he left the Oklahoma City area before police could apprehend him. We got a phone call. I've been talking to the local sergeant. Looks like he's been seen regularly having breakfast at this diner a few hours away." Sikes pointed to the screen with a laser pointer.

"He's just hanging out in the open after making his girlfriend disappear?" Stephen's voice was incredulous. "That's ballsy!"

Sikes nodded. "It's been over eight years since we last knew of his whereabouts. We haven't seen or heard from Mr. Gerritt, until now. After his last trial, Gerritt seemed to go into hiding where authorities were content to let him stay so long as he stopped causing trouble."

"Where's that restaurant?" Mak asked as she pointed to the picture.

"A little town in Southeast Missouri. It's a mom-and-pop restaurant," Sikes answered.

"Charming." Mak studied the photo.

Stephen squinted, stood, and leaned forward slightly. "Hey, I know that place!"

"You do?" Mak asked with excitement.

"Yes, I lived in that area for a year when Anna was a toddler," *with Carley*, he didn't add. "Shit. This guy is practically in my daughter's back yard. It's called Mama's Café."

Both Mak and Sikes stared at Stephen.

"Okay, it's actually about five miles down the road, but still. I have a bad track record with criminals getting close enough to put Anna in danger…" Stephen stopped talking.

"All the more reason for us to go get him and bring him in," Mak insisted. "The sooner the better, right?"

Stephen looked pensive.

"Wilton? Is this going to be a problem for you?" Sikes asked.

"Not necessarily, sir," Stephen said. He'd been challenged on whether he was going to take a case in the past, which is how he'd learned that even though he was considered a rookie in the US Marshal room, Stephen could still refuse to take a case. Especially one that was so close to home. Not his, of course, but his daughter's. He had to wonder if his involvement in a case in that same city would put her in danger.

"Good. Because right now you two are the best marshals for the job," Sikes said.

"I assume you have case files on Anthony Gerritt for me to look at to get caught up to speed?" Stephen asked.

"Of course." Sikes slid a file across the table to Stephen.

"Thanks." Stephen immediately opened the file and started reading. "It says here that he's been in trouble with women, drugs, and cars."

"That about sums it up," Sikes said sarcastically. "Any other questions?"

"Yes, he's probably not living at that café," Mak said. "Did the sergeant happen to follow him to a secret lair?"

"No," Sikes said, "but we have it on good authority that Anthony Gerritt has been having breakfast at that café every morning for the past month."

"Well, he's nothing if he's not consistent," Mak muttered.

"Wilton, questions?" Sikes asked.

"Yes," Stephen answered. "Are we bringing him in for questioning or following him around?"

"Good question." Sikes scratched his head and thought about it. "Normally, I'd say bring him in. He's dangerous and we certainly have cause for questioning. However, I'm curious about what he's doing in town. The sergeant tells us he's been there a while. I want to watch him and see what he's up to. The last thing I need is to spook him and have him on the run again. He skates out of charges when his women disappear. I would like to get something concrete."

"So, we wait until we have enough reason and proof to arrest and charge him. Got it." Mak nodded in agreement, then hit the door as soon as the meeting ended.

Stephen and Sikes stayed back. "He's not Demitri Abbott, Stephen."

"What?" Stephen looked up from the file.

"Anthony Gerritt is not Demitri Abbott, and he's not after Anna."

"While that's true, a dangerous man who needs a bargaining chip can easily gain access to my daughter. Right now, I'm anonymous. The minute I step into that town, it will be impossible *not* to see my daughter, my ex-girlfriend, or her husband. To be seen there will make us all vulnerable. I really don't want to do anything to put Anna or the family in danger."

"Then you better make sure you catch him before that happens." Sikes rapped his knuckles on the table for emphasis.

So much for having a choice, Stephen thought with a sinking feeling.

4

MAK

Mak was home early. She always left the office after lunch when she had an upcoming case that would take her out of town. She loved her home. It was truly her place of solace. Her sanctuary from the hard life on the road. She and John had bought it together after they had Harper. It was a sensible, red-brick home in the suburbs. Inside was where the magic resided. Warm gray walls with pops of blue, yellow, and white accented the home. Hardwood floors stretched underneath her feet, with an open layout that made it difficult to sneak around. Which was precisely what she was attempting to do right now. She'd slipped her shoes off just inside the front door and crept to the living room.

She found her three-year-old daughter, Harper, on John's lap. Mak quietly stood on the other side of the wall peeking around as her husband, the sexiest father in the world, read a naptime story to Harper.

John was tall, broad, and fit. He stayed home with Harper so her mommy could go out and *save the world*, as Harper liked to tell her friends at dance class. It took a secure man to run the home while his wife worked a job that she was passionate about. A dangerous one at that. Though John's consulting work seemed to keep him busy during Harper's nap times.

Harper looked up and caught Mak peeking on them.

"Mommy!" Harper shrieked, her auburn ponytail swinging as she jumped off her daddy's lap and ran to greet Mak.

"Hey, Harpy!" Mak squatted down to pick up her daughter, hugging her tight.

"Now look what you did," John grumbled. "I just had her settling down. Now we have to start all over. You're taking a nap today, young lady."

"Awwww…" Harper pouted. "Will you take a nap with me, mommy?"

Mak laughed. "I wish! You have no idea how lucky you are that you get to take naps, young one."

"Naps aren't lucky!" Harper's voice was muffled as she buried her face into Mak's neck.

"Come on," Mak said, as she bounded up the stairs with Harper still clinging to her. "The sooner you close your eyes, the sooner you can open them back up."

Harper giggled.

It took Mak ten minutes to get Harper situated in bed, and there was no guarantee Harper would stay there.

Mak ran back down the stairs, stripping off her clothes as she went. Her shirt was off and discarded before she even hit the landing. Her pants were partially unbuttoned when she met her husband in the living room.

"Makayla! The blinds are open," John protested lightly with a grin when Mak put her arms around him and started kissing him.

"Close them," she commanded.

John did as she instructed.

Mak was down to a bra and panties in minutes.

"Wow, babe, you been working out?" John asked with a sarcastic smile. It was his favorite joke.

"Always!" Mak smiled. She started tugging at his clothes. "Let's see what you have under there."

Mak peeled John's shirt off and ran a hand over his washboard abs. "Looks like you've been hitting the ab roller."

"Some people are just born with it." He shrugged with false modesty.

Mak moved to unbuckle his pants.

John put his hands on Mak's small waist and pulled her close. "It's not a race, Makayla. If you're here now, that means you've got another case."

"Yes… and?" She ran a hand through his longish black hair with his premature gray strands sprinkled in.

"Should we talk about that?" John asked between Mak's kisses.

"Yes, and we will. But right now, we need to love each other like it's our last night on Earth—"

Because it could be… they both thought it, but they didn't have to say it aloud.

"Alright," John agreed. "Then I suggest we take it in here." John picked Mak up. She wrapped her legs around his waist as he walked them into the bedroom and shut the door.

5

WILTON

Stephen was working late again. Not because he needed to. Because he wanted to. Lately, the thought of going home to an empty house had gotten worse. The silence that greeted him when he walked through the door was overwhelming. He preferred to spend his evenings at work.

If he was really honest, Stephen would admit to himself that he wasn't working tonight. He opened his desk drawer and stared down at the manila envelope that sat on top of a few legal pads and some pens scattered and rolling around the drawer.

The manila envelope held all the answers to the past but gave Stephen nothing but questions for today. Inside the envelope was an eight by ten glossy photograph of a man Stephen had never seen with his brother, Greg. The man was holding a gun to Greg's face. Stephen knew it was minutes before his sibling was murdered. Only, the man holding the gun was not Greg's convicted murderer.

Stephen's jaw set when he thought about the man who had been convicted of killing Greg. Davey Stinnert had been Greg's best friend and worst influence. Stephen had always secretly blamed Davey for taking Greg down the path of popularity and intimidation.

Greg's murder had been an open and shut case. Davey Stinnert had pleaded guilty to murder in the first degree. Davey had been a minor, which had put him in Juvenile Hall instead of prison. They'd released Davey after ten years due to good behavior. Stephen was already a cop by that time. But Davey getting out earlier had only fueled Stephen's passion about the career choice he'd made and reiterated why he'd gone into law enforcement.

When Trevan Collins had handed Stephen a manila envelope a few weeks ago, Stephen barely had time to process what it might be. Stephen had been leaving the funeral of his first partner, Ethan Booker. Trevan had approached Stephen's car, handed him the envelope, refused to answer Stephen's questions, and walked away. But not before giving Stephen strict instructions not to come after him.

Stephen had thrown the envelope on his passenger seat and jumped in his car, driving by Trevan's vehicle to get his license plate number. Stephen had used that number to track Trevan down. He now knew Trevan's last address on file was one from Stephen's hometown in Arkansas. Stephen suspected that Trevan had gone to school with his brother, Greg. This address, along with a background check Stephen had run on Trevan, had confirmed his suspicion. Though Arkansas was home, Stephen hadn't been back there since before the encounter with Trevan. Stephen had called Trevan's phone number, but Trevan either didn't want to pick up his phone or the number Stephen had was old.

Stephen pulled the envelope out of his desk, opened it, and slid out the blown-up glossy photograph. He focused his whole mind and energy on the picture in front of him. He leaned forward and began to note each detail in the picture, his eyes scanning slowly to burn this piece of evidence into his mind.

The focus of the picture was on two faces, zoomed in close. Stephen could clearly see his brother's profile as Greg Wilton's eyes were locked on a man standing in front of him. The look on Greg's face wasn't one of fear. It showed that in Greg's last minutes, he felt anger and defiance.

Interesting, Stephen thought.

A man was standing two feet in front of Greg, his arm stretched out with a gun against Greg's head. The man holding the gun looked to be in his forties with light brown hair. His hair waved long enough to hit his shoulders. It reminded Stephen of a hairstyle he'd seen while googling popular 80s sitcom stars.

Now, Stephen checked the background for some clue that he may have missed. There were other people there. But the camera was so zoomed in on Greg and his murderer that the background was fuzzy. Stephen could only make out the shapes of four people standing in what looked like a circle. If it was a full circle, Stephen could only speculate where the man who had captured this evidence was standing.

Stephen gulped. This was the hard part. From years on a police force, Stephen recognized the technology that had been used to take this picture. This picture was from a still frame of a body cam.

He knew this at a glance because there was a square video watermark timestamp with a yellow border around a series of numbers in the upper left corner. Inside the outlined box was the date, time, and serial numbers with the duration of the video.

Anyone can buy this tech. It doesn't mean it was an officer, Stephen tried to reason with himself. Because if it was an officer, Stephen would have to conclude that the officer didn't turn in this evidence. There were many ominous reasons why an officer would keep information like this to him or herself—coercion to join the bad side, blackmail to keep the officer quiet, or an inability to deliver it. An incapacity—Stephen considered—such as death. But none of that explained how it ended up in Trevan's hands.

Tonight, Stephen changed tactics. He'd scanned the photographic evidence of Greg's murderer into the facial recognition database they used to identify criminals. There had been no match. There had to be a criminal record in order for the database to recognize the picture. Stephen made a fist and brought it down against the desk. He let an expletive erupt.

He was officially at a dead end.

Stephen swiveled in his chair and stared out of his office window, letting his mind wander. He sat looking at the sky that had turned dark, remembering the day he'd met Alyah Smith right here in his office. The pretty DA who'd changed his world. She'd been so mad at him that day. Then he'd won her over. But it hadn't been enough. In the end, she'd left him like every other woman in his life.

But Alyah wasn't every other woman. She was smart, successful, powerful, and beautiful. In the short time they had spent together, Stephen had fallen in love. That wasn't hard for him to do though. In truth, Stephen fell in love too easily. He gave his heart away, often resulting in the painful crush of his spirit when the woman he'd loved left.

Stephen sighed. He had a theory that Alyah had left because she'd been running away. She was scared. The only way to fix that was to show her his consistency. Stephen would wait forever for a woman like Alyah.

Stephen picked up his phone. He turned back to his desk and propped his feet up. He leaned back in his chair and dialed her number. He didn't call her every night. But on the nights when he did, she didn't answer. He always left her a message. For him, it had become a weird form of therapy. Like he was processing his life and thoughts aloud. Tonight was no different.

"Hi, Alyah, it's Stephen," he greeted after her voicemail

picked up. "Just thinking about you. I don't stop thinking about you, really. No matter where I am and what I'm doing, you're never too far from my thoughts. We've been assigned to a new case. It's south a few hours from here. Close to where my daughter lives."

Stephen felt his chest tighten. Was that fear or anger that such a horrible criminal lived so close by his daughter?

"Thing is, if we're on a case, I don't think I should visit Anna. I think it might put her in danger. That's gonna be hard to be in the same town, in the same area, and not pay her a visit. I miss her a lot, you know? Sometimes I wonder if I'm a bad dad because I don't find a job closer so I can spend more time with her—"

Stephen's phone beeped to indicate he was getting another call. He looked at the phone screen and didn't recognize the number. He glanced at the clock on his computer screen. It was 8:15 p.m. Late enough he should head home.

"Alyah, I need to go. I'm getting a phone call. Take care." Stephen hung up the phone and clicked over to the new call.

"Wilton," Stephen greeted.

"Stephen? Is that you?" a female voice asked, sounding unsure of herself.

Stephen took his feet off the desk and sat up straighter. "Yes, this is Stephen Wilton."

"Hey, I'm not sure if you remember me. This is Beth Donovan. I went to high school with you—"

"Beth! Of course, I remember you," Stephen said with a smile. Beth was a year older than Stephen and had briefly dated his brother in high school.

"How are you?" Beth asked. Her voice sounded strained and sad.

"I'm fine, but how are you?" Stephen asked. "If you're calling me, I assume there's a not so good reason?" It was a well-known fact that Stephen had gone into law enforcement right after high school. They'd promoted him to a detective early in his career when they needed him to go undercover for a case. Stephen had always been lucky in his career.

"My baby sister, Lacy, has gone missing," Beth announced.

"Missing, missing? Or is she just not answering her phone?" Stephen frowned. He tried to remember Lacy but couldn't quite recall her.

"She's not answering her phone. It's not like her. Sometimes she ignores mom's calls. But it's because mom calls her all the time. She always answers when I call. I've been calling her for over three days."

Stephen did a quick search in the database. "Lacy Donovan?" he asked.

"Yes," Beth confirmed.

"I don't see a missing person's report out for her—"

"We haven't filed a report yet," Beth corrected.

Stephen frowned. "Then why are you calling me?"

Beth was quiet for half a minute. Then she sniffled. "We don't know where she was living. I'm afraid to put out a report because what if we're overreacting? She desperately wanted her privacy. She wanted to show us she could be an adult and live life without us…" her voice trailed off.

"Beth, I'd love to help, but that's not really my job anymore. I can connect you with Lieutenant Roger Higgins. He's over the Police Station of Little Rock. You can trust him. You all still live around that area?"

"Yeah." Beth blew her nose loudly.

"Okay, then he's your guy. I'll reach out and let him know you'll be calling him soon. The sooner you get a missing person's report and BOLO, be on the lookout, the sooner they can find her," Stephen put the phone on speaker and scrolled through his contacts. He found the number and sent it to Beth.

"Can they look around discreetly? I don't want to her to get mad if we're just overreacting. Maybe she just doesn't want to talk or something," Beth said softly.

"She's important to you and if you feel something is wrong, there's no reason not to check into it," Stephen assured her.

"Okay, thanks, Stephen. I'll give him a call."

"Good luck, Beth. Hang in there. If anyone can find her, it's Higgins and his police force."

"Thank you, Stephen," Beth said with sincerity in her voice.

Stephen said *goodbye*, stood up, and turned off his computer monitor. He headed toward the door. His phone beeped once indicating he had a text message. As he looked at his phone, his heart swelled with warmth and hope.

Alyah: *Goodnight, Stephen.*

6

LACY

Their voices were a soft whisper, but they overlapped like echoes inside a cave. Once Lacy heard their stories, she couldn't unhear them. Each woman's explanation of when she'd vanished was more tragic than the next. Lacy's heart squeezed and broke for them. As she sat with her knees in the cold dirt floor, she focused on each woman's pain, feeling it as if it were her own.

I was going to meet my boyfriend. I'm pretty sure he was going to propose... Emma said. Tears filled her big, blue eyes and a wistful look clouded her features as if her memory could transport her away. Back to that hopeful, exciting time in her life.

I had just gotten off work. I'm a nurse. I was working a night shift. I wasn't as alert because I was tired and upset. A patient had died that night... Isa had admitted. Isa's eyes stared at nothing as she spoke. There was no emotion—sad or angry. *I opened my car door, and he was there. Waiting in the shadows. I didn't even have time to react. I don't know how I got here. I just woke up here.* Lacy knew Isa had shut down her emotions. The cold, dissociative way Isa told her story made Lacy sad.

My little girl was sick. I'd just gone out for cough medicine, and I didn't make it back. I have a little girl. She's six. I wonder how old she is now. I don't know how long I've been down here… I wonder if she's safe. Lauren had balled up her skeletal hand in a fist and let a few tears roll down her cheeks.

With some effort, Lacy made her way through all the stories of the girls and how they'd gotten down there. They whispered that they weren't the only three girls who'd been down in the *earth prison*, as they called it. A man would come and take a girl at random, and they would never see her again. They didn't know where she went once she left. They never talked about what they suspected.

Lacy felt lucky—if it was possible to feel such a thing in this dark, hopeless place. She didn't have a fiancé or a child waiting on her back home. She had a mother and sister who were probably going out of their minds with worry. Lacy didn't know how her dad might be handling it. He had always been reluctant to show emotion or express himself. Lacy never knew what he was thinking.

These girls thought they were the lucky ones, Lacy decided. The ones who had survived down here with minimal food and water. They'd felt sick in the beginning, but it had become their new normal. Now, they were all friends. They only had each other.

As Lacy regarded her lethargic, hopeless friends, she knew she would never accept this as her fate. She would get out. When she did, she'd get them out. She'd save them all. She didn't waste time with reassurances. She needed to keep her mind and spirit strong and ready. When the moment presented itself, she'd react so quickly, the kidnapper wouldn't know what had hit him.

Lacy was going to free them all.

7

WILTON

Stephen hadn't slept well last night. *What else is new?* he thought. Even into the late hours of the night, he mulled over the consequences of working a case so close to the town where his daughter lived.

His first responsibility was to keep Anna safe. Not bring danger closer to her. He tried not to replay the night he'd found Carley shot in the abdomen, dying in front of him and Anna, who was safely hidden. The scene played on a loop in his mind.

He and Mak had conversations about PTSD sometimes. If he thought for a second that he had PTSD, he should recuse himself from the case and maybe take time off to get some help. Lately, strange things seemed to trigger small anxiety attacks. A few of the attacks he'd had seemed to stem from his memories of Carley and unresolved issues from her death.

He got dressed for the day, made sure he packed a light bag, and stepped into the cool, crisp morning. By the time he reached the parking lot where he was due to meet Mak for their road trip for the new case, he'd convinced himself it would be better to sit this case out.

"Hey, Wilton," Mak called out as she loaded up the

unmarked company vehicle. As usual, she had a small duffle bag with her, which she threw into the back seat of the unmarked US Marshal Range Rover. He had to hand it to her. She knew how to pack light and she never seemed to forget anything.

She held a mega-sized coffee cup like it was a present. She turned to him, waiting until he was closer. "You look tired," Mak grinned.

Stephen stopped a foot from her and crossed his arms. The air was chilly, and his coat was only going to keep him warm long enough to say what he needed to say. "I think I need to sit this one out, Mak," Stephen stated.

"Sit what out?" she asked, looking bewildered.

"This case."

"Woah, it's a little late for that now, Wilton. Get in," Mak opened the door to the driver side.

"No, I'm serious, Mak. I can't bring trouble to my daughter's back door." Stephen stood his ground.

"Then don't," Mak responded. She jumped up behind the wheel.

"I live in fear that a criminal—"

"Demitri Abbott, I know," Mak interrupted.

"He could go after Anna any day," Stephen said.

"He hasn't yet. What makes you think he will now?" Mak argued.

Stephen shrugged. "My point is, I can't chase criminals in the same town where she lives. I can't risk endangering her life again."

"It's not the same town," Mak inserted. "It's the next town over. You were a detective. Did you fight crime in the same town where your family lived?"

"That's different," he said.

"It's not." Mak started the SUV. "Look, if we don't leave, it'll knock us off our schedule. The sooner we find him, the sooner we can follow him to his evil lair, get evidence of what crime he's committing this time, and throw him behind bars." Mak brushed her hands together like she was getting rid of crumbs.

Stephen weighed her words.

"Come on," Mak coaxed. "Get in. We can talk about how we can keep everyone safe on the way."

Reluctantly, Stephen grabbed his bag from his SUV and got in the car.

"There we go!" Mak hooted. "You know what I think?"

Stephen buckled his seatbelt. "Bet you're gonna tell me."

"I think you get tired and overthink things," Mak announced.

"How do you know I'm tired?" Stephen asked.

"You were at the office really late last night," Mak said.

"How do you know? Are you spying on me?" Stephen howled in outrage.

"Of course not," Mak grinned. She was cheerful at the beginning of a new case. Something about a new mystery seemed to excite her. "I had to run to the grocery store last night. I drove by the office. Your car was still in the parking lot. What were you doing here so late?"

"It wasn't that late," Stephen protested. There was no way he was going to talk about Greg or the envelope he'd received. "I got a phone call from an old friend from high school. Her little sister is missing. I gave her the number to my old lieutenant in Arkansas. She'll be in good hands."

"Good," Mak responded as she hit the highway.

"The thing is," Stephen pondered out loud. "Do we only take kidnapping cases if they're high-profile celebrities? Doesn't that seem unfair? We should be equal opportunity. Anyone who's missing should have all authorities looking for them."

"We track down criminals who no one else can seem to find. And we take cases when the Attorney General tells us to. That was how we ended up with the last case." Mak was referring to their first case together where two of America's most beloved celebrities had gone missing. Both the FBI and the Manhattan County Police District had been too busy with another case, so they reached out to the US Marshals.

Stephen shrugged, reluctant to acknowledge her point.

"I know what you're thinking, Stephen, but you can't help with a missing persons case in Arkansas when you're working on a case in Missouri. Keep your head in the game. Not to mention, you need to make sure we get in and get out. Before your family spots you."

"That's your plan on how I can avoid my family in such a small town?" Stephen asked. "Get in and get out fast?"

Mak nodded. "You could text them and tell them you're in town and ask them to pretend not to know you."

Stephen thought of the judgement he'd get from Anna's mom, Paige, on that one and shuddered a little. "Hard pass."

"I really think it'll be a non-issue, Wilton," Mak said dismissively, then changed the subject. "What's the missing girl's name?"

"Lacy Donovan," Stephen stated. He'd once been allowed to go help with a kidnapping in Canada, but he knew that was different too. It was during a time when he wasn't working on a case and the office was quiet. Sikes had approved it due to the special circumstance.

For now, he'd left Beth Donovan, Lacy's sister, in good hands with his former lieutenant. Mak was right. He needed to focus on the case in front of him. Mainly, how to keep his life from intersecting with his daughter's while he was in town.

8

MAK

The silence was slowly killing her. Mak reached out and turned up the radio. If there was one thing she hated more than anything else, it was silence. After a few more miles of nothing, Mak sighed and turned the radio back down.

"Alright, Wilton, talk. You've been abnormally mopey lately. I mean, you're always serious, but what's with the quiet soldier thing you've got going on?" Mak blurted.

"Quiet soldier?" The corners of Wilton's mouth twitched, and he raised an eyebrow at her.

"Yeah," Mak shrugged. "You know what I mean. Spill it."

"There's nothing to explain really. This is me. This is my life," Wilton said grumpily as he looked out the window.

"Noooo, this is your life when you're not in a relationship," Mak stated directly.

Wilton groaned. "If I wanted a lecture on being single, I'd call my mom."

Mak grinned. "Still on that *Woe is me, I'm so unlovable* kick?"

Wilton was quiet for a minute. Mak figured his mind was on Alyah. "No. I'm not unlovable. I just haven't found the right girl yet."

"I see. Because the *right girl* packed up and moved thousands of miles away?" Mak poked.

"One thousand fifty-four miles," Wilton corrected automatically.

"I knew it!" Mak cried gleefully. "You can't stop thinking about her, can you? Do you know why she left?"

Wilton had his suspicions. None of which he could confirm. "She got a job as a District Attorney in Washington, DC," he said, repeating the reason she'd given him. "She didn't want to always wonder what her life would be like if she didn't at least give it a shot."

"So you think she'll be back? After she's done *giving it a shot?*" Mak asked.

"I don't know, Mak." Wilton clenched his teeth as he remembered her two-word text response to his long voicemail last night. *Goodnight, Stephen.* It was over. Before it had a chance to begin. Just like all the others.

"Well, something's gotta give with you, Wilton. You can't stay at the office until all hours of the night working on things you haven't even been assigned. It's our responsibility to keep ourselves in peak physical condition. You can't sacrifice your mind, body, and soul for this job. You need to take care of yourself first. That way you can be your best self and stay focused on the job." Mak nodded for emphasis.

"Dr. Phil, is that you?" Wilton smirked.

"No. John has me listening to this new podcast. It's the *Mind, Body, and Soul Guy* podcast. Ever heard of him?" Mak asked, a serious look in her eye.

Wilton's face now sported an all-out grin. "No. I have not heard of that guy. Pretty sure he didn't come up with that all by himself though."

Mak glanced at Wilton and back at the road. "That's what it takes to get you to smile?"

"Yes," Wilton coughed to smother his laugh. "Please, please, tell me more about the mind, body, and soul guy. Why isn't he a woman, by the way? Wouldn't that be more impactful and powerful for you?"

"I believe in equality. Men and women both have the same opportunity to say and do smart things," Mak defended, then threw out a challenge. "Laugh it up, Wilton. We both know who'll be healthier at the end of the day."

"Yes, you're healthy, in peak physical condition, and fast. I'll give you that. It'll help you run away from the bad guy who retaliates when your shot goes whizzing to the right of his head," Wilton joked with an air of superiority.

"Low blow, sir. I think I like you better when you're moody," Mak grumbled, then turned the radio back up.

"It'll be fine, Mak. That's what partners are for. I'll do the shooting," Wilton's voice was full of mock sincerity.

"You really can be a jackass, you know that?" Mak muttered.

Wilton was chuckling. "Good talk, Mak. I feel so much better. You're right. We should do this more often."

9

WILTON

Twenty minutes before they arrived at the café, Mak turned down the radio again.

"Did you read Anthony Gerritt's rap sheet?" she asked, lowering her voice.

"Yes, but I don't think anyone can hear you," Stephen quipped. "You can speak in a normal voice."

"He's a real piece of work," Mak went on, ignoring him. "He has a few charges for possession of drugs. What you won't find in his file is any conviction for drug-trafficking, sex-trafficking, or murder. He was arrested and presented to a jury on more than one occasion for the murders of women he'd been seen with before they disappeared. He has a fantastic legal team because there was *never enough evidence* or there was enough *reasonable doubt*. He was never convicted," Mak's tone was disgusted.

"What do you think is the real story?" Stephen asked.

"He murdered those women. You can't convince me otherwise. Serial killer if I ever saw one. Same thing happens every time. He shows up in public with a beautiful woman who looks exactly like the last one, by the way, blond hair, blue or green

43

eyes, tall, thin… Two months later, that very woman will go missing." Mak tapped the steering wheel in frustration. "They would find evidence that she was there at his house—shoes, clothes, makeup—all with her DNA on them. None of it proved a thing because they were dating. The lawyers all said, *Of course there's evidence she's been at his house. They were in a relationship,*" Mak said in a deep voice, imitating a male lawyer.

"So, he was never convicted. I think Sikes said he disappeared from the public after that?" Stephen recalled the brief. "He went underground."

"Yeah. Which is exactly what I'd do if I were guilty, too," Mak said. "Lay low."

"Remind me to be afraid if you ever isolate from the public," Stephen smiled.

"No, really. This guy is super extroverted. Larger than life—both physically and personality-wise. Everyone knows him. He frequented the same places on the same days. Total creature of habit. Then he just falls off the face of the earth for years. This is the first I'm hearing of him resurfacing."

"Did anyone think maybe he'd been murdered?" Stephen asked.

Mak nodded. "Yeah, that was a theory, but I didn't believe it for a minute."

"Why not?" Stephen wondered.

"I knew he'd resurface someday. He just had to lie low for a while." Mak turned on a blinker.

They entered the tiny town that bordered the one where Stephen had spent one of the happiest years of his life. His gut churned. He and Carley had eaten at this very restaurant on more than one occasion.

"Something brought him out of hiding. I wonder what it is," Stephen said as Mak parked outside the café. He glanced over at the white-washed wooden siding on the tiny little diner. Cheerful, red shutters lined the windows. It had a new black shingled roof. It looked little from the front, but Stephen knew it was roomy inside.

"What indeed?" Mak murmured.

"Hey, do you want Anthony Gerritt to know you're a marshal?" Stephen asked her pointedly.

"No, why?" Mak looked at him blankly.

Stephen pointed to Mak's jacket. "Might want to ditch your fancy US Marshal jacket."

"But it's chilly out," Mak whined as she took it off quickly and shoved it behind Stephen's seat. "You're just jealous because you don't have one yet."

"You're right. I am. I'm going to steal yours one of these days." Stephen jumped out of the car. "Try to act casual. Have you ever been undercover before?"

"Of course. I'm like a chameleon. I blend right in," Mak said as she picked up her pace.

Stephen had to do a slight jog to keep up. Mak had long legs and walked quick and with purpose, which always surprised Stephen.

"What's good here?" Mak asked cheerily as she walked through the door.

Stephen stared at her for half a second. *Good*. She was acting as if they were just getting breakfast. Mak wouldn't be blowing their cover any time soon.

"Sit anywhere you like," a server greeted them with a smile.

Stephen glanced around. It was quaint and clean inside. Thick, plastic, black buffalo-plaid tablecloths draped over each of the circular tables that filled the center of the dining room. There were lamps on the booths lining the walls. The tables were full of people getting ready to start their workdays.

The smell of bacon, cinnamon rolls, and coffee wafted through the air. Stephen heard his stomach growl.

They looked around and immediately spotted the unmistakable large frame of Anthony Gerritt. His once dark hair had more salt than pepper sprinkled in. He was sitting in the far corner talking and laughing loudly with two gentlemen who looked to be his age.

The packed café left Mak and Stephen few choices of where to sit. There was a booth near the front and a table that was open right in front of Anthony Gerritt.

On one hand, they could get close and try to pick up the conversation. But they would risk getting unwanted attention. Today was just about getting eyes on Gerritt and maybe trailing him if they got lucky.

They simultaneously headed for the table up front.

Stephen sat with his back to the table where Gerritt and his men were sitting.

Mak had eyes on the criminal though she was careful not to stare.

They were perusing the menu when Stephen looked up in time to spot James Friesen, Anna's stepfather, walking through the door.

James' eyes fell on Stephen and lit up. He immediately headed for Stephen's table. Stephen made eye contact and gave him a small shake of his head. Then he stood.

"What are you—" Mak started but snapped her mouth shut. She spied James walking toward Stephen and put her face back into the menu.

Stephen tilted his head toward the men's room and stepped in front of James, taking big enough steps to put some space between them. James followed him into the bathroom.

Stephen immediately put his finger to his lips as he met James' questioning eyes. He pushed open the doors to the bathroom stalls. Satisfied there was no one in the bathroom, Stephen clicked the lock on the door.

"Hey, man, what are you—"

"James, I'm sorry," Stephen kept his voice low and urgent. "I'm in town on a case. I don't want anyone in danger. I can't associate with any of you because I don't want you to get in the crosshairs."

"I understand," James responded slowly, his accent thick with a Canadian lilt. "So, you didn't want us to know you're in town and you can't associate with any of us for our own protection, eh?"

"Right," Stephen exhaled. "Now, I need to get back out there—"

"You know you're never gonna hear the end of this if Paige finds out you were in town but didn't see Anna," James articulated Stephen's current fear.

Stephen nodded. "I know. James, I need you to make her understand. We don't need Anna to become a target if things go sideways here."

"Are we in some trouble, Stephen? Should we take a vacation and get out of town?" James asked. "My parents are dying to see the kids."

"That's up to you, man. Right now, all is well. But if it does go sideways, they can't come after you if they don't know we're connected," Stephen explained.

"Got it. Well, I was just picking up an order for the missus. I'll wait a few minutes and come out, snub you, pick up my order, and go," James grinned.

Admittedly, Stephen understood what his ex-girlfriend saw in James. He was funny, good-looking, and extremely likable.

"Good to see you, Stephen. Be safe," James said as he went to the sink and started washing his hands.

"Thanks," Stephen nodded, unlocked the door, and walked out. But the scene at his table stopped him short.

Mak was still at their booth in the front, but she was now standing, looking combative. Anthony Gerritt had apparently left his back corner table and now stood in front of Mak. Mak watched as Anthony Gerritt futilely mopped at a big, brown wet spot on his shirt. Stephen quickly surmised that Mak must have spilled her coffee down Gerritt's shirt. Gerritt's face was red, anger evident in his body language.

Stephen looked around for the other men who had been with Gerritt but didn't see them in the café. Out of the corner of his eye, he saw James pick up a bag and pay the cashier for his food.

As James left the restaurant, Stephen finally found his voice. "What in the world is happening here?"

10

MAK

It wasn't Mak's fault. Right after Wilton got up to go to the bathroom, Anthony Gerritt had made eye contact with her. It wasn't casual eye contact either. Mak had been studying the menu intently. She hadn't eaten before she left, and breakfast sounded like heaven right now.

Today, they were doing recon. She could casually drink coffee, eat breakfast, and pretend not to watch Anthony Gerritt. Only, *he* was watching *her*. With focused intensity. Having decided what she wanted, Mak lowered the menu and found Anthony Gerritt leering at her from his table in the back.

Mak's breath caught as her eyes locked with Gerritt's. Wordlessly, the men at his table got up and left. Slowly, without taking his eyes off her, Anthony Gerritt pulled out his wallet and threw money on the table.

Then he got up. He strolled right to her. Mak was speechless. She tried to smile disarmingly. Then, she took a drink of her coffee and choked a little as it went down the wrong pipe.

Anthony stopped right at Mak's table. He really was a tall, imposing man. His stomach was a little rounder than the last picture they had and he held more weight in his face than before. But his dark, piercing eyes glared at her the same way he looked into the camera for his arrest photos. An angry, light pink scar curved from the corner of his mouth to his chin. Up close, it made him look all the more threatening. Mak couldn't help but wonder where he'd gotten that scar.

He stared at her for a solid minute.

"I know you," he finally broke the silence. His voice was low, but his baritone was deep and authoritative.

Mak squirmed inside. She stared at him without comprehension until a thought occurred to her. She felt instant anger bubble up inside her. Still holding her coffee, she stood up quickly, straightened her spine, put her shoulders back, and lifted her chin in an effort to make herself big. She closed the space between them, eyes narrowing.

"Are you hitting on me?" she raised her voice in offense. Then she lifted her hand with the ring on it. She put it right in his face. "Can you not see this thing, or do you just not care?"

To Mak's surprise, Gerritt started laughing. It was a deep baritone belly laugh. Then he stepped closer. All trace of laughter fell from his face. What was left terrified Mak to her core, and Mak didn't scare easily. She was looking into the face of pure evil.

"You're good. But not that good. I know who you are. I'm gonna pretend it's a coincidence that you're here. In my town. You better not let me catch you here again. I won't be in the mood for pretend tomorrow." Gerritt's pointer finger double tapped between Mak's collarbones.

Mak reacted fast. No man put their hands on her, *ever*, with the exception of her husband. She flung the hot coffee in Anthony's face, but because he was so tall, it saturated his shirt on his chest and seeped through.

Anthony yelped and jumped back. He grabbed a stack of napkins from the table and started dabbing at the coffee.

Mak used it to gain the advantage. "I don't know what you

think you know or who you are. But where I'm from, no man touches a woman without permission. I suggest you walk your ass out of here before I call the cops on you. And *you* better hope I don't see your face in this café ever again!"

Wilton was suddenly at the table.

Nice of you to show up, Wilton, Mak thought, her emotions warring between anger and panic, but she stood her ground.

"What in the world is happening here?" he asked, looking from Mak to Anthony.

"This man was just leaving," Mak answered Wilton's questions without taking her eyes off Gerritt. To Gerritt, she lowered her voice into a menacing growl. "Do we have an understanding?"

Anthony Gerritt threw the coffee-soaked napkins on the table and looked at Mak with pure hatred. Anger lined his words. "You go your way, and I'll go mine. But you better pray to your God that we don't ever run into each other again."

"Learn how to treat a woman, asshole!" Mak yelled at Anthony's retreating form.

Slowly she turned back to Wilton, whose mouth was gaping open in sincere shock. Red crept up the back of Wilton's neck.

Mak shrugged at Wilton and sat back down as if nothing had happened. But inside she was trembling.

Wilton slowly sat down across from Mak. "You want to tell me what just happened?"

"He knows exactly who we are."

11

MAK

Wilton was seething mad, and he wasn't trying to hide it with his stormy silence as Mak drove back to their office in Kansas City. After they ate breakfast in silence, they wordlessly got in the SUV. Only when Mak was navigating onto the highway and heading home did Wilton speak.

"What part of undercover do you not understand?" Wilton spat out.

"Harsh," Mak answered quietly with a calm that only came over her when she felt afraid, and she needed to take control of her emotions. "Watch your tone, please. He approached my table."

"Why?" Wilton asked.

"He said he knew who I was. I thought he was hitting on me. He put his finger on me, and I reacted. I threw coffee on him." Mak wasn't proud of her reaction, but she was more worried about Gerritt's words. What if Anthony Gerritt really did know who she was?

Wilton was quiet for a minute. "He touched you?"

"Yeah, right here." Mak pointed to the place between her collar bone.

"You're right, that is unacceptable." Wilton's jaw tightened. "Let's call Sikes."

When Sikes answered the phone, Mak and Wilton explained the situation.

"I don't understand, Mak," Sikes said. Mak's cell was synced up with the car, and Wilton could hear both sides of the conversation through the speakers. "How did he know who you are? Run me through everything that happened again, slowly. From the time you got to the restaurant, got seated, and Anthony Gerritt came to your table. Don't leave out one detail."

Mak told the story again. She refused to look in Wilton's direction. She knew he thought she'd somehow blown it. She'd thought he was joking when he tried to coach her on being undercover. Now she knew he'd been serious. He'd expected her to blow this, and she had. Only she couldn't figure out how.

"Huh," Sikes replied. "I can't figure out where you went wrong, Mak. Wilton, tell me in detail your interaction with James from the time he walked through the door to the bathroom chat and back out."

Wilton told his story in more detail than Mak ever could have. How that man remembered the color of shoes people wore and what they were eating was beyond Mak. She wished she paid more attention to detail in this job.

"It sounds like you played this right," Sikes said, his voice sounding confused. "Great job, Mak. Putting the focus on him as a womanizer was brilliant. You never broke from that?"

"Nope. To be honest, sir. I actually thought he might be hitting on me. Though we know I'm not his type... It was the only logical explanation I could think of. I mean, we had just walked through the door." Mak signaled to switch lanes and glanced in her blind spot.

"Who knew we were on this case?" Wilton asked suddenly.

"Wilton, you know as well as I do, it's common knowledge

around here who is working what case. If you're suggesting someone in this office is dirty—"

"No one is suggesting that, sir," Mak cut in.

Wilton shot her a dirty look and contradicted her. "It wouldn't be the first time."

"Noted," Sikes said. "It would be the first time in this office under my watch."

"What are the other possibilities?" Mak asked.

Sikes was silent for half a minute.

"What?" Mak tapped her fingers on the steering wheel.

"The alternative is… not good. I just had a realization. You're on your way back here, right?" Sikes asked.

"What are you thinking?" Wilton asked.

Sikes let out a long sigh. "Remember Gerritt's last trial, Mak?"

"Yeah, how could I forget. I was a rookie. I sat in to see the outcome. It was part of my training to assess the evidence and understand how to give the DA everything they would need to close a case and put the bad guy behind bars."

"Right, only Anthony Gerritt didn't land behind bars," Sikes finished the story.

"And?" Mak asked.

"And as much as we like to say times have changed and the world has progressed, a female US Marshal—even a newbie rookie—might have been memorable to him. Maybe he saw you sitting in the courtroom when he left," Sikes said.

Mak gasped over the possibility. "You think?"

"I didn't think about that when I assigned this. Here Wilton was worrying about if he was the best marshal for this case when we should have been worrying about you," Sikes voice held a strict tone.

Wilton shook his head. "Or maybe we shouldn't jump to conclusions and assume he specifically remembered Mak from that moment like seven years—"

"Eight," Mak corrected.

"Eight years ago. Maybe, he's a criminal who does his research on law enforcement in the area so he doesn't get caught with his pants down. He wouldn't be the first one to do this. We all know Scott Milternett, KC crime boss, made it his business to know everyone in the marshal's office," Wilton stated logically.

"Yeah," Mak agreed slowly. "Yeah, you might be right. There's no way he would remember me from way back then. I really don't love the idea of Gerritt knowing anything about us."

"Well, it goes without saying. Come straight back here. We'll regroup and come up with another plan." Sikes hung up.

Wilton turned to Mak. "It doesn't feel good when your job has the potential to expose your family does it?"

Mak didn't answer but as she pictured John and Harper, the panic inside her grew.

No, she thought, *no, it does not.*

12

WILTON

Stephen was driving to Arkansas. After he and Mak arrived back at headquarters, they all agreed there was nothing else they could do about Anthony Gerritt for today. Mak would have loved to go back to that café the next day just to spite Gerritt. But the truth was, Gerritt would likely not be back now that he'd been discovered. They had lost their lead on him. They would have to come up with a new plan.

Should I give this to another team? Sikes had asked after noticing how shaken up Mak had seemed.

No! Mak had answered adamantly. *If Anthony Gerritt knows about me, he knows about every other law enforcement agent in this building. We all have to tread carefully with this guy. We'll find another way.*

Go home, enjoy an early weekend. We'll regroup Monday, Sikes had released them midday on Friday.

That's how their week ended.

Only, Stephen wasn't going home. He'd be damned if he spent another weekend at his empty house alone with nothing but the TV for company. He didn't want to go see his little girl yet either. He needed to let the dust settle with Anthony Gerritt before he felt safe to set foot in that town again.

Instead, he'd called his former lieutenant, Roger Higgins, from the Police Station of Little Rock.

"Stephen! How the heck are you?" Higgins asked with genuine surprise in his voice.

"Good. Can't complain," Stephen smiled despite himself.

"Good to hear from you. What are you up to these days?" Higgins asked.

"I'm making a trip to Arkansas this weekend. Thought I'd say *hi* to the parents…" Stephen let his voice trail off.

"This wouldn't have anything to do with the woman you sent to my office, would it? Beth Donovan. You went to high school with her, didn't you?" Higgins probed.

Stephen was quiet for a second, silently cursing himself. The reason Higgins had let Stephen go from his detective position was because Stephen couldn't walk away from an investigation that had involved his daughter. Higgins thought Stephen should stay out of the case. When Stephen had refused and defied orders, his lieutenant had let him go.

Higgins had allowed one too many instances of Stephen stepping in and working a case where Stephen was personally invested. It was Higgins who had pointed out that Stephen lived in the gray area, and it was going to get him in trouble someday.

"No," Stephen quickly denied. "I didn't know Beth well in high school. She was my brother Greg's age." Beth was only a small part of the reason he was on his way back home. Greg was the real reason Stephen needed to make the trip. He had questions about his brother's death, and he planned to get to the bottom of it.

"I see," Higgins said, his tone doubtful.

"Anyway, are you free for dinner today or lunch tomorrow?" Stephen asked.

"I'm free for dinner," Higgins said jovially.

"Great," Stephen set the time and place. He'd be in town right about that time and judging by the way his stomach was growling, he'd be more than ready to eat.

Stephen hung up the phone and called Alyah. As usual, her phone went straight to voicemail. After the tone, Stephen paused. He wanted to tell her about his day. But he couldn't talk about details of a case, and he certainly couldn't leave them over the phone. Then there was his brother Greg's murder and the contents of the folder she'd encouraged him to open. He didn't want to talk about that either.

In the end, he decided to talk about Mak spilling coffee all over a known criminal they'd been watching. Earlier today, Stephen had felt so angry, but now as he retold the scene he found when he came out of the bathroom, Stephen was actually laughing.

"I'm telling you, Alyah. I can't leave that woman alone in a restaurant for five minutes. The guy was literally across the café from us, in the very back corner when I left. I come out of the bathroom and the guy is standing inches from Mak with hot coffee soaking his shirt to his chest. Of course, our recon mission was over. I'll even admit I was a little pissed—" *Or a lot pissed*, Stephen thought. "But one thing's for sure, a job with Mak at my side will never be boring."

Stephen said *goodbye* and hung up the phone.

"Huh," he mumbled to himself. "I guess I'm not irritated with Mak anymore for blowing our cover."

He could even go as far as to admit he'd found a friend in his new partner.

13

LACY

When Lacy woke from another stiff night of sleep on the ground, she thought about camping. She remembered camping in the hills of Arkansas while she was growing up. Family vacations, or *staycations*, they would say, took place tent camping with her parents and sister.

There was nothing more beautiful than a sunrise coming over the top of the mountain, illuminating the view of trees and hills, with a river way below running through a ravine. The breathtaking view went on for miles with steep drop-offs just below. Lacy would wake to the smell of bacon frying in a cast iron pan over a revitalized fire from the previous night.

Lacy's sister, Beth, was older, prettier, and protective. Sometimes, it felt like Lacy had two moms. She often took turns calming her *two moms* down. If Beth wasn't lecturing her about safety and self-care, her mom was. Lacy had been so tired of it, she'd moved away. Somewhere neither of them would find her. She hadn't given them her forwarding address. Now she was lying on a dirt floor where no one could find her if they tried. Lacy might die on the very property where she had been living in secret.

No! Something snapped in Lacy. She was a survivor. She was mentally strong. Stronger than the girls who lie sleeping on the ground. She wouldn't accept this situation. This wasn't her fate. She would fight. She would save them all.

She pushed her body into child's pose, her favorite yoga position, then to down-dog. She had been working on her yoga certification before this. She knew how to use the poses to stretch and strengthen her body. Though she was captive, no kidnapper could stop her from keeping her muscles warm and limber. A man who had taken her may have control over her physical location at the moment, but no one could control if or when she meditated. She needed to keep herself strong— mentally, physically, and emotionally. The time would come, and Lacy would be ready.

When the girls woke, Lacy would ask them about their captor. Was there more than one? The more information she had, the more chance she had of getting free. She would ask them about all the men they'd seen over the years—the height, build, hair color, sound of the voices. It would be like studying for a test.

Only, passing this test would determine the outcome of their lives.

14

MAK

Mak was still pouting from her run-in with Anthony Gerritt.
Though she was off for the weekend, she wasn't off the case.
Her body was in the house with her attentive, sexy husband and
sweet, hilarious three-year-old but her mind wasn't. Try as she
might, Mak couldn't stop reliving the run-in with Anthony
Gerritt.

I know who you are... he'd said.

Sikes said she'd played it well. The only reason she was still
standing to tell the story is because her surprise over Gerritt
marching across Mama's Café had been real. She was in a male-
dominated field. She wore a wedding ring, and Mak certainly
didn't consider herself pretty by any means, no matter what her
husband said about her. Despite how mad she'd gotten at
Anthony Gerritt in that moment when she believed he'd been
hitting on her, Mak felt something way worse than anger after
he'd walked away. She'd felt fear.

She gazed at Harper who was busily skipping through the
kitchen with a piece of construction paper and crayons in her
hand. Harper climbed a kitchen chair, pulled her bare feet under

her, and placed the construction paper beside ten others she'd already colored, cut, and pasted.

Mak still felt afraid.

John came up to stand behind Mak. He wrapped his hands around Mak and hugged her to him, resting his chin on top of her head. He cuddled her close. Mak felt goosebumps rise on her skin. She hoped she would always have that reaction to her husband.

"Makayla," John's deep voice rumbled lowly. "What's going on with you?"

Mak sighed. "I'm just wondering if it's all worth it. You know? What good is putting away bad guys and saving the good ones if I'm leaving you both here vulnerable and in danger?"

John stiffened. "Woah, woah, woah!" He turned Mak around and gazed into her eyes, searching the depths of her soul. "I've never heard you talk like this. He really got to you, didn't he?"

Mak had told John a vague version of the whole story. Upon hearing that Mak had thrown her coffee at a criminal, John had laughed hard.

That's my girl! No one puts a finger on my woman without consequences! he'd said, shaking his head.

Mak had shrugged and grudgingly smiled. John trusted her and loved hearing her stories. But she could tell this one was about to become his favorite.

Mak stared into John's eyes. "If anything happened to you guys, I'd never be able to live with myself. You know, I run around like I'm superhuman and don't stop to consider the consequences. But something like that happened to Wilton and he barely got his little girl back before it was too late. And look at what happened to Booker—"

"Makayla, stop. This isn't you. What you do is brave and courageous. You're experienced and know how to take care of yourself. And I know how to take care of me and Harper. Being a US Marshal is what you do. It's who you are. It's all I've ever known you as. But if you let fear get in your head, you're right, it won't be worth it. Fear can get you killed."

Mak shuddered. He was right. She needed to stop worrying about the future and live in the here and now.

The doorbell rang.

Mak's eyes widened in surprise. "Who's that? We aren't expecting anyone."

"Calm down," John smiled. "This will make you feel better."

Mak trailed John to the door.

"Dad!" Mak gasped when she saw her dad standing on the doorstep. She flung herself into his arms.

Larry "The Epic" Taylor still looked great at sixty-four. Unlike some of his buddies, Larry hit the gym five days a week. He was six foot two, strong, and tan. His hair was a variety of grays from dark to light gray, all mixed together. It only made him more distinguished. His brown eyes were like Mak's and Harper's. If only mom were still here to see how well he'd aged.

"Pop-pop?" Harper squealed from the kitchen and the sound of little feet running pounded loudly on the floor.

Larry released Mak and bent down just in time to pick up his granddaughter.

"Come in, come in!" Mak invited, shutting the door behind him. "It's freezing out there! What are you doing here?"

Larry laughed as he followed them into the warm kitchen where Mak and John had been talking.

"I have a race tomorrow night, and I thought I'd stop here to spend the night before I head out in the morning. If that's okay with you?"

"Yeah!" Harper yelled. She hugged her Pop-pop's neck harder.

"You're always welcome here," Mak smiled.

"I was just about to order dinner," John said. "Who wants pizza?"

There was a resounding chorus of agreement from around the room.

"Where are you racing?" Mak asked.

"Southeast Missouri," Larry answered.

Mak's eyes widened as he went on to describe the area. "Camera crews or is this one secret?" she asked.

"You know I don't go race anywhere without a camera crew around, darlin'. It's in my fancy Hollywood contract. Larry 'The Epic' Taylor won't step foot near a car without makeup and a camera panned in on his face," Larry grinned widely as he teased her. He framed his face with his hands. "This is the money-maker, right here!"

"Dad!" Mak smiled and scoffed at his antics. "So, this one is publicized?"

"Do you think I'd tell my US Marshal daughter where a secret street race was if we were doing it illegally?" Larry razzed.

"Good point," Mak said.

"When will we get you behind the wheel again?" Larry asked. "I need someone to take over my legacy and this one is a little too young." Larry set Harper down at the kitchen table and started tickling her.

"Harper got her driver's license two weeks ago. Didn't you, Harper?" John teased.

"Uh-huh!" Harper agreed, gasping between giggles.

"What?" Larry howled in mock anger. "You aren't officially a great driver until you've practiced with Pop-pop."

"I'll show you!" Harper slid off the chair and out of his grasp. She ran from the room.

Mak was suddenly serious while thinking, her brows furrowed in concentration.

"I know that look," Larry said.

"Yeah, I just got a terrible, awful idea," Mak said.

John grinned as he picked up the phone to order pizza. "She's been thinking a lot today."

"Thanks for the warning," Larry said. "It must be something serious if my act-first-consequences-be-damned daughter is sitting around thinking."

"Ha, ha," Mak said sarcastically.

John made the order and hung up the phone.

"Maybe I should get behind the wheel again. Just one race. For old times…" Mak said. Did facing her fear mean putting herself right in the middle of an adrenaline-charged adventure?

Larry clapped his hands together. "That's my girl!"

The whir of a small engine and crunching of fat tires sounded as Harper rode a pink plastic Lamborghini at top speed and barely slowed down before she hit a wall.

"See, she got her driver's license," John said.

"Oh, she *is* just like her mama," Larry stated with pride.

Mak was enjoying every moment of this and found herself present and engaged. But in the back of her mind, she was brewing a new plan. One that might get her a solid reason to be back to the area where Anthony Gerritt was doing something illegal.

Maybe she could bring Gerritt to her.

15

WILTON

Stephen walked into a diner in Arkansas with a pang of nostalgia. He found his former lieutenant, Roger Higgins, in the back at their usual booth. This was the place where Higgins had introduced him to Brix, the US Marshal who had set Stephen on this career path.

Stephen's mind flashed back to that day. He remembered he was in such turmoil because Anna was missing, and he didn't feel he could make the decision to jump careers until he'd found her. When he dug deeper, Stephen had realized it was his unresolved feeling for Anna's mom, Paige, who was single back then. Those feelings had been what had held him back.

Stephen shook his head. It was hard to believe another person could have kept him from starting a career he'd only dreamt about. He thought of Alyah. He knew deep in his heart it was why he hadn't tried to convince her to stay and why he hadn't followed her to Washington, DC. He couldn't be the person who held her back.

Higgins was already standing up when Stephen got to the table. Stephen offered him a hand, but Higgins grabbed his hand and pulled him in for a hug. Stephen swallowed his surprise.

"Stephen! Long time no see. How are things?" Higgins said as he sat back down. His thick eyebrows were all gray now. His once brown hair was peppered with more gray than the last time Stephen had seen him. He'd always been a tall, broad man. While it was no doubt Higgins had aged, he was still strong.

"Great! Things are good," Stephen admitted.

"Glad to hear it. You look good. Marshal work appears to suit you," Higgins said.

"Yeah, I love the job," Stephen admitted. "How about you? You still happy with yours?"

"They finally promoted me to Captain."

"That's great!" Stephen exclaimed.

Higgins shrugged nonchalant. "Nah, they know I'm retiring in five years. Should have done it years ago."

Stephen grinned. "Yeah."

Higgins pulled out a set of readers to study the menu. "Doc says I have to eat healthier. Gotta admit, I've never looked at that side of the menu."

"Wait, is everything okay?" Stephen asked, feeling concerned. He'd never known Higgins to be one who cared about what he ate.

Higgins waived a hand dismissively. "Just some high blood pressure and cholesterol stuff. Call it aging. I'm fine."

Stephen didn't know if he believed him, but he gave Higgins the dignity of not pressing the issue.

"How about you? Anything new? Girlfriend, perhaps?" Higgins asked, glancing at Stephen over his glasses.

Stephen laughed lightly in wonder at this new turn in their relationship. Stephen had always been close to Roger Higgins when he was Stephen's lieutenant. Because the job had been Stephen's whole life, Higgins had always known about everything, from the cases Stephen was working on to what was happening in his personal life. Admittedly, for years, those two things—work and personal—had intertwined. If he were honest, they still did.

Stephen shook his head sadly and admitted, "Single as can be right now."

The server came and took their order.

"Give it time," Higgins said. "You always did have a way with the ladies."

Stephen snorted. "That's what people think. It got me an annoying little nickname at the office. Get this, I'm *Love 'Em and Leave 'Em, Wilton*."

Now Higgins laughed and practically choked on his drink. When he could breathe again, he wiped his eyes. "So, what's the real story?"

"I can't get them to stay," Stephen admitted. "I've been advised that I come on too strong and they see it a mile away because I want a wife and family."

Higgins speared him with his gaze. "It's really hard to balance a family in this line of work." Stephen knew Roger was speaking from personal experience.

"I thought so too, but I've got this partner who's married, and her husband stays at home with their daughter. They make it look easy. I think it's possible, I just haven't found the right girl yet." Stephen liked this new theory. It gave him hope.

"Well, I can't tell you if she's the *right girl*, but I can tell you Beth Donovan is quite the looker," Higgins said. He reached for something he had sitting on the booth seat beside him that Stephen hadn't seen. Higgins put a file on the table and pushed it toward Stephen.

"A looker? Careful, Higgins, your age is showing," Stephen chuckled, teasing him. "Besides, there's more to it than looks. Not to mention, she dated my brother in high school. That might be weird." His fingers were itching to open the folder in front of him. Instinctively, he knew what he would find.

"Lacy Donovan," Higgins said as he tapped the information in front of Stephen.

"The girl who vanished." Stephen opened the manila folder and shuffled through the papers. "There's not much in here."

There was a picture of Lacy, her driver's license, make and model of her car, and the copy of employment records.

"She's squeaky clean with no priors, no real enemies, and best friends who love her and are worried about her. Her mother might be the last person she talked to on the phone. Though they say they're close, neither Lacy's mother nor Beth have any idea where she moved to. They say Lacy wanted her privacy and they were trying to give it to her."

"I see," Stephen said. "Why are you telling me this?"

"Two reasons. I assume you've already made plans to see Beth while you're here. Don't try to argue. When you say you'll stay out of something, you don't. The other reason is because Lacy is not in Arkansas. She's in Missouri. At least, that's where they found her car and responded to an APB. Fished her car out of a lake yesterday," Higgins stated.

"Oh no!" Stephen groaned. That did not sound promising. "Does Beth know?"

Higgins nodded. "Called her immediately. She was devastated."

"You know I can't exactly take cases unless they're assigned to me," Stephen said, though his mind was trying to figure out a way to get involved.

"Well, talk to Beth. Obviously, we've got the county police department working on the case. They're all looking for Lacy now. Combing the area."

Stephen felt sad for Beth. A car in a lake didn't give a good vibe that Lacy was still alive.

"There's another reason why I want to see Beth," Stephen surprised himself by opening up to Higgins. He hadn't been planning to talk about it. "You remember I told you my brother, Greg, was murdered?"

"Of course," Higgins said as he stroked his beard. He leaned back in his seat.

"I was at a funeral when this guy—his name is Trevan Collins—finds me and hands me a manila envelope. Turns out, Trevan went to school with my brother, Greg."

"What's inside the envelope?" Higgins asked.

"An eight-by-ten glossy picture of some man holding a gun to Greg's face. That man was not Davey Stinnert, the teenager who went to prison for Greg's murder."

"Who's the guy and how do you know it's a picture of the day Greg was shot?" Higgins asked.

"The picture was time stamped. It was taken on the day of the murder, seconds before Greg was killed. That's why I assume the man in this picture was the actual murderer who pulled the trigger. I've run it through my databases and there's no facial recognition pulling up."

"So, you're in town to do some investigating?" Higgins took a sip of his iced tea.

"I want to talk to Beth to see if she remembers anything," Stephen finished.

The server put two plates of food in front of them and topped off their drinks.

Higgins leaned forward. "Let me take a look at the picture. Maybe I know him. It was around here, right?"

"Yeah. Let me grab it from the car." Stephen stepped outside to collect the manila envelope. He brought it back in, sat down, and looked around to make sure no servers were close by. Then he pulled out the picture.

Higgins grunted as he studied the picture. "Male, Caucasian, long, wavy, light-brown hair, approximate age in this photo is forty, which would make him about fifty-five now…"

Stephen pointed to the time and date stamp in the corner of the picture. "Body cam technology."

Higgins looked at Stephen and held his gaze. "I know what you're thinking, and I wouldn't jump to conclusions. This tech is accessible to everyone. Not just law enforcement. Just because the police force had it doesn't mean it was exclusive to us. What we can assume is that someone held this over the perp here," he tapped the killer's face. "For around fifteen years. Why release this now?"

Stephen shrugged. "I'd start with who the man is."

"Can I take a picture of this?" Higgins asked.

"Sure," Stephen agreed.

Higgins took a picture with his phone and slid the photo back in the envelope. "I'll look into it from my end. But Stephen, this was a long time ago. You know what happens to cold cases—"

Stephen shrugged. "I also plan to track down Trevan Collins, and if I can find him, I'll talk to Davey Stinnert too," Stephen changed the subject, not willing to acknowledge this might never be solved on account of the amount of time that had gone by.

"That seems ambitious for one weekend, Stephen," Higgins said. "But if anyone can do it, you can. Why don't you call me before you go see Stinnert? He might not be happy to see you. You could use some backup."

Stephen shrugged. He'd thought long and hard about his brother. It was time he got answers.

Even if they were answers he might not like.

16

MAK

Mak waited until dinner was done, the dishes were put away, and her dad had gone to bed. Harper had crawled into bed all by herself on account of being up later than bedtime because the adults were busy talking.

Mak paced a bit down the hallway, debated for half a second, then pulled out her phone and called Sikes.

"Hello?" Sikes sounded sleepy.

"Hey, boss," Mak greeted.

"Hey, everything okay?" he wondered. "It's late, Mak."

"Yeah, everything is fine. Sorry. I just had this idea I needed to run by you. I want to make sure it will work," Mak got right to the point.

"Wait, are you actually coming to me instead of rushing into something?" Sikes joked.

"Yes. It might sound far-fetched at first, but just hear me out." Sikes promised.

"Okay, I might have found a way to get back in town with Anthony Gerritt for a perfectly logical reason to confuse Gerritt and make him think he knows me from somewhere else. My dad is Larry 'The Epic' Taylor from—"

"No way!" Sikes interrupted as he named the famous street racing show. "*Street Southwest?*"

"Yes. He has an event tomorrow back in Brighton—where we ran into Gerritt. Didn't it say in his file that he's into women, drugs, and cars in no particular order?"

Sikes was quiet for a second. "Yes, he's had illegal activity revolving around those three things."

"What if I go support my dad at the race on the off chance that Gerritt shows up? It's the biggest event of the year."

"Biggest?" Sikes sounded skeptical.

"Yes. I think this town is a tiny town. Nothing happens there. Trust me, I think it might be why Gerritt is hiding there," Mak promised.

"*If* he's still in town," Sikes said. "If he knew you were a marshal, then he also knew you knew his identity. It might have spooked him."

"True," Mak agreed.

"So, let me make sure I understand. You want to get eyes on Gerritt, but you also want him to see you there? You think if he sees you, it will give you a more logical reason to be in town so he thinks you aren't after him and what—he takes his guard down?" Sikes asked.

"Yeah, when you put it like that, it sounds pretty far-fetched," Mak back peddled.

Sikes was quiet for a minute. "It's not that, exactly. I'm not sure it will work. Who knows if he would be there—"

"Or be watching it on TV," Mak interrupted.

"Right," Sikes paused. "Listen, Mak, what you do on the weekends and when you're off duty is your business. It's not up to me to tell you what to do. I can't give you permission to be there in an official US Marshal capacity. I should also warn you that things could get dangerous, but that would insult your intelligence. You could be going a long way for no reason," Sikes said.

"Nah, I'll be hanging out with my dad. We never do this together anymore," Mak smiled. She had run the idea by John earlier and he had encouraged her to go with her dad to the event.

"If he is there, how will you make sure Gerritt sees you? Throw coffee at him?" Sikes asked.

"Ha, ha," Mak rolled her eyes, wondering when she was going to hear the end of that one. "No. I'm going to race."

17

WILTON

Stephen knew better than to come to town without visiting his mom and dad. Though he'd made a coffee appointment in the morning with Beth Donovan and had made it clear that he didn't want to be up too late tonight, his parents had talked him into a *quick* card game.

"Just one," he'd promised with a smile. He should have known better.

He fielded all the questions they typically asked while they attempted to distract him from winning this hand.

"How's my granddaughter?" his mom, Linda, asked with a pout. She pushed her shoulder-length blond hair back from her face and studied Stephen with blue eyes that resembled his. "It's been too long since I saw her."

"You know you can go see her any time or invite her here for the weekend. Anna would love that!" Stephen replied.

"Do you still like the job, son?" Bruce, his dad, asked. Bruce was aging well with a few strategically placed gray hairs mixed in with his brown hair. He had a kind face. Bruce's eyes locked with Linda's as they often did, love evident in them. It was like his dad couldn't take his eyes off his mom. Even after all these years, Stephen could see and feel the love.

"Yes," Stephen answered.

"Are you staying safe, Stephen?" his mom asked. She always asked that.

"As safe as I possibly can," Stephen assured her even as he caught the hint of worry in her eyes. There was no way he would tell her about his close call on the last case when a shooter had targeted him and his partner, Booker. It had cost Booker his life. It still served to sharpen Stephen's focus. A reminder that he was not invincible.

One game quickly became three before he finally cut them off. Unfortunately, he'd had coffee a little too late in the day and he could feel it kicking in as he walked toward the spare bedroom.

Before he veered off to the room, Stephen stopped and stared at a picture of him and his brother, Greg, hanging in the hallway. One photo in particular was taken two years before Greg was killed. It felt like a lifetime ago. Stephen's arm was slung over Greg's shoulder in a carefree way. Even then, Stephen's blond hair had been curly and unmanageable when it got too long.

Greg's hair, on the other hand, was more like Stephen's dad's, brown and straight. It laid perfectly in place. Greg was smirking at the camera with that expression that Stephen remembered most on him.

His mom approached as Stephen studied the picture and put an arm around Stephen's waist. She laid her head on Stephen's shoulder and studied the picture with him. "Not a day goes by that I don't miss this memory."

"I know," Stephen said. "Me too."

Greg was about as different as he could be from Stephen when they were growing up. Though his brother had a reputation as a stereotypical, popular problem child, Stephen saw him differently. Where Greg got in trouble with teachers for being mouthy, Stephen knew Greg was actually just smart and bored.

More than once, Greg had been accused of cheating on tests because he would ace them with no real effort. Stephen, on the other hand, had to study hard to get decent grades. Greg was inches taller than Stephen and better looking, which meant he always had a date, where Stephen was shy and awkward around girls in high school. Unlike his brother, Stephen always managed to say the wrong thing.

Then there was the bullying thing. Stephen had never seen it, but many rumors flew around school about Greg stuffing kids in lockers, giving them swirlies, and fighting. Stephen assumed those were just rumors. Until the day Greg was killed. Davey Stinnert had gotten on the stand and confessed. Davey said Greg had bullied him for years, and Davey had just lost it and killed Greg.

That's not how Stephen remembered his brother. He had good, fun childhood memories. A memory like the one that came to him as he gazed at that picture of the two of them.

Come on, Stevie, let me show you how to skip rocks, Stephen could still hear the way Greg's voice crackled, going high-pitched and lower during that change into puberty. They'd ridden bikes out to the creek a few miles down the road from the house. It had taken several tries before Stephen was a pro at skipping rocks. In an effort to keep practicing, Stephen went home and skipped a rock into a neighbor's window, breaking it.

You actually didn't look where you were skipping your rock before you threw it? Greg had laughed until tears streamed down his face.

Unfortunately for Greg, their mother had overheard them, and they both had to earn money to pay for the broken window. The day this picture was taken, they had just finished with *chore prison* as they called it. Chore prison was when their mom made them work as punishment for their bad behavior. They were stuck completing chores until their mom released them.

Stephen stared hard at the picture and swore Greg was looking right into his soul.

I'm gonna figure out the truth about what happened to you, Stephen vowed silently.

"Well, goodnight, mom," Stephen gave her a side hug.

"Goodnight, son," she squeezed him back.

Stephen made his way down the hall to the spare bedroom, trying not to feel guilty that his parents had no idea that Greg's murderer still might be roaming free out there. He might have been for the past fifteen years.

18

LACY

It was quiet in the earth prison. It was clear from the hole above them that night had descended. Only, no one was sleeping. Lacy felt stir crazy. Despite the reduced amount of food she'd been eating since she'd arrived, she had random bursts of energy from time to time. This was one of those times.

"Have you ever tried yoga?" Lacy asked her companions.

The women stared at her with dead, lifeless eyes. It was clear that they were beyond the days when they had extra energy stored up inside of them.

"I used to love yoga," Isa mustered a smile.

Lacy was sure Isa had seen Lacy practicing her favorite poses since she'd been down there, but Isa had never attempted to join in. Lacy thought the lack of energy, and maybe lack of hope, had discouraged Isa's involvement.

"Okay, look," Lacy began. "I'm sure you're all tired and most likely you feel sleepy much of the day. But yoga isn't just about movement. There's a way to keep your brain strong, even if your body isn't."

Lacy looked around. Isa, Emma, and Lauren all looked interested in what Lacy had to say.

Feeling encouraged, Lacy continued. "For instance, sitting right here as you are, you can cross your legs and sit sukhasana. Cross-legged, like me."

All three women adjusted their legs to mirror Lacy.

"Good. Now, sit up straighter and rest your hands on your knees. Palms up or down. It doesn't matter," Lacy guided them. The women adjusted their positions.

"Let's start with meditation," Lacy suggested. "Close your eyes, take a deep breath in and breathe out slowly. Quiet your mind and relax into the nothing—"

"I can't," Lauren said, frustration lining her words. "Every time I close my eyes, my brain is a squirrel cage. I'm so anxious about my daughter. Where is she now? Does she think I'm dead?"

"Good," Lacy encouraged. "Acknowledge your thoughts, feel your feelings, and focus on finding peace in the middle of all that."

"Yeah, I have a hard time, too," Isa admitted. "I worry about my patients and who they got to fill in my shifts. I had some regulars I was very close to. Not knowing if they got better is like torture."

"Wow, Isa." Lacy was momentarily stunned. "You're thinking about your patients while you're down here? That's kind. But... It's okay to just think about you and this situation you're in." Lacy heard a sniffle but kept her eyes closed.

"It's just that being down here... not knowing how much longer or if we'll ever get out..." Isa was crying now. "Well, I'd rather focus on my patients. At least they had a chance they were going to make it."

Lacy heard more crying. "Super honest, Isa. That's awesome. I'm going to help you get out of here. I don't know how. But I will never stop trying. Emma, how's it going for you?" Lacy noticed Emma had been quiet.

"At first, I really missed my boyfriend," she spoke in a quiet voice. "He was my world. I thought I couldn't be happy without him. I'm not happy now, of course. But at some point, I let him go. Right now, I need to focus on me. I don't have the energy to try to escape. But I want to be at peace before I die."

Now, Lacy felt tears well up behind her eyelids. She reached over and grabbed the hands of the two girls nearest her. She peeked through her eyelids to see them do the same. They were now all holding hands in a circle of support.

"A meditation circle," Lacy said with contentment. "We are all stronger together."

They were in an impossible situation. But just for tonight, they all had each other.

19

WILTON

Stephen's phone beeped, waking him up. The sun was streaming through the cheerful blue curtains in the guestroom. He felt disoriented. He never slept this hard. What had woken him up? His eyes fell on the nightstand. His phone was not there.

What time is it? he wondered. He searched the bed and under the pillows. No phone. Finally, Stephen got up and spied the phone just under the bed. It must have fallen off the nightstand last night. He grabbed the phone and checked the text message.

Beth: *I'm running a bit behind. Go ahead and grab a booth and I'll be there soon.*

"Oh, shoot! I've gotta go!" Stephen said to the empty room. He quickly jumped in the shower and dressed. His hair was still wet when he walked out the door. It was early enough he didn't run into his mom or dad on the way out.

Stephen slid behind the wheel, started the engine, and floored the car. Though he was late for his coffee meeting with Beth, he wasn't too far away, and her running late had afforded him the time to get there. Now he just needed to pretend he hadn't just rolled out of bed.

Both he and Beth walked in at the same time. They were both so focused on getting inside that they reached for the door at the exact same time. Her touch against his hand shot a warm spark of electricity up his arm.

"Sorry," Beth said as she pulled her hand away. Her fingernails were perfectly polished, and she wore a simple birthstone ring on her right hand.

"Ladies first," Stephen said gallantly. But as he looked into her large blue eyes and noticed her thick, shoulder-length, black hair, he could see the resemblance of someone from his childhood.

"Beth?" Stephen asked, peering harder.

She looked up and laughed. "Stephen! Ohmigosh, you look the same as when you were a kid, only taller."

"That's debatable." Stephen ran a hand through his wet curls. He had a barber now, and when he was young, his mom had cut his hair. "You, on the other hand, are—"

"The same height?" she smiled a little through the lingering sadness on her face. "I didn't get much taller, did I?"

Stephen followed her into the coffee shop and got in line with her. "I was going to say you are beautiful."

"Oh." Beth's cheeks turned pink, and she turned forward, quickly making a show of studying the menu.

"What's good here?" Stephen asked to pretend he hadn't created awkwardness. He called himself an idiot for letting that pop right out of his mouth. They were getting together for professional reasons, not for a trip down high school boulevard. Beth's sister was missing. This wasn't a date. But as he waited for her answer, he felt the familiar quickening of his pulse. He wanted to know more about her.

Stephen listened as Beth explained her favorites. While she spoke, he studied her face. Her large blue eyes studied the menu. She had a small, upturned nose. Though she wore makeup to cover them, a light smattering of freckles covered her cheeks. Her lips were stained dark pink, accentuating her plump natural pout.

Higgins was right. Beth was pretty—classically pretty.

Stephen waited for her to order her coffee and then did the same. As they stood waiting for their drinks, Stephen turned to scan the coffee shop and found it to be loud and crowded. Stephen pointed to an open table in the back corner.

"I'll wait for the coffees if you want to go grab that table?" he suggested.

Beth nodded and walked to the table. Stephen admired her curvy backside and toned build as she walked away. Minutes later, Stephen heard his name. The coffees were up.

"That was fast," Stephen mumbled to himself. He made an effort to snap his attention back to the job at hand. His mind wandered to Alyah. Though he and Alyah weren't together, he felt guilty for checking Beth out just now.

Stephen took a coffee in each hand and walked back to the table. He put Beth's coffee in front of her. He put his coffee down on the table. He reached in the messenger bag he was carrying and pulled out her sister's file. The tab said *Lacy Donovan*.

Beth's eyes immediately filled with tears upon sight of her sister's name. "I'm sorry," she immediately apologized. "It's been an emotional week. I'm just so worried!"

"I know," Stephen looked at her with compassion. "I met with my old lieutenant—well, he's a captain now—from the police station. He filled me in. I know he also told you what's going on and I would like to ask you some questions." Stephen knew it wasn't his place. He also knew, unless the Attorney General made a special exception and appointed a case, kidnapping didn't really fall under his jurisdiction.

Beth wiped her tears and nodded fervently. "Absolutely. Anything you want to know."

"This may sound like a ridiculous question, but does Lacy have any tracking devices on her phone? Location settings and social media can be turned on without us knowing they are—"

"No, she used to be on an app with us, but she turned all that off when she moved," Beth shook her head.

"Do you know why Lacy went to such lengths to move away and not tell anyone where she was?" Stephen asked.

Beth shook her head again. "We just thought she wanted privacy. Like a newly independent person who wants to do everything on her own."

"Okay, and her relationship with you and her mother is good?" Stephen asked.

"Of course. Yes. Lacy and I have always been close. Mom is a bit of a helicopter mom. She's completely blaming herself for this. She feels so guilty!" Beth admitted, emotions clouding her eyes.

"What about your dad? Does Lacy have a good relationship with him?" Stephen wondered.

Beth bit her lip and tilted her hand. "So-so. There's this weird, unexplained animosity between them. They just sort of started avoiding each other at some point in Lacy's teen years. It was like a mutual silence that they both seemed to tolerate. I never understood it and we couldn't get it out of Lacy or dad. Not for a lack of trying. But I don't think it's related to this. Someday, she and dad will figure it out. Someday, if—"

"Does Lacy have any enemies?" Stephen asked before Beth could go down the road of emotional shut down.

"What?" Beth gasped. "No! Why do you ask? Do you know something—"

"Beth, please," Stephen reached forward and rested his hand over hers. He realized his mistake too late. That same spark he'd felt earlier shot right through him. Beth looked surprised as she gazed into his compassionate eyes. This time, she kept her hand where it was. "I don't know anything yet. I know what you know. It's just a standard question."

"No," Beth shook her head. "Lacy has never had enemies. She's bubbly and outgoing. She's beautiful—a tiny little thing but she's freakishly strong."

Stephen laughed. "Okay, good."

"Stephen, be straight with me. This doesn't look good, does it? They found her car in a lake! And if your old lieutenant is handing the case to you, it means he's given up, doesn't it?"

"Beth," Stephen squeezed her hand. "The reason I have your case file is based on where they found her car. Captain Higgins doesn't believe Lacy is in Arkansas. He doesn't have jurisdiction in Missouri. I don't have jurisdiction in this case either unless the Attorney General appoints the case to us—which I can't make him do. But as a marshal, I *can* consult with the officers. As luck would have it, I'll be there on a different case. I can try to stay in the loop and communicate with the police who are working the case."

"Could you?" Beth's eyes lit up and she looked a bit more cheerful.

"Yes, I can. But no promises. Sometimes the police get territorial and weird," Stephen explained. It was always best when local law enforcement worked with them, but there was no guarantee.

"If anyone can help, I believe it's you, Stephen," Beth said and squeezed his hand back.

"If you don't mind me asking," Stephen hesitated. "Why do you think that?"

Beth looked surprised. Then she smiled. "You were Greg's younger brother. The *good* one. Even though you were younger, you just had that vibe about you. You were going to do big things."

"Yeah, well," Stephen felt embarrassed. "The reason I ended

up where I am is because of Greg. I wanted to prevent that sort of senseless violence, and this was the only profession that made sense." Stephen took a sip of his coffee. "You two dated, didn't you?"

"Yes," Beth's eyes got big. "I lost my virginity to your brother."

"You did?" Stephen pulled his hand back slightly.

"No," Beth smiled. "I just wanted to see your reaction."

"Ha, ha," Stephen grinned, feeling relieved. He could feel the heat creeping up his neck.

"No, but I do have good memories of Greg. Before... what happened." Lacy looked sad.

"Yeah, me too. Everyone said he was such a bully and a real bad guy. But to me, he was just my brother," Stephen admitted.

"Yeah, I never knew him to be a bad guy either. In fact, he ended up taking me to prom because my date bailed on me at the last minute. That's when we started dating. Just went out on a few dates after that though. Nothing serious."

"Last minute prom date, huh? That was nice of my brother," Stephen said but his mind wandered. Greg had never gone without a date. He was surprised Greg hadn't already had a date by that point.

"I remember you on prom night too," Beth smiled at some memory.

"Me? I was what, fourteen or fifteen?" Stephen didn't remember that.

"Yes, it was after your mom had taken all her pictures but before we left the house. You brought me a piece of notebook paper. It was a cross with our initials in it. You were quite the little charmer." Beth smiled.

"Huh! Younger me is humiliating older me as we speak," Stephen groaned. "I made a play for you with my brother in the other room?"

"Yep. You told me you would take me to prom next and that someday you were going to marry me," Beth smiled.

"Are you messing with me again?" Stephen asked.

"Only about the marrying you part. The rest is true," Beth winked at him, but her smile faded a little. "Wow, it feels nice to smile. It's hard to do when your sister is missing."

"Yeah, I understand. But I can tell you that everyone working on her case is taking this seriously. Especially after they found her car. Something like this is a very big deal to law enforcement," Stephen promised.

"Thanks, Stephen. I appreciate that," Beth said.

"I'll do whatever I can. I'll communicate with the area police officers Monday and get updates," Stephen said.

"And you'll keep in touch?" Beth looked hopeful and for half a second, Stephen had to wonder if that went beyond communication about her sister.

"Of course. Hey listen, while we're revisiting the past, would it be awkward to ask you questions about Greg?" Stephen tried to keep his voice light and casual.

"What about him?" Beth's voice was compassionate.

"You said you have good memories of him. I do too. I don't want to paint a picture that isn't true. Memories at that age can be unreliable. But what if he wasn't that bad of a guy?" Stephen asked, feeling emotional and vulnerable.

"What are you hoping to hear right now, Stephen?" Beth asked. "I don't have any solid memories that he was a terrible person. I was sad to hear that people thought that after he was... gone. I always wondered if people came up with a story to fit the circumstances of his death, ya know?"

"Not sure. What do you mean?" Stephen asked. He leaned forward, focused on her words.

"I mean," Beth sighed and paused as if trying to find the right words. "I always felt like Greg was actually a good guy caught in a bad situation."

"What situation do you mean?" Stephen asked.

Beth shrugged, her eyes wide with innocence. "Greg chose the wrong guy—Davey Stinnert—who had been his best friend at some point. *Wrong place, wrong time,* the cops said. They thought Greg had been bullying Davey for years and Davey finally had enough. I think I agree. Davey must have just snapped. I don't know that I believe it was all Greg's fault though, the way they painted it. I wonder if there was something wrong with Davey, here," Beth tapped the side of her forehead.

"Hmm, I wonder if Davey ever had a psych eval?" Stephen asked.

Beth shook her head. "I have no idea. That whole situation... It just never sat right with me."

Her words echoed the words of Trevan Collins, the man who'd given him the envelope with his brother's picture. *It never sat right with me...*

"I ran into an old friend of Greg's a few weeks ago who said something really similar. His name is Trevan Collins—"

Beth bobbed her head. "Yeah, I know Trevan."

"Have you guys ever talked about this?" Stephen wondered.

"No," Beth said. "Trevan and I aren't close. We lost touch after high school. But he does live in my neighborhood, a mile down the road from me."

"Oh!" Stephen exclaimed. "That's great news. I'm planning to go see him while I'm in town. Maybe I'll stop by and draw you another picture while I'm in the neighborhood?"

Beth laughed and Stephen watched transfixed as her smile lit up her face and her eyes seemed to sparkle. "I would like that."

Before Stephen could respond, his phone vibrated on the table and Alyah's name flashed on his screen. He could see the message without opening his phone.

Alyah: *Thanks for the laugh. Mak is one of a kind.*

"Well, thanks for your time, Beth," Stephen said abruptly, gently pulling his hand away. "Let's keep talking."

"Sounds good," Beth responded.

Stephen felt genuinely bad when he saw the emotion flash in her eyes. Disappointment. He knew one text from Alyah had been enough to make him pull back. Still, he wasn't looking for just anyone. He was looking for the *right* girl.

20

MAK

Mak watched as her dad double checked where the enclosed racing trailer hitch connected to his Ram 3500 truck. When they got on the road, it was early enough that the sun was barely peeking over the horizon. Mak knew she needed to say something before they got too far. It was important to Mak that she clear up any misperceptions she'd given her dad about this trip.

"Dad, I need to be honest. I'm excited about spending time with you. I'm also excited to run down the track again," Mak started.

"But...?" Larry knew her well.

"I also have an ulterior motive. I'm tracking a criminal in that area. There's no guarantee that he'll be there or anywhere in the vicinity. But if it comes down to it—"

"You have to do your job," Larry summed up.

Mak nodded, feeling relieved that he got it. Her dad always seemed to get her.

"Well, I'm not gonna lie. I hope it's not a friend of mine. We might compete but at the end of the day, we kick back with a cold draft of beer and shoot the shit. Can you give me some heads up before it all hits the fan so I can make myself scarce?" he asked, ruffling his hair before he put on a ball cap that said *Larry the Epic*.

"Of course. Only I don't think it will come to that. I'm sort of undercover. In an unofficial capacity. Just keeping an eye out on his whereabouts," Mak admitted.

"Well, thanks for the honesty, as always, darlin'. I guess I always knew your job might bring you to the track sometime," he winked. "Bunch of delinquents who race cars."

Mak chuckled. The car ride was a good time, as was every time Mak had with her dad. She was glad she wasn't here under false pretenses. Though she knew that her dad's love was unconditional and he wouldn't take it personally.

They arrived at the track and excitement immediately shot through Mak. She could see the rustic dirt parking lot, single paved race strip, and high judge's tower. Larry stopped at the entrance gate, and they waved him through. He drove to the spot they'd directed him to and parked his car.

Mak stepped outside and stretched up on her tiptoes with her arms up overhead. She took a minute to breathe in the air at the track. She could smell gasoline, oil, and nitrous fumes. That was all it took for her adrenaline to peak. Mak remembered this well. Her dad had her behind the wheel before she had her license. He had her under the hood of a car shortly after that. On her sixteenth birthday, he took her to race at the track for the first time.

Back then, Mak had her fair share of wins and losses. But she hadn't been down the racetrack since Harper had been born. It might have even been around the time she became a US Marshal. But Mak knew there were some things that were just like riding a bicycle. You never forgot. She couldn't wait to curl her fingers around the wheel of her dad's 1969 Camaro.

She could see the competing cars in various stages of setting up their booths. The car was only a part the display the racers put on for fans. It would be a matter of time before the gates would open and the fans would come in to buy t-shirts and hats and have pictures signed.

Mak knew that drill very well. Back in the day, Mak had her own eight by ten glossies of her posing in front of a car. She had her own small little group of fans who thought it was cool that a young teenage girl drove race cars down the track. Mak would be lying if she said she didn't miss this just a little.

Noticing her dad backing out of the trailer and into his space to display his car where his booth would be set up, Mak sprang into action. In a matter of fifteen minutes, their booth was set up and they had the Camaro for *Team Epic* out on display.

The 1969 Camaro was fully restored and rebuilt to run perfectly with a nice turbo under the hood. The classic car gleamed in the sunlight with black sheen and red stripes down the middle. She spied the matching helmet and knew that the roll cage inside the car would keep her safe if anything went wrong. Her dad was the epitome of safety. Not that he hadn't had a wreck or two in his career, but he'd always walked away from them just fine.

"Excuse me, Mr. Epic. You ready for your interview?" A man with a large mid-section approached wearing a backwards hat and a large, toothy grin.

"Hey!" Larry let a laugh erupt as he shook the man's hand. He turned to Mak. "Mak, this is the producer of *Street Southwest*, Bobby Markle. Bobby, this is my daughter, Mak."

Bobby turned to Mak, grin still in place, and reached for her hand.

Mak couldn't help but grin back as she shook Bobby's hand. "Nice to meet you."

"Pleasure's all mine. You race too?" Bobby asked.

"She'll take the car down the track today," Larry answered before Mak could.

"Splendid!" Bobby said. "Well, let's get you both on camera."

"Oh, I don't need to—" Mak started to protest.

"Get in here, Mak. Just a quick little bit, then you can take the car for a spin." Larry pulled out a few camping chairs and waved for Mak to sit.

Mak knew better than to argue with her dad. Reluctantly, she sat.

"Okay, this is live," Bobby told them. "We won't be able to edit anything out on this one. If you flub, keep going. You ready? In..." Bobby looked at a cameraman who had been standing by quietly.

The man nodded at Bobby.

Bobby put up three fingers, then two, then one. "We're here with Larry the Epic, one of our favorite racers at *Street Southwest*, and we have a special appearance by Larry's daughter, Mak..."

Bobby asked a quick series of questions that ended up sounding more like a natural conversation between Mak and Larry. It was over almost as fast as it had started.

"You ready to take the track?" Larry asked as a nice ending to the interview.

"Absolutely," Mak smiled for the camera, waiting to drop the grin until they called *cut*.

"Cut! Thanks, guys. That was great!" Bobby called out as they packed up and scouted other talent to talk to.

Then Mak spoke quietly to her dad. "You sure you're ready for me to take the car?" Mak's pulse was jumping.

"Yeah, we have a small window of time to make a practice run or two. Do you remember how to do this?" Larry asked.

"Yeah, I do!" Mak answered excitedly.

"Ok, I want you to get a feel for the car and the power that's underneath her hood before you really put the gas on. You can take a second lap and then apply the gas pedal."

Mak nodded and got serious as he handed her a helmet. She put it on. This car was her dad's baby and he'd talked about nothing else for the last seven years.

She would not be the one to let harm come to it.

Mak sat down behind the wheel and sunk into the comfortable driver's seat. She shouldn't have been so surprised that her dad valued luxury. He had sure earned it at this point in his career.

Checking the interior of the car to get her bearings, she found everything she needed relatively quickly. The gears, the brake shift, and the emergency brake. She could see the button for the parachute when she passed the red line so the car could start slowing down once the race finished. She wouldn't hit that this time around since it was just a practice run. But she certainly would when she was done with her race. She applied pressure to the gas pedal and found it a little jumpier than normal cars she was used to.

No problem, she thought as she adjusted her expectation for the car. She lined up with the other racers waiting for their turn to go down the track. Her pulse accelerated the closer she got to making her debut in this race. At this point she knew her competition would be checking her out. No problem there either because she would keep it chill for now and blow them away later.

Then, it was her turn. With no more time for feelings or emotions, Mak shut them down and focused on the track in front of her. She waited until she got the "all clear" and hit the gas. She immediately felt the back end of the car fishtail, so she let off the gas and quickly tapped the gas pedal under her toe. Her dad had taught that to her early on. She clearly recalled his words.

If the car goes squirrelly, let off the gas and feather it.

Feather it? Mak had laughed. *What does that mean?*

Let off the gas and tap the pedal six times until the backend of the car straightens up, her dad had explained with a grin. *Then push the gas pedal down as far as you can to make up for lost time.*

Just as she predicted, the car straightened out and she was able to give it a little more gas. She saw the red line and let off the gas. With a repetitive tap to the brakes, she rode it out into the open field behind the track. She'd checked her speed and knew she'd hit ninety miles per hour. Which wasn't that fast, considering she'd likely get up to 120 when she raced tonight. But it gave her a good feel for the car. Thanks to the time her dad had put into rebuilding the car and his expertise of racing over the years, his car was smooth and easy to drive.

Her dad met her at the end of her practice run. "How did that feel?" Larry was grinning as he yelled over the engine.

Mak brought the car to a stop and killed the engine. She took the helmet off.

"Amazing!" she exclaimed as she shook out her hair.

"You looked good out there!" Larry exclaimed. "Like an old pro. Like you've been racing your whole life."

"Well, driving gets in the blood," Mak responded with a smile.

Her smile faded when she caught sight of the big broad criminal walking her way. Not walking casually, Anthony Garrett looked like he was on a mission.

Mak forced her heart to calm down. She took guys like this down for breakfast. In a small but subtle move, she put her shoulders back and stood up taller. She looked him right in the eye as he approached.

Anthony Gerritt looked pissed off, as was evident from his reddened face. The scar that ran down his chin was also more pronounced in this visible display of anger.

Two men flanked each of Gerritt's sides. They were the same guys from the café the other day. One man was tall—maybe six foot six—and thin. The other man was well under six feet tall and dumpy.

Bodyguards, perhaps? Mak wondered as her gaze flicked to them and back to Gerrit.

"You not racing this race?" Anthony Gerritt sidestepped Mak and approached Larry directly.

Larry laughed and shrugged. "Oh, I'm racing, but I'm gonna let her go down the track once or twice. This is my daughter, Mak."

Anthony Gerritt's eyes swung to Mak with the same hatred she'd seen the other day. "We've met," he said irritably without offering her his hand.

Larry tilted his head to the side and looked between Mak and Gerritt.

Mak's pulse sped up. *Dad's a smart guy,* Mak reminded herself. *He knows what's happening. He's also smart enough to keep his mouth shut.*

"All my money's on you, not *her*," Anthony Gerritt pointed his finger first at Larry, then at Mak with venom in his tone. "Make sure you're behind the wheel and that you win tonight."

Larry saluted Gerritt with a smirk as Gerritt and his guards turned and walked away.

"I'm gonna ask you this question and I need a quick, simple answer." Eyes still on Gerritt's retreating back, Mak gritted her teeth. "Are you involved with Anthony Gerritt in some way?"

"I don't like that look in your eyes," Larry commented.

"Oh, that's not an answer, dad." Mak's heart sank as she knew before he said the word.

"Yes."

"How involved are you?" Mak hissed. She was still watching the man's retreating back followed by his men.

"He recently became a sponsor," Larry admitted, looking troubled.

"That's it? He sponsored your car?" Mak asked. Her mind raced. How much did Gerritt know about her? Did he know Larry the Epic was her dad before he sponsored his car? If so, how? A deep chill settled in her core as she considered the possibility. Maybe, in the same way he'd known who she was in the café, perhaps he'd done his homework and looked into her family as well.

Larry nodded and confirmed. "Just a sponsor."

Mak felt some relief. "How recently?"

"Yesterday," Larry stated. His eyes were full of doubt and confusion. "I just thought this business owner had heard the race was coming to town and he wanted to look like a big car guy. You know, I get one-off sponsors from time to time who are looking for out-of-the-box ways to market."

Mak grasped for the connection, trying to make the pieces fall together. Was Anthony Gerritt trying to fuse himself into her life through her dad by doing him this favor? By becoming important to her father, Gerritt could pretend to be a good guy while alienating Mak. What kind of narcissistic trip was this criminal on?

"Is he sponsoring you under Anthony Gerritt Associated?" Mak grabbed a fictitious name out of the air with sarcasm.

"Gerritt Construction and Property Management," Larry said.

Mak processed that for half a second. Mak spied Larry's crew walking their way. "Dad, we're gonna talk more about this, but we can't right now."

"What's going on, Mak?" Larry asked tersely. "Am I in some kind of trouble?"

"No," Mak answered. "He is. You need to stay as far away from him as possible."

"Helluva time to be telling me!" Larry stated.

The overhead announcer called racers up on deck. There were several rounds before racers qualified for finals later tonight. Each racer qualified based on the time it took for the car to go down the track. The first ten racers would go down in the next hour. Then they would take a break and the next ten would race. Larry was number five. Grimly, he put his helmet on and got in the car. Mak walked beside his car as he rolled into position.

Eyes up Mak, she gave herself a pep talk. *You can't afford to blink the whole day.*

21

WILTON

Stephen drove to the address he'd found for Trevan Collins. It was a basic duplex with tan siding and dark brown accents. He parked his car in the parking lot and turned it off. He could hear loud, pumping rock music coming from the duplex.

The door was slightly ajar. Stephen knocked, which only made it swing open wider. He put a hand on the doorknob to prevent it from moving and knocked again.

There was no response. He could smell cigarette smoke. Someone was definitely home.

"Hello?" Stephen called out. He wasn't here under the capacity of his badge, but Stephen still knew better than to walk into a home without being invited.

"Hey!" Stephen yelled louder and banged harder on the door.

Trevan Collins, with this dark, curly hair, his green eyes, and light skin peeked around the corner, his eyes wide in surprise. They widened further when they spotted Stephen.

"Oh, hell no!" Trevan shouted. He turned, bolted for the back door, opened it, and ran, not bothering to shut it behind him.

"What the—" Stephen instinctively ran after him. He ran through the front door, past the living room, and out the back door. He got outside in time to see Trevan effortlessly jump over a fence in his back yard.

Stephen sprinted to gain momentum and placed his foot on the back rail of the fence as a springboard to jump his body over the way he'd seen Trevan do it. But Stephen's foot caught on the fence panel, and he found himself pitching forward toward the ground.

He landed facedown, but not before tangling with a prickly bush. The air left his body in a whoosh, and he was left gasping for air. His face and his pride stung as he lay there. Stephen pushed up to his knees but before he could jump up, a foot connected with his stomach. Pain exploded in Stephen's abdomen. The motion rolled him to his side.

Stephen could see Trevan's foot pulling back to take another shot and he caught it before it could connect, twisting Trevan's ankle.

"Ahh!" Trevan shouted in pain. His body fell to the ground with a loud thump.

Before Stephen could get up, the man scrambled to his knees, crawled over, and tackled Stephen. Trevan had Stephen pinned. Stephen registered the large fist coming toward his face before he felt the pain of the hit explode into his eye socket.

"Stop!" Stephen managed to get out before Trevan punched him again. This time, Trevan's fist hit Stephen's chin, busting Stephen's lip open. Stephen could taste the metallic tang of blood. "I just want to talk!" Stephen grunted.

"When I gave you that envelope, I told you to forget I gave it to you," Trevan panted. "As in, don't find me!"

Stephen managed to roll his head to the side as Trevan swung another punch. Trevan's hand connected with the ground this time and he howled in pain. Stephen used this to his advantage to roll them both and fling Trevan off him at the same time.

Stephen jumped to his feet and put his hands up by his face in a defensive pose. Trevan stayed on the ground for a minute before he slowly got up. All fight seemed to have left him.

"You put me in danger coming here like this, Wilton." Trevan's eyes flashed angrily. His chest rose and fell as he tried to catch his breath. He had won the fight merely by throwing quick punches, but as Stephen regarded him, he realized Trevan was out of shape. Stephen bet Trevan had been slimmer in high school but now sported a paunchy stomach. On the ground, Trevan outmatched Stephen due to his body weight. But judging by Trevan's unwillingness to fight standing up, he knew Stephen would outmatch him in stamina.

"What the hell, Trevan?" Stephen said as he wiped the blood from his busted lip.

"I can't be seen talking to you, man. It's not safe. You need to get your ass out of here and out of town, if you know what's good for you," Trevan said. He reached over his fence and unlatched a door.

That would've made things easier, Stephen thought without humor.

Trevan walked through the gate and waited until Stephen came through to shut it.

"I'm gonna let you out through the front door and you better hope this doesn't blow back on me," Trevan said through gritted teeth. "It's one thing when I track you out of state. It's another for you to find me in my own home. There are eyes everywhere man. You need to go—"

"Wait," Stephen said, his voice pleading. "You know the truth. Whose eyes are watching? Just tell me what you know."

"All I know is that picture I gave you. I got nothing else, you hear me? Nothing!" Trevan pushed Stephen toward the front door.

"A name. Just give me a name. Who is the man in the photo?" Stephen asked.

"Get out!" Trevan's voice went up a notch as he repeated his command and pushed Stephen again. The front door was still cracked open. The music continued to play loudly in the house.

"I could subpoena you to testify to what you know," Stephen bluffed.

Trevan lowered his voice and got in Stephen's face. "I'd lie on the stand. Besides, I'm not the one you want. Subpoena Stinnert."

"Your picture proved he served time for something he didn't do," Stephen argued. He doubted Davey Stinnert, the boy who was convicted of and served time erroneously for Greg's murder, would talk to Stephen about the real murderer.

They were at the front door now. Trevan kept manhandling Stephen until Stephen had no choice but to step outside. The sunlight streamed into his eyes, which is why Stephen missed the way Trevan pulled his hand back and let his fist fly again. Stephen didn't have time to react.

Trevan's fist hit Stephen square on the jaw and the power of it sent Stephen flying. He connected with the asphalt as the front door slammed shut with anger and power.

Stephen gingerly lifted himself off the ground and limped pathetically to his SUV. He'd left his gun in the car. He hadn't been here on official officer business. Which was why he didn't have any desire to fight Trevan back.

Maybe I should have defended myself a little better, he thought as he worked his jaw back and forth.

Stephen got in the vehicle and locked the door in case Trevan decided to come at him with a baseball bat. He texted Beth.

Stephen: *I'm in the neighborhood. Thought I'd stop by...*

Beth: *Great. I'm at 1254. A mile down the road from Trevan on the opposite side.*

Stephen: *Do you have any ice?*

Beth: *???*

22

MAK

The engine rumbled so loudly her whole body vibrated from the sheer force but also from the excitement she felt. She wanted to walk away with a decent time. She could smell car fumes and felt the thrill infuse into her veins as she waited. She could see the black skid marks that lined the track and stretched for a mile.

Mak sat in the beautiful, sleek, black 1969 Camaro, with laser focus, revving her engine, waiting for the arm to drop. She envisioned the finish line. She looked up at the scoreboard that currently showed zero seconds on the pixelated billboard. She pictured the time she wanted. The car had run great all day. Not only for the runs Mak had made during practice, but also for her dad, who'd pulled into the number one spot. Larry the Epic was officially the fastest racer of the event.

She saw the arm lift and then drop. Mak pushed the pedal to the floorboard and felt the Camaro leap forward. Her adrenaline surged as the inertia of speed took over the car. She could see the scoreboard getting bigger in her sights. She was vaguely aware of the digital numbers ticking up but was going too fast to see what they said.

Then she realized she couldn't see the board because something was blocking her view. She couldn't see anything at the moment. Movement of red, orange, and yellow crawled and then leapt in her line of site. It took seconds to register what was obstructing her view. Smoke was rolling up from under the hood.

Fire! Mak's brain shouted. Fire was coming from the engine! She shut down her emotions and went into crisis survival mode. Mak immediately took her foot off the gas.

It's a straight shot, Mak, she told herself. *You have fifty feet to get stopped after you run out of asphalt.* Just to be sure, she gently tapped the brakes again. The heat from the flames lapping up on the window was starting to make her dizzy. Mak applied more pressure to the brakes. Then she did the one thing that probably saved her life. She pulled the chute.

Mak could feel the car slowing. She hit the brakes with more force. She applied them harder as the car slowed down, and felt the vehicle come to a stop. She breathed a sigh of relief. The deeper she breathed, the more lightheaded she felt. She was losing oxygen fast. She could feel sweat dripping from inside her helmet. It was then that she realized she hadn't put her helmet visor down, which is why she was inhaling so much smoke into her lungs. At least with the visor down, she might have been protected a little while longer from the smoke that was now filling the car.

Hand on the door handle to open it, Mak turned her head, intending to dive out of the car. Just as she clicked the door open, the front windshield cracked. The force of the windshield broke inward and shards of glass blew toward Mak. One tiny piece caught Mak's forehead under her helmet. Mak threw herself out of the car and landed on the grass.

Mak ripped off her helmet and gasped for air, aware of the car on fire just a few feet from her. Warm, viscous fluid flowed down her face. Mak knew if she opened her eye, blood would seep in. She felt dizzy, then she felt nauseated. She thought she saw people running toward her out of her peripheral. Before Mak had time to panic or throw up, she passed out.

23

WILTON

Stephen found Beth's house and knocked on her door. Beth opened the door with a reserved smile on her face until she saw Stephen.

She gasped and covered her mouth. "Oh no! Your beautiful face!"

Stephen grimaced when he tried to react to her words, which only resulted in more pain from his busted lip. He knew the sight he made. He'd checked out his wounds in his rearview mirror, trying to decide if he should keep right on driving back home. He saw the scrapes from the fall into the brush on the left side of his face. The purple bruise over his eye was swelling and making it hard to keep his eye open. There was another bruise on his jaw and under his eye, and he had a busted, bleeding lip. He decided he needed an ice pack and some ibuprofen before he drove back home.

He should have been embarrassed to see Beth when he was in this condition. He was a US Marshal for heaven's sake. But he had no indication that Trevan Collins was going to run and then jump Stephen.

Beth pulled him into her duplex. She gently pushed him to

sit on her oversized, very comfortable couch. "Stay right there," she instructed. "I'll get you some ice."

"Do you have any ibuprofen?" he asked, watching her wander out of the room with his one good eye.

"Of course," Beth called back from another room, her voice sounding compassionate.

Beth returned juggling ibuprofen, a water bottle, and an ice pack. Stephen swallowed the pills and put the ice pack over his face.

It was then that Stephen really looked at Beth. Her black hair was pulled back into a ponytail. She was wearing black leggings and a long t-shirt that did nothing to hide the curves of her body. Her feet were bare. It felt oddly intimate for someone he'd just re-met. But then, he had surprised her in the middle of her day. He'd been accused of falling too hard for a woman, then planning a wedding in his mind without knowing how to be vulnerable or open enough to get her down the aisle.

"I sure know how to sweep a girl off her feet, huh?" he joked.

Beth smiled with concern in her eyes. "Stephen, what happened?"

"It's nothing—"

"Stephen," Beth gave him a stern look. "You can't come over here looking like this with no explanation."

Stephen nodded. "Okay," he started but stopped again. Not only did he not want to answer her, Stephen had no idea where to start. He took a deep breath.

"Trevan Collins found me a few months ago and handed me a photo in a manila envelope," Stephen began. He winced, the pain in his lip intensifying as he talked.

"Oh no! Did that hurt?" Beth sat next to him and gently took the ice pack from Stephen's eye and put it on his lip.

Stephen nodded.

"What was the picture of?" Beth asked.

Stephen took the ice pack off his face. "It was a picture of Greg. Minutes before he was killed."

Beth gasped. Her hand came up to her mouth.

"I think they put the wrong guy in prison," Stephen admitted.

"Oh no!" Beth whispered, her blue eyes big in horror. "Are you okay?"

He shrugged. "Yes, but I don't know who the man is, so I went to see Trevan."

"And you got in an accident on the way there?" Beth looked so genuinely confused, Stephen smiled until his lip hurt again.

"No. Let's just say Trevan didn't want to talk," Stephen admitted. He felt the back of his neck turn red.

"Trevan did that to you?" Beth looked surprised.

"Mostly," Stephen said, not willing to admit he'd jumped a fence and face planted into a bush.

"You poor thing! I can only imagine what you're going through. On top of that, Trevan has the nerve to fight you?" Beth stood up angrily. "I'm going to talk to him."

"What?" Stephen barked. "Beth, sit down. Trevan isn't a safe person. Trust me, if he could do this to me when I just wanted to talk, I don't want to think about what he'd do if you actually provoked him."

"It's not okay, Stephen. He assaulted an officer!" Beth was looking around the room. "Where are my shoes?"

"Beth, sit back down. I wasn't there in an official officer capacity. This is personal. I needed information. I approached Trevan the wrong way. I need you to let this go. For your own safety. Trevan might be unstable and he's clearly hiding something." Stephen reached out for her hand when she sat back down.

"I just wanted to help," Beth said, looking dejected.

"I know," Stephen attempted another smile. "You're very sweet.

Unexpected tears sprang to her eyes. "They won't let me help find my sister either."

"Come here," Stephen said with a sigh, his eyes softening and his focus switching to her.

Beth scooted over to Stephen, and he put an arm around her shoulder and hugged her into him. She laid her head on his shoulder. For a few comfortable minutes, they sat in silence.

"I'm sorry about Greg," Beth whispered. "I hope you find the man in the picture."

"Me too," Stephen said. "And I'm sorry about Lacy. I'll do what I can to help."

"Thank you, Stephen. I believe you will. I'm also sorry about your face," Beth said as she turned and put a soft hand against his jaw. She pulled her knees under her and gently kissed the scratches on Stephen's face.

"Thanks," Stephen said. He wasn't sure how he felt about this new experience with vulnerability, but it sure felt nice to have someone who cared. Even if just for this moment.

"Should we watch a movie?" Beth asked suddenly.

"A movie?" Stephen asked. Now it was his turn to feel confused.

"Yes, Stephen. When is the last time you were able to relax? I know you'll be back on a case—maybe even my sister's case—Monday. Today, why don't you just relax and enjoy the weekend?"

Relaxing and watching a movie was so foreign to Stephen. He agreed and snuggled closer to Beth. Shortly after the movie started, Stephen fell asleep, snoring deeply. He couldn't remember the last time he'd slept so soundly.

24

MAK

Mak could feel her body moving. Someone was dragging her across the soft earth. The events of the car fire came back to her then. She could hear the ambulance siren and she jerked awake.

"I'm fine," she shouted, energy flooding her veins. "I can walk."

"No, you can't." It was her dad's voice, but he sounded so far away.

He is going to be so mad about the car, Mak thought. She felt herself being hoisted up and then laid flat onto a stretcher. She could hear a crowd of people clapping as they loaded her into an ambulance.

Is that for me? she wondered. She attempted to open her eyes as an EMT put oxygen over her nose. Viscous liquid blurred her vision. That's when she remembered. She'd cut her face on flying windshield glass.

"Take a deep breath for me," a woman said. "Can you hold this on her face?" A female EMT was talking to someone else Mak couldn't immediately see.

Mak breathed in and out a few times. She still felt lightheaded.

"Okay, I'm Carol and this is Jim. I'm going to clean up your cut. Then we'll determine if it needs stitches."

"No stitches," Mak said immediately. She felt no pain. She wondered if that meant she was in shock. "Where's the cut?"

"It's over your right eyebrow." The EMT swiped the side of Mak's face and dabbed something cold over Mak's forehead.

Mak winced and sucked in air. "That hurt."

"I know. I'm sorry. I just needed to clean it and see if we can get the bleeding to stop." To her protégé, Carol gave a command. "Can you hold this? I need to check the rest of her."

After a moment, Carol said, "Good, now apply pressure," Carol instructed Jim. To Mak, Carol said, "Can you tell me if anything hurts?"

"Okay," Mak agreed.

She felt the EMT poking around on her. "If anything feels sharp or sore, let me know."

Mak felt the oxygen drop from her face. She filled her lungs with natural air.

"Did anything hurt when you took that breath?" Carol asked.

"No," Mak told her.

"Good," Carol pressed lightly under Mak's ribs. "Breathe in for me again."

Mak obeyed.

"Any pain?" Carol checked.

"No."

"Good," Carol repeated the process three more times and listened to Mak's lungs. "Everything seems okay, but you'll need to get a checkup by your regular doctor when offices open up," Carol told her.

"Okay," Mak agreed easily, but knew she wouldn't. "How's the cut?"

"Let me see it," Carol instructed Jim.

Jim pulled the ice away.

"Hmm, it's still bleeding. You might need a stitch or two," Carol said, prodding it gently with gloved fingers.

"No stitches," Mak said again.

"Okay, I can put a few butterfly bandages on it, but blood dripping into your eyes is going to make your life difficult," Carol's voice was laced with sarcasm.

"Let's try bandages," Mak requested.

"Okay, take a deep breath in. This will pinch a little," Carol warned.

Mak sucked in air. It did hurt but only for a minute. Carol repeated her action two more times.

"Okay," Carol announced. "You are good to go."

"Thank you, Carol," Mak said, feeling relieved but still a little shaken. "Thanks, Jim."

"It's what we do," Carol dismissed Mak's gratitude. "Keep the ice pack. Fifteen minutes on and thirty minutes off."

"Be careful out there," Jim said with a smile.

Mak helped herself out of the back of the ambulance. She saw her dad's car being towed down the track side road.

Her dad stalked over to Mak with a thunderous look on his face. Mak felt like she was thirteen years old and about to hear it from her father who was one of her favorite humans, runner up only to John and Harper.

They met in the middle of a grassy hill.

"Are you okay?" Larry asked Mak.

Mak nodded because she didn't want to admit how shaken up she felt.

"Good. We're loading up the car and getting out of here."

"But the awards—"

"We're leaving. Awards aren't important today," Larry snapped.

Mak followed her dad, questions brewing that would need to be answered later. Her dad wouldn't be accepting his first-place trophy on a nationally-syndicated show, and she had a feeling it was all her fault.

25

WILTON

"Stephen? Wake up."

Stephen felt his body moving and wondered if he was on a boat floating out to sea. He moved back and forth as an urgent voice dragged him out of his slumber.

"What?" he was sleepy and disoriented. "What time is it?" He bolted up and looked around with no recollection of where he was. A soft sun was rising in the sky. He looked around the room until his gaze fell on Beth, the culprit of his sleep interruption.

"Sorry to wake you," she whispered softly.

Stephen could see she'd been crying. "Beth? What's happened?"

"Brighton Police Department called. They dragged the lake where Lacy's car was found. They've been looking for the past thirty-six hours and there's no sign of her. They're gonna stop looking there."

"That's not necessarily bad news, Beth." Stephen knew he needed to be careful and not paint a sense of false hope. "It just means she didn't drown."

"Yeah…" Beth nodded and wiped the tears from her face. "This is just so hard, ya know? The not knowing."

"Yes, I know," Stephen agreed.

"I can't sleep," she admitted. "I'm so jealous of you. You fell right to sleep last night—"

"Last night?" Stephen's eyes widened in surprise. "I slept all night? Why didn't you wake me?"

"You looked so peaceful, and I thought sleep would be the best way to help you heal. Speaking of which," Beth leaned forward and peered at Stephen's face. She tsked her tongue. "You look a little worse today, Stephen."

"Not even gonna sugar coat it are you?" Stephen smirked, then flinched. "Ow…" He grimaced. "Beth, I have a stop to make before I head back home. I really need to get going," Stephen said.

"I understand," Beth looked disappointed. "Will you let me know if you find anything out about Lacy?"

"Of course," Stephen agreed. He stood when she did and leaned down to kiss her cheek. He smiled at her unexpected sweetness and hospitality. Then he took a step back, knowing this would not be the last time he'd see her.

Stephen waved to Beth who was standing on the doorstep, hair looking slightly unkempt and little makeup on. She made an adorable picture. It was hard for him to say *goodbye*, but he had found Davey Stinnert's address before he'd left. He needed to find the man who'd served time unjustly for his brother's murder. Which meant if Davey took the fall, he likely knew who he'd taken the fall for.

Stephen drove his Tahoe until he was heading out of town. The area became more rural with less houses than land. That meant one of two things. One, isolation for a man who'd served a prison sentence, which was probably smart. Two, a visitor would have a hard time getting help if things went wrong out here.

Unbidden, Stephen's mind returned to Trevan's unexpected attack. He pulled out his phone and called his former lieutenant.

Higgins answered the phone with a gravelly voice. "Wilton? Do you know what time it is?"

Stephen checked the time. "Seven fifteen on a Sunday. Sorry, I didn't know you actually slept in. Aren't you on call?"

Higgins chuckled. "Not this weekend. But it's okay. What's going on?"

"I'm on my way out to see Davey Stinnert. He's pretty far out here. I just thought I'd give someone a heads up. In case it doesn't go well," Stephen admitted.

"What the—Wilton! What are you thinking?" Higgins' voice sounded alert again. "When you said you planned to see him this weekend, I didn't know you were going alone. Why don't you stop right where you are and let me go with you. You have no idea what to expect."

"I'll be okay," Stephen stated. "I'm armed and I'm on guard. Trevan Collins jumped me yesterday. I had my guard down. I won't do that again."

"I don't miss trying to manage you, son," Higgins grumbled. "Why don't you send me the address and if you don't call me in an hour, I'll come out there."

"Deal," Stephen said. He hung up and texted the address to Higgins. Another mile up the road and the GPS announced, *You have arrived.*

A small trailer that looked like it was in need of some repair loomed ahead. It sat on acres of land. In fact, Stephen couldn't see another home around. Acting more confident than he was feeling, he got out of the car and walked up to the door. He knocked loudly.

He'd hoped getting there so early would catch Davey off guard and he'd either still be in bed or barely awake. There was no car in the driveway. Still, Stephen knocked longer and harder.

Either Davey Stinnert wasn't home, or he wasn't coming to the door. It was time for Stephen to admit defeat. He was at a complete dead end. He was nowhere closer to getting answers about his brother. He slowly got back in his car. He texted Higgins.

Stephen: *He wasn't home. I'm gonna hit the road and head home.*

Higgins: *Look me up the next time you're in town.*

As he drove, Stephen realized maybe he couldn't solve his brother's mystery, but he could help Beth by solving her sister's disappearance. He had a few hours to switch his mindset back to the missing Lacy Donovan case.

26

LACY

Lacy had done her homework. In the underground cave where she currently lived with the other women, they had nothing but time to talk. There didn't appear to be any listening devices. The first time they spoke, Lacy whispered, knowing listening devices were always a possibility. When nothing happened, she decided there weren't any.

There were three men. The girls had given them nicknames. *Tall Beanpole* was easily six foot five. He was rail thin which made him look like he could fall over on his feet.

"Don't underestimate him though," Lauren shivered. "He's freakishly strong and fast."

"You know this from experience?" Lacy asked, feeling a trickle of fear crawl down her spine.

"Yes," Lauren's eyes welled up with tears. She indicated a scar on the side of her face. "He was angry that he had to *put me in line*. Said I was devalued now."

Lacy shuddered.

Another of the three men, *Average Joe*, they told her, was most likely five foot nine inches tall with a tubby belly and a strong grip. "Don't underestimate him, either. He looks out of shape but he's scrappy. Once he has you in his grip, he won't let you go. If he catches you after you get away from him, he'll make you regret it."

"Got it," Lacy nodded with a deep breath in. "The third?"

Temper Titan, they'd dubbed him, was the boss. He was tall and broad. A bit of a stomach but mostly a mass of muscle and bulk. He had a scar on the side of his face. It seemed to make a C down to his chin. Lacy was sure that was who had carried her into the underground earth prison.

"Don't look him in the eyes. His eyes are dead. Soulless, beady eyes that pierce through you if you attempt to make eye contact. He straight sold his soul to the devil and is working directly for him."

"Yikes," Lacy muttered. In all three cases, she felt like her best shot at escape would be speed. She needed to slip out of their grasp and run without looking back. They would expect her to be weak after all the time underground. But she would surprise them all.

"Okay, now I need you to tell me what happens when they take you out," Lacy had saved this question for last, not sure if she was brave enough to hear the answer. She was sure she wouldn't be able to handle knowing the torture these girls had likely been through.

"After a week, sometimes two, of your capture, they will take you out and walk you blindfolded into a house. It's cold in there —it feels like you're in a freezer. Not sure why they keep it so frigid. They'll take you down to a basement. Then they'll put you in the golden cage—"

"Wait, like an actual cage?" Lacy interrupted.

"Yes, an actual cage, painted gold. Then they—" Isa trembled.

"Go on," Lacy encouraged her. "I can handle it."

"They'll put you in the shower and clean you up. Then they'll take photographs of you. They'll tell you to pose sexily and if you don't, they'll beat you in places that won't be photographed. Trust me, it's not worth it to fight. Then they'll drop you back in the crate when it's all over."

Lacy had scratched a mark in the wall each day she'd been there. She'd been gone four days. In three days, she would be taken to be photographed. She wasn't stupid. She knew what they were doing. She'd heard about the illicit black market. Girls were being trafficked via the dark web. Once the right bidder chose a girl, the girl would be shipped off to their new owner.

Lacy knew what to do when it was time for her photoshoot. She was developing a plan in her head. Fight. Get away or die trying. She knew if she got shipped away, she would never be found again.

"One more question. How many women were here when each of you got here?" Lacy asked.

"There were four when I got here. I've been here the longest. I've seen other women come and go," Emma said as she brushed her stringy, brownish-blond hair out of her eyes. She was so frail from lack of eating, her bones showed through her skin.

Lacy averted her eyes.

"There were two others when I came to live here," Isa said. Lacy noted her use of words *live here*. She was paler than her blond coloring and light skin had naturally been. Her blue eyes seemed to protrude from her face. Her cheek bones were rigid.

"I got here after Emma did," Lauren stated. It looked like it took all her energy just to say the words. She was a dishwater blond with a complexion that would have been darker had she not been living underground. She also had sunken features and bones showing through her skin.

This will not be me, Lacy resolved. *I will not give up hope or resign myself to eventual death at the hands of predators.*

"I'm going to get us out of here. If it's the last thing I do."

27

MAK

She'd been right. Her dad was mad. But not about the car. He had his own theories that involved Anthony Gerritt rigging his car with an explosive. For once, Mak took the high road.

"Dad, when could he have done that? One or both of us were with the car all day," Mak said. They were, weren't they? Mak tried to move backward through the whole event like Wilton would have. He was the details guy. If Mak could tap into that ability, she'd be a much better marshal.

"Didn't you see the look in his eye when he approached you?" Larry seethed.

"Yeah, I had a run-in with him this week. We aren't exactly friends," Mak's snarked sarcastically.

"He wants to kill you, Mak," Larry said with conviction.

Mak's blood ran cold for a second. Then she recovered. "I'm sure a lot of criminals want to kill me, dad."

Her dad grunted but continued driving. "I don't like it. I'm kicking him off my sponsorship the minute I get home."

"Dad, wait," Mak tried to think it through. But her head was really throbbing and the cut above her eyebrow ached. "I've already made an enemy out of this guy simply because I'm in law enforcement. I don't want to provoke him further. Why don't you just let it be for now? I'll think it through and talk it over with my team. I can let you know the best course of action. Above all, I need to keep you safe."

Larry raised his voice. "He blew up my car. With you inside it. What if—" his voice broke.

"Dad, I'm fine," Mak patted his arm while he drove.

"You got damn lucky, kiddo. I don't know what I'd do if I lost you. I'd probably be in jail right now…"

"Well, you didn't. I'm fine and you can't prove he had anything to do with it," Mak said firmly.

"Do you know how much time, effort, and money has gone into that car?" Larry hit the steering wheel now. "He needs to pay for that."

"You know what, dad? If I can somehow prove that he had a hand in that, he will pay. If I can't, well, you know the risks involved in racing. We all do. You'll just have to start over."

Larry was silent and brooding the rest of the way home.

Mak had succeeded in locking down her emotions with her dad, but one look at John when she walked through the door and she felt her emotions rise. When she saw the dark storm cloud in John's eyes as he viewed her cut, Mak lost it. Thankfully, Harper was in bed when she got home. John led her to the couch as she explained the fire.

"I didn't know where the glass had cut me. I just saw blood and felt the gush of it pouring down my face," Mak wiped the tears that rushed out in a torrent. "I felt this blinding pain and I wondered if it had cut my eye."

"Baby!" John breathed as he pulled her head into his broad, muscular chest. "Are you okay?"

"Just shaken," Mak admitted. She didn't admit to John that though she'd played it chill with her dad, she'd agreed that

Anthony Gerritt might have tampered with the car after her dad's race. If that was the case, Larry was right. Gerritt had tried to kill her. The possibility left her cold. The fact that he'd come so close to succeeding was terrifying. That, she could not tell John.

28

WILTON

Mak and Stephen arrived in the conference room at the exact same time bright and early Monday morning. They walked in to find Deputy Sikes already sitting at the table. Upon sight of the two marshals, Sikes' mouth dropped open.

Stephen sat down next to Mak and both of them faced their superior officer like they had been called to the principal's office for fighting. Both of them certainly looking the part.

Sikes was speechless for half a second as he stared. "What the heck happened to you guys?" he finally sputtered.

Stephen and Mak looked at each other. Really looked. The swelling in Stephen's face had gone down. But he still sported a black eye, a bruised jaw, and a scratched-up cheek. Mak looked considerably less beat up, but the three butterfly bandages barely concealed a nasty gash over her eyebrow.

Neither of them spoke.

"Did you do this to each other?" Sikes pointed back and forth between them. Then he crossed his hands over his chest.

They shook their heads.

"Well, do we want to talk about it?" Sikes' tone was impatient.

"No," Stephen said.

"Yes," Mak said at the exact same time.

"Well, thank God someone is willing to talk about this weekend," Sikes nodded to Mak and sent Stephen a look of annoyance.

Mak cleared her voice. "As you know, sir, I hit the racetrack with my dad this weekend—"

"You did what?" Stephen interrupted. His mouth gaped open.

"My dad surprised me with a visit, and it turned out he had a televised race at a track very close to where our hometown villain is hanging out. So, I joined my dad for a trip to the racetrack."

"Did you race?" Stephen asked, clearly trying to wrap his brain around Mak's story.

"Yes, but that's beside the point," Mak answered quickly. "I ran it by Sikes here to let him know I would keep an eye out for Anthony Gerritt while I was there. Well, Gerritt walked right up to my father's car the minute we pulled in. He was not happy to see me, I can tell you that. He had sponsored my dad's race car the day before the race. Which I do not think was a coincidence. When he thought I'd be racing, he threw a fit in front of my dad. Gerritt said his money was on my dad, not on me, and that my dad had better win."

"Did he?" Stephen asked.

"Yes."

"How did you do?" Sikes asked.

"I ran the car down the track after my dad's race to walk away with a final race time. After they tally up the points in each bracket and declare a winner, they allow racers who want to determine their finishing time to go down the track one more time. So, I'd just started down the track when my car caught on fire—"

"It what!" Sikes leaned forward. His eyes were huge.

Stephen stared at Mak in horror.

"Caught on fire with me in it. Anyway, I kept my calm and went through all the motions of slowing down the car. When it rolled to a stop, I opened the door just as the windshield exploded. I'd forgotten to put my visor down and a piece of glass cut my eyebrow." Mak pointed to her butterfly bandages.

"Is that true?" Stephen demanded.

"Yes, Stephen. I couldn't make that up if I tried. I got pretty lucky too. It was only a small piece and an inch lower, and it would've cut my eye." Mak didn't admit that had been her worst fear.

Sikes' mouth was hanging open. "Honest to God, Mak, when you called me and told me your plan, I didn't think Anthony Gerritt would even be at the track. What do you think it means that Gerritt sponsored your dad's car when he did?"

"I think he's messing with me. He knows exactly who I am and he's trying to send me a message. He can get to me, and he can get to my family. That, or he's a raging narcissist who is trying to make himself important and wedge himself between me and my dad." Mak's brown eyes flashed with anger.

"And the fire in the engine?" Stephen asked. "Do you think he—"

"My dad is livid mad. He believes it was Gerritt. Dad thinks his car was in mint condition before I ran it down the track and believes there was no way a fire could've started spontaneously. But I feel like we were around the car the whole day. There's no way Gerritt could've gotten into the engine without us knowing," Mak answered the question Stephen was going to ask.

"You really knew about this?" Stephen asked Sikes.

Sikes nodded and put his hands up. "Again, I thought there was no way Gerritt would show up. The guy's hiding in plain sight."

"Oh, and get this, he sponsored my dad under a company

named Gerritt Construction and Property Management. He's masquerading as a real businessman now," Mak snorted.

"That's good." Sikes snapped his fingers and cast his MacBook to the big screen. He typed in *Gerritt Construction and Property Management* and grinned when a website pulled up. "This, we can work with. We can investigate his business to see if there's anything shady going on there."

"At what point do we have enough to bring him in? Do you still want us to watch him?" Mak wondered.

"Absolutely. This is a great start. But we need hard evidence. This guy's notorious for walking away from crimes we all know he committed. If we can get a concrete piece of evidence to pull him off the street, we should be able to hold him. Then we can get a warrant to further investigate his business and personal property to see what else we can turn over. Good job discovering the name of his business, Mak." Sikes nodded.

"Yeah," Stephen smarted sarcastically with a look in Sikes' direction, then to Mak. "Good job not dying in a car this weekend."

"Somebody's gotta do it. Happy to take one for the team. Now, do you want to talk about your weekend?" Mak pointed to Stephen's face.

"No!" Stephen snapped.

Mak shrugged. "I'll get it out of you eventually."

Stephen didn't bother to argue. But he felt his brother was a private matter and he didn't need Mak, or anyone else at his office, mucking around in it.

"In the meantime," Stephen turned to Sikes. "What's our next move?"

"The next move for you and Mak, the dream team?" Sikes asked.

"Hard *no* on that nickname," Mak mumbled.

"You're going back in. Apparently, Gerritt is too arrogant to hide, even with you showing up in town," Sikes said. "But I need you close in case we get wind of illegal activity. Why don't you make friends with the local authorities and see if you can work out a collaboration."

"With all due respect, sir," Stephen started. "Our collaboration in New York had unwanted side effects—"

"Yeah, for the former Chief of the MCPD," Mak snorted.

"Not every agency is dirty, Wilton," Sikes responded. "You'd do well to keep an open mind. It's not like you see on the movies. Most police departments welcome a little backup. Especially these days with the workforce being what it is."

"Okay, friends it is," Stephen agreed. He looked at Mak. "Maybe you could try not to provoke the perp this time?"

Mak rolled her eyes. "Gee, I'll try really hard to ignore Gerritt when he approaches me in public this time around."

Stephen gave her a hard look. Then he remembered his promise to look into Lacy Donovan's disappearance. Going back put him in a perfect position to check in on that investigation. There would be no easy way to do so without letting Mak in on the case. There would be plenty of time for catch up on their nice, long ride back to the country.

29

MAK

It was fifteen minutes before Mak decided to break the silence. If there was one thing Wilton was better at than Mak, it was staying silent.

"You gonna talk about what happened this weekend?" Mak asked, one hand on the wheel and the other hand making a circle around her face.

Wilton stared out the window for a minute. "What I can tell you about this weekend is that I went back to Arkansas. Remember that friend of mine who called about her missing little sister?"

"Lacy... I can't remember her last name." Mak tried but came up blank.

"Donovan. Well, I went back home to talk to her sister, Beth, and my old boss. I learned that Lacy's car was fished out of a lake ten miles from where we're going, and it falls under the jurisdiction of the very police department Sikes asked us to make friends with."

"That doesn't sound promising. I'm sorry to hear that. But you know missing persons isn't our jurisdiction," Mak reminded him quietly. But saying the words out loud took her back to when she had said that to Wilton on their first case together, a kidnapping case they'd taken in New York not long ago. Wilton's instincts had told him that while the rescue had been a success, the case wasn't over. Mak had insisted the job was done and they needed to move on. She had been wrong. She still felt some guilt about that and how she'd treated him when Sikes had to send them back to New York to tie up the loose ends.

"True, it doesn't sound good," Wilton agreed easily. "I just promised Beth I'd connect with the police force and keep her posted if anything came up about Lacy. Since we're connecting with them to take down Anthony Gerritt, I thought I'd inquire about Lacy."

"I see," Mak was quiet for half a second. "I don't have a problem with that."

"You don't?" Wilton asked, sounding surprised.

"No, well, I would normally tell you it's not our case and therefore not our issue, but the last time I told you that, if you would have listened to me, our kidnapped victim might have ended up—"

"Yeah, I know," Wilton said. He looked deep in thought. Pensive, even. "You've been honest with me—like when you admitted you tend to rush in—and I need to be honest with you. There's something I tend to do in this job as well."

"What's that?" Mak asked.

"I've been known to get personally involved in cases. My old boss, who had become like a mentor to me, had no choice but to let me go in the end because I kept investigating cases that involved the people I cared about. On my last one as a detective, he ordered me off a case, but I refused to stop investigating."

"What was the case?" Mak asked.

"It was when my daughter went missing," Wilton answered.

"Wow. Appreciate the honesty, Wilton, but I gotta say, if Harper went missing, no one could stop me from trying to find her either. He fired you over that?" She shook her head, feeling surprised.

"Yes, but he called it 'promoting me to my next opportunity,'" Wilton threw up air quotes. "He connected me with a recruitment marshal and then he gave me a glowing letter of recommendation."

Mak snorted. "Promoted you to your next opportunity?"

Wilton nodded and smiled. "Yeah. It sort of took out the sting."

"Is that the same lieutenant you went back home to see?" she asked.

"Yes," Wilton admitted.

"And did you guys get in a bar fight while you were gone?" Mak gave him a sly look.

"No," Wilton's neck turned red.

Mak noticed his tell-tale sign of agitation and decided not to push him further. "Fine, just tell me one thing. Are you telling me all this because Beth is another *Love 'Em and Leave 'Em, Wilton* victim?"

Wilton let out a sound that was close to resembling a bear growl. "Is that nickname *ever* going to die?"

"It's too soon to tell." Mak grinned.

"No. Beth and I aren't involved," Wilton admitted.

"What, did she gain fifty pounds and grow a mustache since high school?" Mak teased.

"No. If you must know, she's beautiful. We had a great connection—"

"But?" Mak asked.

"She's not Alyah," Wilton admitted. "Wow, I cannot believe I just said that out loud."

"Yeah, I gotta say, you are being very transparent in this car ride right now, Wilton," Mak grinned at him. Though she knew he was still holding back and there was something he wasn't admitting, she chose not to push it. "When's the last time you talked to her—Alyah?"

Wilton shook his head. "Other than an occasional text response to long rambling voice mail messages I leave her, I haven't."

"That's rough," Mak said sympathetically.

"Yeah," Wilton agreed. "Someday, I'll meet the right girl."

"Well, maybe Alyah's not the wrong girl exactly, she's just in the wrong location," Mak tried to cheer him up.

"Maybe. Maybe we'll get a case in DC," Wilton said with hope on his face.

"I see what you mean about how you mix personal with professional," Mak laughed.

"Back atcha," Wilton said. "Team Epic racer."

"How did you know that?" Mak asked.

"YouTube, Mak. Your car fire with a back story on your teenage racing days wasn't too hard to find."

Now it was Mak's turn to grumble. "Great. Just great."

"The camera loves you. No wonder Anthony Gerritt can't stay away," Wilton teased.

"Seriously, though…" Mak dropped her voice though there was no one else in the vehicle. "I think I get how you feel about tracking a criminal in your daughter's back yard. When I found out Gerritt knew me and could get to my father so easily? Everything about this became personal. We have to take him down, Wilton. I can't risk my family."

Wilton nodded. "I could not agree with you more."

30

WILTON

The Brighton Police Department was a tiny, two-office hole in the wall with a conference room and a two-person jail cell. If that wasn't an indication that crime didn't happen much in these parts, Stephen didn't know what was.

Mak and Stephen walked through the door and found themselves in front of a heavy-set woman wearing a police uniform. Her dark brown hair was pulled tightly into a bun at the back of her head.

She extended her hand. "Hi, I'm Sergeant Huntington. Was just heading out to make the rounds. What can I do for you?"

Mak and Stephen flipped their badges and explained they were with the US Marshal's office.

"Is there somewhere we could talk?" Stephen asked.

"Absolutely," Sergeant Huntington said. "Let me call in my deputy. Sturgis?" She turned to look around the room.

There was no movement in the room. Sergeant Huntington shrugged and motioned for them to follow her to her office.

"It's lunchtime around here and my receptionist is gone. Sturgis must have crept out for lunch too. Well, what can I do for you all?" Sergeant Huntington sat down hard at her desk.

Mak and Stephen followed her lead and sat in the chairs across from her.

"We're here to watch a well-known criminal with hopes of arresting him. We'll be looking for evidence to put him away. He went underground for close to eight years and has resurfaced in this area," Stephen began.

"Let me guess," Sergeant Huntington leaned back in her chair. "Anthony Gerritt? I'm the one who alerted your boss."

"Okay, so you know a woman he was dating recently went missing—from Oklahoma City? Shortly after that, Anthony Gerritt, who has been arrested for the disappearances of other women in his life, fled the area. We suspect his involvement in all of the vanishings, but he's always gotten out of the charges," Mak added.

"I did not know. I just responded to the APB. So you think Gerritt has come to hide out in our little quiet town?" Sergeant Huntington asked with one eyebrow raised skeptically.

"Yes," Stephen placed a file on Sergeant Huntington's desk in front of her. "He owns a company called—"

"Gerritt Construction and Property Management," Sergeant Huntington finished with a shake of her head as she opened the file and began to scan the information. "Yep, I know him and the company. Shame too. He popped that business up fast and brought quite a few jobs to the area. But I've been keeping an eye on Gerritt since he arrived. The minute I saw the APB though, I notified your boss. While Gerritt's business has been in the area for a while, he wasn't physically here in town until after the company was up and operating. He arrived here around three months ago."

Stephen shared a look with Mak. So, it was true. Anthony Gerritt *was* trying to reinvent himself as a legitimate businessman and bring in people who would be loyal to him.

"Why were you keeping an eye on him?" Mak asked.

Huntington shrugged. "I always watch when outsiders come

to the area. We don't have a lot to offer big, fancy corporations. Call me suspicious or curious but I always wonder if they have ulterior motives."

So, this sergeant had also suspected that Gerritt was up to no good.

"For now, we're just letting you know our end goal. Are you available if we should need backup?" Mak asked.

Sergeant Huntington nodded. "Yep. Whatever you need. We're understaffed but we have a few holding cells here if it comes to that. This is a quiet little town. Not much happens. We'll be available to help."

"Good deal!" Mak exclaimed.

Stephen nodded. "There's one other thing I'd like to collaborate on, if you're willing."

"Whatcha got? Wilton, was it?" Huntington asked.

"Yes. My friend's sister, Lacy Donovan, is missing—"

"Yeah. We fished her car out of the lake last week." Huntington shook her head. She leaned forward. "We dragged that lake. Few deep spots we had a hard time getting to. But there was no sign of her body."

Stephen nodded. "Yeah, I heard. Not sure if it's a good sign or a bad one."

Huntington shrugged. "It's not good or bad. It's just a car in the lake with no *sign* of the owner. She's still a missing person. We'll keep looking, but for now, the trail has gone cold. We looked through that car for anything current to tell us her place of residence. Nothing. It was all papers registered to her parents with their address. We don't know where she lives or where she worked. Like she was trying to be a ghost. I don't know about you, but I never went to such great lengths to hide from my parents when I left home. They think it was her exerting her independence. I think it was more than that."

"You think someone was after her?" Mak asked. Now she was leaning forward.

"Dunno," Huntington said. "It's just pretty weird is all. I keep thinking there has to be a connection between that and her going missing. I'm no profiler, but if someone out there really likes to target women, someone who's a possessive, domineering type who finds out she lives alone, and no one knows where, she becomes an easy target. Her mom told her that, too, but it didn't change anything."

"What do you make of her parents?" Stephen asked. He racked his brain for a memory of them but came up short. He didn't actually date Beth after all, his brother had.

"We did a conference call with them. Told them there was no need for them to come to town at this point. The mom was borderline hysterical. She couldn't seem to pull herself together. The dad, well, extreme opposite. Stoic and unemotional. Can you imagine? I know there are strong, silent types, but he had nothing. I found that odd," Huntington admitted.

"Truly," Mak said, nodding her head.

Stephen knew Mak was thinking about Harper again. He knew that because anytime someone's daughter went missing, he couldn't help but think about Anna. He made a mental note to call his daughter tonight. He'd underestimated how hard it would be to work in the same town and not see her. Guilt tugged at his heart. He missed Anna.

31

MAK

As they were leaving the station, Mak sped her steps. Clearly, Wilton was starting to anticipate this and kept up just fine this time. Once in the car, Mak fumbled around for sunglasses before she started the Range Rover.

"What do you think about all of that?" Mak asked. "Do you know Lacy and Beth's parents?"

Wilton shook his head. "I never met them. Beth is a year old than me, and she briefly dated my brother—"

"I didn't know you had a brother," Mak interrupted. "I have a couple brothers."

Wilton paused and decided not to correct Mak. He didn't have a brother. He *had* a brother. "Anyway, Beth and I weren't close growing up. I'm actually surprised she remembered me."

"Hmm," Mak pursed her lips, deep in thought. "It might be helpful to interview their parents. Maybe even in person if you're planning another trip back there anytime soon."

"I don't know when I'll go back," Wilton sighed. "It depends on this case."

"Of course," Mak agreed. "Speaking of this case, I have an idea."

"Well, we're at a standstill at the moment, so I'm listening." Wilton gave her his attention.

"Let's go back to the racetrack," Mak grinned.

"What?" Wilton asked incredulously. "Are you seriously thinking about racing at a time like this?"

"No, silly. I don't want to race. I want to see if there's camera footage anywhere that caught Anthony Gerritt messing with the car before I raced. That would produce evidence Sikes was talking about that would get him a conviction."

"Huh," Wilton grinned at her. "Look at that. Very creative, partner."

32

MAK

Mak and Wilton stepped out of the car and walked toward the asphalt track where Mak had spent the past Saturday. They had called ahead and learned that the owner and the racetrack manager were working today. As it turned out, there was a lot of work to be done after an event, but they agreed they would be happy to talk to Mak and Wilton.

Mak headed straight for the control tower, knowing that was where any office at a track would be. She tapped lightly on the door that was a few inches ajar. A couple of ladies sat in the office. One was on the phone, and one was counting money.

The money counter looked over her shoulder and called out, "Just a minute."

Mak and Wilton waited patiently until the money counter finished her chore, put the bills in a bank bag, and locked it in a safe. The woman was curvy and tall with curly blond hair and blue eyes.

Mak gave her a bright smile. She stuck out her hand. "I'm—"

"Well, hey there! I know who you are. You're Larry's daughter. I'm Bernie." She peered closely at Mak's face. "You scared the shit outta us Saturday with that car fire. You okay?"

Mak touched the butterfly bandage self-consciously. "I am. Just a little cut."

Bernie tsked her tongue. "You better thank your lucky stars for that one. That was a big fire!"

"True," Mak said. "Bernie, this is my partner, Stephen Wilton—"

"Well, aren't you easy on the eyes?" Bernie said as she pumped Wilton's hand up and down.

"Nice to meet you," Wilton smiled.

"What can I do for ya'll?" Bernie asked.

"Well," Mak laughed a little, sounding embarrassed. "Dad was worried that someone tampered with the car. Once he makes up his mind, I can't talk him out of it. He's on the road to the next race as we speak, and since I stayed in the area, I promised him I'd stop by and see if you have any camera footage from that day. Something that would show our booth?"

Bernie chewed on her lip, seeming to consider Mak's words. For a brief moment, Mak thought she might tell them to jump in a lake. But then Bernie turned back into the office and waved them in.

"Hey," the woman who had been on the phone turned to stare at them with curiosity.

"Kristin, this is Wilton and Larry the Epic's daughter. Sorry, what was your name again?" Bernie asked.

"Mak," Mak said with a winning smile and handshake to Kristin.

"Oh, yeah, how are you?" Kristin asked with big eyes.

"I survived," Mak joked.

"I see that!" Kristin said.

"They want to check camera footage from Saturday. Larry thinks someone messed with his car, which may have started the fire," Bernie explained.

"Might have," Kristin shook her head. "Rough crowd, these racers."

"Can you get them set up with what we have?" Bernie asked.

"Absolutely," Kristin agreed. She pulled up the laptop and accessed security footage. "If you find anything, let us know. We don't take that stuff lightly. We'll bring charges."

"Thank you," Mak said as she plunked down in front of the computer.

Bernie put a seat beside Mak so Wilton could sit. "Make yourself at home. We'll be in and out of here cleaning up." Bernie shuffled out of the office.

"Thank you," Wilton responded for Mak who was already looking at camera pictures from every angle.

"Kristin, can you point out where our booth was in reference to what I'm looking at on the screen?" Mak asked.

"Sure," Kristin said as she pulled a map of the grounds out of a desk drawer. She leaned over Mak's head and pointed in the corner of one screen. "You would have been in this area."

Mak leaned closer. "Is there a way to enlarge that camera view?"

"Let me see," Kristin said. Still leaning over Mak, she pushed a few buttons and the camera widened over the whole screen.

"Perfect!" Mak cried.

Together, she and Wilton watched hours of footage. They even figured out a way to speed up the video. But the video showed nothing out of the ordinary.

"Was there any time you were lined up that he could've gotten to the car?" Wilton asked.

Mak thought for a minute. She even closed her eyes like she was replaying the day. "I really don't think so. Kristin?" Mak asked.

"Yeah?" she looked up from her phone.

"Are there any camera angles from here?" Mak pointed to

the place where the lineup of cars seemed to hide from sight on the other end of the announcer's tower.

Kristin zoomed the screen back out and looked through all the camera angles. "I'll be darned. I don't think there is."

"Huh," Mak said. "Okay, then I think we've seen all we can."

Wilton stood as Mak did. They shook hands with Kristin and said *thank you* one more time. They were almost out of the office when Mak stopped abruptly.

"Kristin, remind me of your title?" Mak asked.

"I'm the owner of this racetrack," Kristin puffed out her chest proudly.

"Wonderful!" Mak said. "Dad and I had a great experience— other than the fire at the end. Seems like a big job to put on an event like that. Do you run it all by yourself?"

"Oh, mostly. We have a few partners, but I do most of the heavy lifting. Me and Bernie."

"Good job. I'm curious, were your partners at the race on Saturday?" Mak asked.

"One was. Anthony Gerritt was here but Bill Brash wasn't. Why do you ask?" Kristin tilted her head to the side.

Mak's blood ran cold as Kristin confirmed her suspicion. She was kicking herself for not thinking that through before she'd come in here asking to see the footage. "Oh, dad and I were just comparing notes about the tracks he's been to. Thinks he wants to own one someday."

"I'm surprised he doesn't already," Kristin winked at Mak.

"True," Mak bobbed her head with a forced smile. "Well, we'll leave you to it."

Mak and Wilton walked quickly to the car and got in. Once the doors shut, Wilton turned to stare at Mak.

"Why didn't you show them your badge?" Wilton wanted to know.

Mak started the car. She shrugged. "Just a hunch that we'd get further on my connections than on a badge."

"I guess there's nothing illegal about it if they allow you access to the footage," Wilton said. "Are you worried about them mentioning that you were here to Gerritt?"

Mak shook her head. "Let them. He knows I was at the race. He knows my car caught on fire. He probably knows I suspect him. He doesn't care. He might even be covering his tracks. If he knew where the cameras would be angled, he could have planted something without anyone seeing a thing."

"I see. Listen, we need to call Sikes about the fact that Gerritt is an owner of this track." Wilton let his words trail as he dialed Sikes on speaker.

Once they relayed they had come to the track to check race-day footage, Sikes was silent for half a second.

"Trying to get proof of Anthony Gerritt tampering with a car," Sikes mused aloud. "I like it. Good thinking, Mak. Did you find anything?"

"No, but there's a blind spot in the footage—like a gap in the security camera's coverage. If something happened there, we wouldn't have evidence," Wilton informed Sikes.

"Let me guess. You think someone who knew the camera angles might have chosen that spot to mess with the engine?" Sikes asked.

"I do," Mak said with a nod of her head. "Turns out, this very racetrack is another one of Anthony Gerritt's businesses. At least, he's a partial owner."

"Well, I'll be…" Sikes said. "We have a team looking into the businesses we could find that Anthony Gerritt started or is involved in. We didn't find his involvement with the racetrack. There might be something bigger than tampering going on here—"

Wilton and Sikes said the words at the exact same time.

"Money laundering."

As they finished the call and Wilton hung up the phone, Mak backed the vehicle up, then pulled away from the racetrack.

Neither Mak nor Wilton was aware of the dark, black eyes of the man who watched their every move.

33

MAK

As they drove away, Mak pulled out her cell phone. "My turn," she said to Wilton. "Call dad's cell," she said to her phone which was connected to the car. They listened to the rings so many times, Mak thought it would go to voicemail.

"Hello?" the rough, gravelly voice of her dad finally answered.

"Hey, dad!" Mak greeted. "You still asleep?"

There was a silence before the answer. "Hey, Mak. Yep, still sleeping."

"Ah. Big race last night?" Mak smiled at Wilton knowing an all-night race most likely meant it was an illegal one.

On a Sunday? Wilton mouthed with eyebrows raised in surprise.

Mak shrugged and nodded.

"I cannot confirm or deny to my US Marshal badass daughter..." his voice trailed and Mak thought he might have fallen back to sleep.

"Dad?" Mak asked.

"Huh?" he sputtered. "Yeah, I'm here."

"Has your team had a good look at our footage from the race?" Mak asked.

"Yeah, why?" he grunted.

"Did they see anyone suspicious tampering with the car?" Mak wondered.

"No," now Larry sounded more alert and pissed off. They could hear rustling. Maybe he was sitting up in bed. "I had them look through everything. We got effing nothing."

"That sucks," Mak hissed, feeling disappointed. "We went to the racetrack and looked at footage. Nothing there either. Did you determine what caused it to catch on fire?"

Larry cursed angrily. "Electrical fire. As in, there was a sliced wire in just the right place, which means the *wrong* place. Would have taken seconds when we had the hood up for someone to come by, snip it, and keep walking."

"Seriously?" Mak asked. Her heart sank. Gerritt was bolder than she'd given him credit for. He worked his schemes in plain sight. "Do you think we could get footage from the show producers?"

Now, Larry laughed. "Wow, Mak. That's a tall ask. I think you'd have to subpoena that. Do you think Hollywood producers would let you take a peek at a behind-the-scenes footage without one?"

"No, probably not," Mak said, trying to think of a new angle. "Why don't you send me the contact information you have for the producer just in case?"

There was a long silence on the other end again. "I can do that. You met Bobby Markle at the race. But you need to promise not to burn this contact. I know you're smart and you'll figure out a way to ask nicely or play by their rules. My career isn't over, you know, and I still need the *Street Southwest* team to be friendly."

"Of course, dad!" Mak agreed readily. "You know how charming I can be..."

Wilton smirked at her.

Mak grinned back at him.

"But you also know if anything is amiss, I can find it. You want to know what happened just as much as I do," Mak said.

"Yeah, I do. I'll text it over to you. Now, if you don't mind, I got a few more hours of beauty sleep to catch up on."

"Sure, dad. Sweet dreams." Mak ended the call. Minutes later, she felt her phone vibrate with a text of Bobby Markle's number.

"You are aware that the amount of footage they likely got for the whole day could take hours to sift through, right?" Wilton asked.

Mak shrugged. "What else are we doing right now?"

"We could be eating," Wilton replied.

"Yeah, let's do that," Mak agreed. "But first, let me call this producer."

Mak spun her tale to the producer as Wilton listened, shaking his head. She explained that she was the driver of the car that caught fire and she was hoping to look through the footage of when her car blew up to figure out if anyone had tampered with the car. Mak knew she had a way of making these big asks look like little favors. Markle promised to send footage over to them within the next couple hours. All Mak had to do was sign a non-disclosure form, which meant they could sue her if she broke confidentiality.

"Sure thing," Mak agreed, rattling off her email address. "Send it on over."

"Will do. And how are you doing, Ms. Epic? That was a nasty fire. They said you would be okay. How are you feeling?" Markle asked.

"I'll live," Mak said, laughing a little over the new nickname. "I got pretty lucky. Just a cut over my eyebrow."

"Yeah, that is lucky," Markle agreed. "Well, take care of yourself. Oh, and I'd love to interview you if you're ever interested. Viewers love female racers—you're a real minority in a race car."

"That's a shame, too," Mak said. "Tell you what. I'm in the middle of a big project right now but if it closes and I make it back to the race track, I'll give you an exclusive interview."

"Great!" Markle seemed genuinely excited about the prospect.

Mak thanked the man and hung up. She reluctantly met Wilton's gaze after she parked the car outside Mama's Café, remembering the last time they were there. "What?" she sighed.

Wilton grinned widely. "Well, if things go south with the US Marshals, you can always race cars for a living."

"I don't plan to quit my day job any time soon, Wilton." Mak got out of the car.

34

LACY

Lacy was shaking uncontrollably. She wasn't sick. In fact, she'd woken up earlier than the girls just like every other morning. She'd been so strong the whole time she had been in captivity, refusing to let men who meant her harm, who wanted to use her for their own gain, determine how she felt.

Today was different. Lacy woke feeling panic and fear. But it wasn't for her own life. It was for them. The three other women who had been stuck down here for far longer than Lacy had. They deserved to be set free. Lacy had made them all a big promise.

What if she couldn't deliver on that? Was it foolish to believe that she could single-handedly save three other women who were frail and weak from three men who were large and strong?

Lacy knew the answer. It was highly unrealistic. Yet, she had given them her word without having a plan for how she would keep it. If she was so capable, how did Lacy end up here, anyway? She was no different than they were. Even in the best physical shape of her life, during the height of her independence, Lacy had been captured from her own home.

That's when the shakes set in. The uncontrollable shaking inspired by fear. Fear was immobilizing. That one simple emotion was shutting down her brain. Ice flooded through her veins.

Lacy was so disappointed in herself. She had been so strong. It was she who had been instructing the others to keep their mind, body, and spirit strong.

But look at you now, Lacy's brain mocked her. *Not so strong anymore, are you?*

Lacy let her body slide back down the wall until she was lying in corpse pose. *Fitting,* she thought.

As Lacy lay there, a small voice fought through the negative, fear-filled emotions.

Fight.

Lacy worked to clear her mind. But panic still gripped her hard.

Be strong.

Lacy felt hungry, angry, lonely, and tired.

Feel your emotions.

Lacy let sleep pull her further into the darkness.

35

MAK

After breakfast, she and Wilton had gone back to the Brighton Police Department and borrowed an unused laptop. They'd watched the episode of *Street Southwest* from last weekend.

Mak had to roll her eyes when the commercial cuts to break away for sponsors showed dramatic footage of her car catching on fire and her dad dragging her out of it. Though she had to admit, she'd keep watching for that bit of drama too. She just wished it hadn't been at her expense.

After the first show tease, Wilton turned to Mak with eyes full of disbelief. "Seriously, Mak! You must be the luckiest woman alive. How did that not go worse for you?"

"Shh! It's back on," Mak shushed him and turned up the computer. They'd watched the whole show but didn't catch one moment of suspicious behavior near her dad's Camaro. Mak understood now that the producer had been serious about giving attention to women in racing. There was quite a bit of footage with her and her dad. She had to admit, minus the fire at the end, she and her dad made a great team.

The footage from *Street Southwest* showed up in a secure Dropbox by noon. All six hours of it. Why they needed that much footage to put together one two-hour show, Mak would never understand.

Mak suggested they split the footage so she and Wilton would only spend three hours a piece watching. Wilton readily agreed. The deputy on duty, a very serious, mostly frowny young guy named Sturgis, offered his laptop for the second viewer.

An hour later, Sturgis came over to watch footage over Wilton's shoulder after Wilton explained what they were doing. The first time he saw Mak's face appear on screen, Sturgis took two steps backward and peered over at Mak, who was watching her own screen intently with headphones over her ears.

"That's her!" he said, his voice high with excitement.

"Yeah." Wilton said. "Her dad is Larry the Epic from *Street Southwest*."

"No way! He was just in town!" Sturgis exclaimed. "And you think Anthony Gerritt tampered with the car?"

"I do," Wilton nodded. "We're just trying to prove it."

"Right," Sturgis said as he set his eyes on Wilton's screen with renewed enthusiasm. "Sarge briefed me on why ya'll are here."

"There she is again," Wilton commented.

"Camera loves her!" Sturgis exclaimed.

"I can hear you, you know," Mak said, feeling annoyed, mostly because she wasn't seeing anything to help her case.

"No disrespect, ma'am. I'm just saying they seem to really like showing you and you photograph well." Sturgis let his face fall back to the frown he seemed born with.

"Apparently, women in race cars aren't common—even in this day and age. They're probably looking to find new viewers," Mak commented, her eyes never leaving her computer screen.

Wilton didn't respond. He pointed to his monitor. "See that space right there?"

"Yeah," Sturgis said, leaning forward.

"That's where we think it might have happened. We paid a visit to the racetrack this morning and checked their footage. There's this area, right here by the pit, where the cars line up, that seems to have no cameras on it. Whoever did this knew that. Anthony Gerritt is a part owner of that racetrack."

"Really? That must be fairly new," Sturgis commented. "I know the owner and I didn't think she had a partner."

"Maybe he's a silent partner?" Wilton suggested.

"Uh uh," Sturgis said. "I went to high school with the owner's son. He was awful proud that his family owned that racetrack. Gerritt just pulled into town a few months ago."

"You knew Gerritt was here?" Mak asked, pausing her footage and pulling off her headphones.

"I did," Sturgis nodded. "When someone new comes into town and starts new businesses or buys old ones, it hits our radar. This isn't a town where people come to make money, you see. Not exactly a thriving community. We have the bare necessities and that's how we like it. We can drive into the next town if we need something special. So, I looked him up. I know all about Anthony Gerritt—pretty shady guy."

"What did Sergeant Huntington say when you told her your concerns?" Mak asked, unaware that the door had opened on the other side of the reception desk.

"She said, *let's keep an eye on him*. We can't arrest him unless we catch him doing something illegal," Sergeant Huntington answered as she walked into the room. In her hands, she held three pizza boxes. The smells that wafted out of the boxes made Mak's stomach grumble. "Sturgis, the marshals might get paid to watch TV all day, but you don't."

Sturgis rushed to take the boxes out of Huntington's hands and placed them on a vacant desk. He flipped open a lid and grabbed a slice of pepperoni pizza.

"Sure, help yourself," Huntington said with sarcasm. She turned to Mak and Wilton. "Ya'll want pizza?"

"Sure, thanks!" Mak said as she rose to her feet. "So, you had Sturgis watching Gerritt too?"

Sergeant Huntington grabbed a pizza slice and plopped down in a chair. "This town doesn't see much crime. We aren't staffed to handle it if we do. We also know everyone and everything that happens around here. It doesn't take long for word to travel—"

"Even gossip to and from strangers. We don't know an enemy around here," Sturgis jumped in.

"Until now," Huntington admitted. "I told you I was hoping Gerritt was a legit businessman here to revitalize the community. Despite my suspicious mind, I like to give people the benefit of the doubt. Still, I felt unsettled by him. In truth, I don't have the resources or the protection to go poking into Gerritt. Didn't even see the APB at first. Called your boss the minute I did. I knew enough to see he's bad news, but figured out he knows how to get out of trouble and clean up his messes. I thought if he's someone the US Marshals were looking for—that's what you do, you hunt known criminals—I'd just pass it along the line."

"So, you called Sikes?" Mak asked.

"Yep. Emailed a photo I'd snapped of Gerritt outside the café. This man is a businessman in my community. So, I never attempted to pull him in for questioning," Huntington explained.

"I get it," Mak said slowly. "Well, I appreciate that you're willing to help us bring Gerritt in."

Huntington nodded. "Of course."

"Is there anything else you need to tell us about Gerritt?"

"Yeah, he and his *construction crew* are having lunch at the pizza place down the street. Truth is, I went in to have lunch but saw him there and changed it to a to-go order. You're welcome, by the way."

"Thanks!" Mak said with a mouth full of hot cheese.

"Wilton, should we take a break to follow Gerritt around town?"

Wilton looked skeptical. "Do you think you can follow a man through this town without being obvious or getting caught?"

"Well, we can try," Mak said, grabbing her jacket and throwing it on. She held the keys out to Wilton. "Maybe you drive. He knows me. I can sit in the back. The windows are tinted on our vehicle."

Wilton took the keys from her carefully. "You aren't going to backseat drive the whole time, are you?"

"Wilton, I'll be in the back seat. That's the only thing I can do."

"I could leave you here. There's still a whole lot of footage to go through," Wilton suggested, looking hopeful.

"I'll watch the footage," Sturgis volunteered quickly, glancing at Mak with a look of adoration in his eyes.

Mak glared back.

Wilton coughed to cover his laugh.

Huntington's eyes narrowed. "You know the drill, Sturgis. Your first obligation is to this job. I'll let you play detective until it's time to do the rounds. But the minute someone calls with a cat stuck in a tree, you're going to the house call."

"Yes, ma'am," Sturgis agreed.

Mak and Wilton left the station and hopped in the car.

When they got to the pizza restaurant, there was no sign of Anthony Gerritt.

"Damn it!" Mak exploded.

"Woah, calm down," Wilton said. "We'll get him. Sooner or later. He's not going anywhere, and this is a small town."

Mak sighed. "I know. I'm sorry. I'm just feeling tired and cranky. Most likely because I haven't called home in a while."

"Okay, let's get you a coffee before we go back to the station. You can call John and Harper any time," Wilton said.

"Thanks. Coffee would be great. The coffee at the station is awful," Mak complained.

"Agree," Wilton seconded. "I have to say, I don't think we're going to find anything in that footage."

Mak made a noise of frustration. "I know," she groaned. "It seems like a waste of time, but we need to be thorough. We only have a couple hours of footage left."

"Each," Wilton glanced at her in the back seat before he eased the car back onto the road and grinned. "Hey, what does this kind of work remind you of?"

"Being a rookie marshal getting all the worst assignments," Mak grumbled, not seeing the humor in this.

"Right. Me too. Only, I was a rookie cop, of course," Wilton said. "You ever miss those days?"

"No," Mak said quickly. "I do not."

"I do," Wilton said. "They were simpler times. I was young and in love. I didn't stay a rookie for long though. They promoted me to detective and put me on an undercover assignment to *date* a girl. They suspected she and her mother were a mother-daughter murder team."

"What? For real?" Mak asked, feeling more engaged in the conversation again. "Was she?"

"She wasn't, but her mother was."

"Did she find out who you were?" Mak asked.

"Yeah, she did," Wilton sighed.

"What did she do about it?" Mak wondered.

"She broke up with me," Wilton admitted.

"But you weren't actually together, right?" Mak asked.

"We were. I bought her a ring and everything. What she didn't know was I'd gone and recused myself from the case when I realized I'd fallen in love with her. But because I never had the courage to tell her the truth, and she found out in the worst possible way, she never trusted me again," Wilton pulled into a grocery store.

"Why are we here?" Mak asked.

"There's a coffee kiosk in here that makes a great cup," Wilton informed her.

"Oh," Mak said. "Wait, don't tell me this girl is Anna's mom?"

Wilton grinned as he got out of the car. "Yep."

"Your life is tragic, Wilton," Mak said. She actually found herself feeling sorry for him. She followed him out of the car and into the grocery store.

They were almost to the coffee counter when Wilton heard a woman's voice behind him.

"Stephen?"

"Speaking of my baby mama..." Wilton whispered.

Mak's eyes got big as she took in the pretty brunette with long, straight hair and bright green eyes. "I'll just go order some coffee."

"I'll try to keep her out of danger," Wilton responded. He turned and walked toward the woman.

"Hi, Paige."

36

WILTON

Stephen met Paige in the middle of a grocery aisle, made eye contact, then turned abruptly to study the shelf in front of him.

"Paige, I can't be seen with you in town. I'm on a job," Stephen said in a low voice as if he was talking to the can he plucked off the shelf.

Paige sighed and took his cue. She, too, began studying the shelf. "I know that, Stephen. James told me. But you also promised him you would call Anna and you haven't. We need to know what's going on."

"Well, you know I'm limited on what I can tell you," Stephen said lowly.

Paige chanced a glance at him. "What happened to your face? Are we in danger?" she hissed.

"I promise I'll call you at the end of this day," Stephen said. He put the can back on the shelf and picked up another one.

"Yeah, that's what you told James last week," Paige huffed.

"No, I told James I would call. I didn't say when," Stephen corrected her.

"Well, your daughter misses her daddy," Paige snapped in a quiet voice.

Stephen inhaled. "I'm sorry about that. You're right. I've been distracted." There was no way Stephen was going to share that his distraction went further than this case. It went to his friend's sister who was still missing and his brother's real murderer. "I'll call her tonight. I promise."

"Thank you," Paige said and spun on her heel.

He watched her walk away. Stephen found Mak right where he'd left her. Only, Mak now had two coffees in her hand and offered one to Stephen.

"Black coffee, right?" she asked.

Stephen nodded and took the hot cup. "Thanks."

"You're welcome," Mak said easily. "Everything squared away?"

Stephen nodded again as they turned to leave.

Once back at the station, Stephen stopped in to see Huntington.

"Hey," she greeted. "Any luck?"

Stephen shook his head. "Any luck finding another clue on Lacy Donovan?"

This time, Huntington shook her head.

"Okay," Stephen accepted her answer with heaviness. They really had stalled out.

"I'm afraid Sturgis had to run out on a call, so he didn't get any further with your footage," Huntington informed him.

"Okay, thanks for the update," Stephen went out to the office to find Mak already sitting at the computer with her big headphones on. He followed her example and un-paused the footage on his screen.

A few hours later, they still had nothing more than when they started. Mak and Wilton agreed to call it a day and headed back to a small hotel just on the outskirts of town.

As Mak opened the door to her hotel room, Stephen heard her greet John from her cell phone.

"Hey, babe!" she said. "Just a long, unproductive day... You?"

Stephen opened his own door and waited until it closed behind him to dial Paige on his cell phone.

"Hey, Paige, sorry about earlier," Stephen immediately started.

"Stephen, what's going on?" Paige asked. The background noise grew quieter, which meant Paige had walked into another room.

"We're tracking a criminal who has set up shop in the area," Stephen began. "There's no reason to assume you're in danger. He knows who my partner Mak is but not me. Which means, as long as we pretend not to know each other, there's no reason he would use you guys to retaliate or manipulate me."

Paige sucked in a gasp. "That doesn't sound promising to me, Stephen. He could easily find the connection to us—"

"I don't think so. Yes, Anna has my last name, but you and James don't. Anna doesn't have a social media presence and mine is too far outdated. Plus, schools would protect her information." Stephen relaxed on the bed.

"Okay, I'm going to rely on you to tell us if or when that changes," Paige said. "James' parents are dying to see the kids. We could jump on the red eye to Canada."

Stephen knew Paige was referencing a time in her past when she'd done just that. She knew about this flight from experience. "I'll let you know. Can I talk to Anna?" he asked.

"Wait. How do you know we haven't already had contact with this criminal?" Paige asked.

"Good question," Stephen answered. "I can give you his name, but you need to swear to keep it quiet. We cannot afford for this guy to get spooked and leave town. It's Anthony Gerritt."

There was a dead silence on the other end of the line.

"Paige?" Stephen asked. "You still there?"

She swore softly. "Gerritt Construction and Property Management just reached out to James to offer him a job."

"When?" Stephen promptly stood up and started pacing.

"Two days ago," Paige answered.

"What did James say?" Stephen asked.

"That he'd think about it. James doesn't really need the job, but he does miss construction. So, he's thinking," Paige admitted.

"Okay, good. Paige, I've changed my mind. You and James need to go. Quietly. Don't tell anyone you're leaving. Surprise his parents. Just get on a plane and let me know when you get there," Stephen's voice conveyed his urgency. Anthony Gerritt knew who he was and now he was learning everything he could about Stephen, just like he had Mak. Since when did criminals stalk law enforcement agents?

"Okay, let me talk to James. I'll put Anna on but please don't scare her. I need her to think this is just a fun, surprise visit to the grandparents."

"Okay," Stephen agreed. When he talked to Anna, he was glad to hear she was her silly, funny self. After he hung up the phone, Stephen took a long, hot shower. He put on a clean pair of cargo pants and t-shirt. He knew he wasn't going to be able to sleep knowing Anthony Gerritt might be stalking his family.

Stephen knocked on Mak's door less than an hour later. She held the door open wide to let him in. She had changed into sweats and her hair was wet, much like Stephen's.

"Gerritt is now trying to infuse himself into my family, too. His construction company offered Paige's husband a job," Stephen explained. "They're making arrangements to fly to Canada to see James' parents as we speak. I'm gonna do an overnight stakeout. I can't afford someone getting to my daughter again."

"I'll go with you," Mak said, looking around the room. She

grabbed a pair of jeans from the floor and went into the bathroom.

"No. One of us needs to sleep tonight," Stephen yelled at her through the closed door.

"We're stronger in numbers, Wilton. What happens if you get too tired to keep your eyes open?" Mak asked when she popped back out. She slipped her shoes on and was already tying the laces. Her eyes were wide with excitement.

Stephen knew it was the thrill of the chase for her. He also knew Mak had a good point. He'd fallen asleep during the most important night of Carley's life. It made him too late to save her.

"Okay," he finally agreed.

They went out the door together because as Mak said, two marshals were stronger than one.

37

LACY

Lacy's head was pounding. She twitched but didn't open her eyes. Instead, senses heightened, she took in her surroundings. She did not know where she was or what to expect. She wasn't in the earth prison anymore. That was the only thing she knew for sure.

The surface under her was hard and cold. She had one hand pinned underneath her and the other hand was flat against the ground. She rubbed her index finger back and forth. The floor was smooth and slippery. Metal, she decided. Not the red dirt floor where she had been for the past eight days.

She could hear voices. They were muted as if they were far away. She strained to hear. Deep, male voices sounded like they were arguing. She could hear loud eruptions of shouts and laughter. Then she heard numbers. None of it made sense. The numbers were going higher and higher. They were bidding. A group of men were bidding.

Lacy couldn't chance that their attention was elsewhere, so she barely opened her eyes and peered out from under her eyelashes. What she saw caused her heart rate to spike. She snapped her eyes back shut and tears puddled in the corners.

She didn't dare move to wipe them. She had no choice but to just let the tears fall.

She was in a cage. The golden cage.

How had this happened? Her plan had been to fight and then run. She didn't even remember being lifted from the earth prison. She lay very still now, attempting to meditate, to lower her heart rate and relax.

Remember, she commanded herself. Then she waited.

Little flashes came back to her.

She was in the prison with the other girls. A noise sounded above them. Lacy looked up. She saw moonlight and a man's face. The thought flitted through her mind, *Which guy are you?*

Then she felt herself being lifted. He had lassoed her too quick for her to run or make it difficult for him. Her feet had no more than settled on the ground when she felt a painful jab into the side of her neck.

Run, she'd told her feet. They did not obey. Instead, her knees buckled under her, her legs gave out, and she felt herself falling into blackness.

They had drugged her. Of course they had. This wasn't their first time. They knew ambitious girls like Lacy had plans. They weren't going to give her a chance to put them into play.

What am I wearing? Lacy asked herself, her mind coming back to the present. Her hand, the one stuck under her body, had begun to go numb. She moved it, feeling the resulting tingles. Her fingers felt the foreign material that covered her. She was wearing some silky dress. Was it a negligée? The realization hit her like a ton of bricks and made her want to vomit. They had dressed her up, or down, judging by the cold breeze on her legs, in a tiny little slip that was likely very revealing.

And now they were bidding. Were they taking bids on her? That would mean they'd taken pictures of her. Right? No, Lacy was sure she'd been unconscious this whole time. Would they have taken pictures of an unconscious girl? She couldn't know for sure. Either they had taken them, or they were going to. Regardless, Lacy had one more shot to escape. The walk back to the earth prison.

Only now, she knew their system. She'd have to fight them before they stuck her with the needle full of sleeping drugs again. Which means she'd have to fight more than one.

Lacy felt her heart sink. She wasn't sure she could take all three of them.

38

WILTON

As Mak drove to Stephen's daughter's home, his phone rang. It was Paige.

"We booked a red eye for tonight," Paige told him, sounding breathless. "Do you know how hard it is to pack three kids?"

Stephen flinched at the reminder of how little responsibility he had for Anna. He knew Paige hadn't meant it that way, but being this close to his daughter without being able to see her was a constant reminder that he wasn't spending enough time with her. "I'm sorry."

"What?" Paige asked. "No, Stephen, you're doing your job. James is helping me. I'm just complaining. Anyway, I wanted to let you know we will be safe in Canada by morning."

"My partner, Mak, and I will be parked outside watching the house tonight. Let's not take any chances. We'll escort you to the airport, wait for you to go in, then I'll come in separately to say *goodbye* to Anna—"

Mak's eyes cut to his in surprise.

"We'll wait in the airport until you're through TSA. You text me when you're safely on the plane," Stephen continued his instructions.

"I'm sure we'll be fine—"

"That's not a risk I'm willing to take," Stephen cut her off. "Now, just be casual and go about your night as if it's a normal night until the minute you leave for the airport. Just know we're out here if anything goes wrong."

"Got it, Stephen," Paige said.

"Good. Now put Anna on, please."

"Daddy!" Anna's shrill little girl voice sounded over the receiver. He couldn't believe she would be five soon. "We're going to Canada on an airplane!"

"Woah!" Stephen said as he pointed to the exit Mak needed to turn on. "Canada sounds fun!"

"Yeah! And we're going after my bedtime!" Anna giggled.

"No way! You're going on an airplane, *and* you get to stay up past bedtime?" Stephen played into Anna's enthusiasm but really, his stomach was in knots. Who was to say that just because they got out of town, they would be safe? How far-reaching was Anthony Gerritt's network?

After he hung up the phone, Stephen voiced his concern to Mak.

Mak was quiet for half a second. "I was actually thinking about how John and Harper are sitting over at my house unprotected right now."

"Good point," Stephen said. He seemed lost in thought for a minute. "It's late, but I think we need to check in with Sikes."

"Sounds good," Mak agreed.

"Park just up here," Stephen pointed to a place just down the street but under a tree in the shadows. "You can see the house from here."

Mak pulled the car in and turned off all the lights. She dialed Sikes, putting the phone on speaker.

"How's it going there?" Sikes asked.

"Not great, boss," Mak began. "Turns out Gerritt might be

targeting Stephen's family here as well. We're watching the house until they can get on a red-eye to Canada tonight."

"Good, that sounds like a great plan. Did you get anything with the footage?" Sikes asked.

"No," Mak gritted. "Sikes, back to the family protection plan. Do you think John and Harper are safe from Gerritt?"

"Hmm, are you concerned?" Sikes asked.

"A little," Mak admitted.

"Why don't I see if I can get a patrol car circling the block regularly until this is over?" Sikes suggested. "I can put in a call to Kansas City Metro PD."

"Thanks, boss." Mak sagged with relief.

"Now, we wait," Stephen said when she hung up the phone.

"What time are they heading to the airport?" Mak asked.

"Nine forty-five," Stephen answered.

Mak laid her seat back, put her tennis-shoe clad feet up on the dashboard, and put her hands behind her head. "Wake me up if anything happens."

"Seriously? Some partner you are," Stephen grumbled.

"Don't be jealous because I can sleep anywhere." Mak smiled, adjusted the seat again, and closed her eyes.

Stephen had thought she was joking but was shocked when he heard her breathing deeply. He stared at her with envy. That was a skill he needed to learn. He could use more sleep.

Stephen fiddled with his phone. His mind drifted to Alyah. He wanted to be open with her. It wasn't easy. Still, he got out of the car and stepped outside into the cool night.

Leaning against the car, he called Alyah. As he suspected it would, his call went right to voicemail. Maybe that made it easier to be vulnerable. Maybe he just needed to talk to someone about what was weighing on his mind. A one-sided conversation might just do the trick. When her greeting finished, he spoke after the beep.

"Hey, Alyah. I hope things are going well for you in DC.

Actually, that's a lie. The truth is, I miss you. Every day, I secretly—not so secretly—wish you would realize DC isn't for you and come back. Because I'm here. I'll always be here. But that's not why I called. Remember that envelope you encouraged me to open? I did. After you left. It was a picture of my brother. See, my brother, like your sister, was older than me. He was also a strong-willed troublemaker," Stephen laughed a little, then continued.

"It got him killed. The story was that he'd mouthed off to the wrong guy. The guy pulled out a gun and shot him. But that envelope held the picture of a guy holding a gun my to brother's head. It was time stamped and dated the day my brother was killed. The guy holding the gun in that photo wasn't the guy who was convicted of his murder. Part of me wishes I'd never opened that envelope. But you were right to encourage me to. Only, I have no idea what to do with that information now.

"I tracked down the guy who gave me the picture and I ended up with a swollen black eye, a couple of scrapes, and some bruises. I'm nowhere near closer to the truth than I was before I went poking into it." Stephen sighed, ran a hand through his hair, and tilted his head up to look at the stars. He wondered if Alyah was looking at the same stars in DC tonight. But then he figured his stars were likely clearer in this country setting than they would be where she was in the city.

"What happened with my brother is the reason I joined the police force, you know. I wanted to prevent things like that from happening. There's no way I can let this go. I can't unknow what I know. Not being able to do something is killing me. I saw my parents when I went back home. I couldn't bring myself to tell them. Not until I have more answers.

"Anyway, I wanted to thank you for challenging me to face my fear of opening that envelope. And sort of blame it on you because I'm losing a lot of sleep over it. Well, let's be honest, I lose sleep thinking about you, too. Wow, that was cheesy. I'm gonna go. Feel free to reach out anytime." Stephen hung up, feeling like an idiot. He'd already hung up so it was too late to erase that message. He was in a one-sided relationship. But for some reason, Stephen couldn't make himself move on.

When Stephen got back in the car, he noted that Mak was still breathing deeply. What he failed to notice was that Mak wasn't fully asleep.

Hours later, Stephen poked Mak to wake her up.

His eyes were on his family as they quietly loaded up the car in the dark, like they were the vonn Trapp family sneaking out of the country. It wasn't too far from the truth.

Mak opened her eyes. She stared at Stephen for a minute.

"Are you awake over there?" he asked.

Mak nodded and noticed the car in front of them leaving. She put on her seatbelt, turned on the car, and started driving to the airport.

Stephen's phone lit up with a text message. He waited to read it until they were all safely parked at the airport.

Alyah: *Hey, thinking about you. Thanks for what you shared. It means a lot that you would trust me with that.*

39

LACY

Lacy was running. Her bare feet screamed in pain when she first slipped through the sliding glass door. The earth was barren of soft grass. The rocks under her feet were sharp daggers into her high arches. Still, she did not hesitate.

Run. Run as if your life depends on it. Because it does.

Lacy shut down her brain, refusing to acknowledge the discomfort and obeyed her thoughts. She ran straight into the forest. There, she stumbled twice. Once when her foot caught a tree root, causing her to pitch forward. She had to cover her own mouth to stop from shouting out in pain. The second time was when a tree branch smacked her across the face. Hard. She stumbled for a minute, thinking she might pass out. She quickly recovered.

Keep running!

She felt like she was a good half mile away when she finally heard them come stomping outside. They were loud oafs who were shouting and cussing and desperately looking for her. But they seemed slow. She knew the silky golden dress would be easy to spot if there had been a moon tonight. There wasn't.

While the darkness worked to conceal her, it also made it harder to see in front of her.

She heard a rip and knew a branch had caught a piece of thin fabric she wore on her body. She didn't care about that. She just kept running. Her lungs should be burning and perhaps they were, but she made no note of it. Nor did she acknowledge that the night was crisp and cold, despite her pounding heart and rolling sweat. Adrenaline coursed through her, warming her entire body.

Run for your life.

She ran until she was in an open field. Then she stopped short. It appeared to go on for another quarter mile. She'd be vulnerable running out in the open. Especially if they had guns. There would be nothing to keep them from shooting her in the back. That was a risk she had to take. With newfound energy surging through her body, she sprinted across the field.

When she thought her legs might give out under her, she saw the lights just beyond a short row of trees. She could hear a highway. She thought she might cry from relief. But she knew she could not. She didn't have the luxury of emotions right now.

Just a little further. Just keep going. You're almost there.

She stepped into the short row of trees and paused. Now that she had stopped, she could feel her hot, flushed face. Her heart beat roared in her ears. Her breath was loud and ragged. She leaned against a tree and looked down. There were bloody scratches all over her arms and legs. She could only imagine what her face looked like. Her barely-there golden dress not quite covering her thighs had been ripped in several places and the hem dangled lower than the short skirt. Her left toe was swollen from where she'd smacked it on the root.

None of that mattered. What did matter was *why* they hadn't followed her. She'd ascertained from how loud and raucous they had been back at the house that they were likely drunk. That might have been the sole reason she'd gotten away.

When she'd heard the door of the golden cage open, she'd waited with her eyes closed until a man reached in and grabbed one of her legs. She let herself be dragged out. She allowed it until she knew she was out the cage. She had the element of surprise and she used it. She brought her knee up and hit his nose with such force, blood instantly began pouring onto the floor.

The man didn't seem to know what had hit him, and Lacy hadn't given him a chance to figure it out. She sprang to her feet and kicked him in the stomach as hard as she could. Then she connected the sole of her foot to the side of his face.

She hadn't waited to see how he would respond. Luck, or something else, had been on her side because the man had taken the assault with a series of grunts and gasps. She tiptoed quickly to the room on the side of the house opposite the loud, yelling men who appeared to still be bidding.

She'd found a sliding glass door, unlocked it, and let herself out before anyone knew she was gone. That's how she'd gotten so far before she'd been discovered. Why one man had come to get her out of that cage and not the whole pack of them, she'd never know. Or perhaps her brain didn't want to think it through.

But now, as she stood working to catch and quiet her breathing, she realized something else. If they hadn't followed her through the woods, they'd gotten in their cars. She listened to the noises of the highway beyond. They knew something she didn't know.

They knew where she would exit the property. They were on the other side waiting for her. Even slow, drunken criminals were still masterminds at their dark arts. She had outwitted them for now. But they were waiting for her. She knew they would kill her if they found her. She had to find another way out of here that they wouldn't suspect.

Lacy looked at the tree she stood against. She looked up the trunk. It was risky, but she remembered her childhood of scampering up trees *like a monkey*, her mom used to say.

This tree was an easy one to climb. It was tall and even if she couldn't stay up there forever, she knew she'd have a better chance of seeing the highway, beyond the tree line, and coming up with a new plan. Besides, she could use the time to calm herself down and think more clearly.

That was how Lacy came up with the plan that ultimately saved her life.

40

WILTON

Stephen and Mak watched as Paige and James juggled babies and suitcases. Anna, who had always been mature for her age, took care of herself. She walked in front of her parents, rolling her little suitcase behind her. Watching her, Stephen felt a lump form in his throat. She was his everything.

Once the small family entered the airport, Stephen and Mak got out of their car and followed them in. It took exactly three minutes for Anna to look behind them and spot her dad.

"Daddy!" Anna shrieked. She forgot about her suitcase and ran to him. She jumped into his waiting arms.

Stephen scooped her up and cuddled her tight.

"Are you coming to Canada with us?" Anna asked. Her big blue eyes were bright with excitement, or maybe exhaustion. Her hair was a mass of long, blond, curly frizz. She was wearing pjs that did not match. Stephen knew Paige let Anna pick her clothes because making choices at this age was important, and the type and color of clothes didn't matter.

"No, honey," Stephen said. "I came to say goodbye and tell you to be a good girl for mommy and James, okay?"

"I will, daddy," Anna nodded. Then she pushed her bottom lip out. "I wish you could come with us."

Stephen smiled. "I wish I could too." He noticed Mak standing awkwardly by herself. He waved Mak over to join him and walked with Anna back to Paige and James.

"Hi, Stephen," Paige greeted. She smiled but her smile didn't reach her eyes. She looked frazzled and worried.

"Hey, man," James clapped Stephen's shoulder hard.

"Hey, guys!" Stephen greeted back. He turned to Mak. "This is my partner, Mak. Mak, this is my family."

"Hi," Mak smiled warmly as she shook hands with Paige and James.

"Wow!" Anna smiled at Mak with surprise. "You're a police lady?"

Mak laughed. She hesitated. Then she nodded, deciding not to correct her. "Yep, I am."

"You're pretty!" Anna said with adoration.

Mak laughed again. "Thank you. So are you!"

Anna wiggled down from Stephen's arms to reclaim her luggage. "We're going to Canada," she told Mak.

"I know," Mak said. "Your daddy told me."

"Sometimes I miss working with the police department," Paige sighed.

"You were in law enforcement?" Mak asked with surprise, looking at Paige as if it was the first time she saw her.

"CIO, Civilian Intelligence Officer, up in Winnipeg," Paige said proudly.

James juggled a baby in one arm and put an arm around his wife. "It's how we met," he spoke with a thick Canadian accent.

"Oh! Did he make you quit your dangerous job?" Mak leaned in and asked Paige.

Paige looked surprised, then a little offended. "No, I had to let go of the job when this one," she gave Stephen a pointed look, "put me in j-a-i-l." She spelled the word with a whisper.

"What?" Mak asked with a smile. "Is that a joke?"

"If only," Stephen sighed. "Kinda thought you'd let that go."

Paige shrugged. "It's a more interesting story than what I do now—juggling babies and animals."

"Oh, I'm sure Stephen will tell me all about it," Mak said with a look that told him he was going to have to do just that.

"Well, hey, you guys need to go through security to catch the plane," Stephen said, changing the subject. He clapped James on the back this time. "Hey, man, hope you learned your lesson about not taking rides from strangers at airports—"

"Not funny," James said with a wide grin, contradicting his statement.

Mak shook her head. "Stephen, I can't wait to hear all these stories."

Stephen didn't answer as he went for a round of hugs. "Be safe, guys. Text me the minute you land. Proof of life pics and everything."

"Promise," Paige said.

"Bye, daddy!" Anna said, giving him a loud, smacking kiss on the cheek as he gave her a final hug.

"Be good for mommy and James." Stephen squeezed her tight.

"I will," Anna waved, took hold of her little suitcase, and they all walked away.

Mak and Stephen stepped out the door of the airport into the crisp night air. It was a dark, moonless night. The only lights tonight were coming from the airport.

"I can't wait to hear all these great stories. How many times have you come to the rescue for your family?" Mak asked with a smile. "Or made trouble for them…"

Before Stephen could answer, his phone rang. It was an unknown caller. Stephen answered more to avoid Mak's question than anything else. "Wilton."

"Hey, it's Huntington. I think you and your partner need to

come to the station. We have someone here you might like to meet."

Stephen was silent for a moment. Dare he hope? "Lacy Donovan?"

"In the flesh," Sergeant Huntington stated.

Stephen hung up the phone with a dazed look on his face. He turned to face Mak.

"What is it?" Mak's face looked apprehensive. He understood. Sometimes the news was bad.

"They have Lacy Donovan at the police station."

41

WILTON

Using her driving expertise, Mak broke every speed limit law and made a twenty-minute trip in a little less than ten. Stephen used that time to call Sikes and fill him in. The phone was connected to the car so Mak could be a part of the conversation.

"I have a story to tell you," Stephen led.

"I'm listening," Sikes stated.

"I got a call from an old friend from high school around the time we started trying to track down Gerritt. Her little sister, Lacy Donovan, had gone missing. I went back to Arkansas last weekend and had a conversation with my old lieutenant. They found Lacy's car and it had just been fished out a of a lake—"

"You'll never believe where!" Mak interrupted.

"Let me guess. In the same area as where Gerritt is hiding out?" Sikes asked.

Mak deflated a little. "I feel like you already knew that."

"Sergeant Huntington from the Brighton Police Department called me after you arrived to make sure you two were legit and there on assignment. She mentioned your questions about Lacy Donovan," Sikes explained.

"So, you knew?" Stephen felt surprised by this. This was

exactly the sort of thing that would have gotten him in trouble when he was a detective working for Lieutenant Roger Higgins.

"Yes, but I figured as long as it didn't take you from your current assignment, there was no harm in keeping an eye on the case," Sikes answered. "Besides, it sounded like it had already ended—not well. I thought it might be a matter of time before they found her in the lake."

"Well, they did find her, but not in the lake. She's alive and at the police station. We're on our way there now!" Mak's voice was loud with excitement and the adrenaline she was getting from so driving fast.

Stephen shot Mak a look of disappointment. *Must she always deliver the punch line?* he thought.

"Wow, that's a shocking twist," Sikes mused. "Those things don't always end well."

"Right, we're on our way there now," Stephen concluded the story. "We figure we can at least provide backup."

"Yeah, from what Huntington said, they're short staffed. I think this is the most action her station has seen in a long time," Sikes agreed.

"We can see the station, sir. We'll keep you posted," Mak said before Stephen hung up the phone.

Mak threw the car in park and shut off the engine. Stephen and Mak rushed inside at full speed, excitement coursing. They paused once inside the station, looking around for Lacy Donovan.

Stephen spotted her sitting in a conference room with the door open. He could see her from where he stood. She was pale and clearly shaken up. She was wrapped in a thick blanket, sitting on a chair looking dazed, and staring at nothing in front of her. Officer Sturgis stood just outside the door of the conference room.

Huntington met them before they could walk any closer, stopping them like a protective mother bear. "Now, hang on a minute there, guys," she warned in a hushed tone. "Don't go rushing in guns a blazing and scare the girl. Poor thing was shaking from head to toe when we got to her. She'd managed to walk into a grocery store before she passed out on the floor. She's clearly in shock. She couldn't tell anyone where she'd been or how she'd gotten there."

"Did you take her to a hospital?" Mak asked.

Huntington shook her head. "Normally we would have, but rather than traumatize her further, I put a call in to a doctor to come here. A hospital can be a lot of stimulation, and I wanted to avoid her waiting all night in a room. Not to mention, we have a local doctor who makes house calls. She's on her way here."

"Okay," Mak acknowledged. Upon spotting Lacy in the conference room, Mak's eyes softened considerably.

Stephen's heart was beating quickly in his chest, but he knew that Sergeant Huntington was right. He needed to be calm and approach Lacy like she was a scared rabbit.

"Has she told you anything yet?" Stephen asked.

"Not really. We wanted to have her on record when she spoke. She told us she'd been kidnapped. Kept saying she needed to go back for her friends. She didn't have time to find them. She feels guilty about leaving them behind," Huntington told them.

"There are more women?" Mak whispered, the color leaving her face.

"That's what she said. We brought her straight here to give her privacy. Once the media finds out about this, they're going to be all over her—"

"No!" Stephen cut her off with a slash of his hand. "No media and no phone calls home until we know exactly what happened. If she saw her kidnapper's face and she got away, she's going to need more than anonymity, she's going to need protection."

"Especially if she can lead us to other missing women," Mak agreed.

"We need her statement, but not until she's ready to tell us her story. I'll stay all night if that's what it takes to get it." Huntington crossed her arms over her chest.

Mak bobbed her head. "Me too."

"Then it's agreed," Stephen said. He led the way as he approached Lacy slowly. He waited until she lifted her eyes to his. He hated the fear he saw in them. Up close, Stephen could see the sharp scratches all over Lacy's face. One of them was bleeding pretty badly. Her blond hair had blood, dirt, and leaves tangled into it. He could only imagine what her body looked like. There was a blanket wrapped around her and two bare feet peeked out from underneath. They were caked with dirt and red clay.

He took a seat across the table and propped his elbows on top, his hands clasped together in an unassuming pose. He saw Mak and Huntington follow his lead and sit down at the table. Huntington sat beside Stephen, and Mak took a seat next to Lacy.

Sturgis shut the office door to give them privacy and stayed guard outside the office.

"Hi, Lacy," Stephen fiddled with the badge he'd pulled out. Then he handed it across the table to Lacy. He was encouraged when she took it from him and studied it. He could see dirt caked into a few of her fingernails. "I'm a US Marshal. My name is Stephen Wilton. This is my partner, Mak Cunningham. And you've met Sergeant Huntington?"

Lacy nodded and handed Stephen back his badge. Her eyes flitted to Mak's badge when Mak laid hers on the table as well.

"Lots of people have been looking for you," Stephen began.

"How do you feel?" Mak asked.

Lacy swallowed hard. "I'm scratched up. I'm tired. I'm—afraid. Mostly, I feel so guilty." Tears welled in her eyes.

"Understandable," Mak murmured. "We're here for you. Whatever you need, please let us know."

Lacy nodded.

"Can you tell us why you feel guilty?" Mak asked.

Tears fell down Lacy's face now, creating a river of dark stains through her dirty face. "There are more women in the earth prison. Three of them. They're my friends. I left them—" A broken sob came out in a loud heave.

Mak's eyes welled up too. "I'm sorry about your friends. The good news is you lived to tell us where they are. That's the best way you can help them now. We're going to find them."

"Okay," Lacy whispered. The tears lessened and she seemed to pull herself together.

"Are you okay to continue?" Mak asked, her eyes searching Lacy's.

Lacy nodded and brushed the tears away.

"Here's what needs to happen in the next few hours," Stephen said, hating that they needed to walk her through the process when what she really needed was time to grieve her experience and heal. But he'd done this before in his job as a detective. There was a fine line to balance with victims. They needed to clearly know what to expect. There needed to be no surprises. "We have a doctor on her way here. She's going to examine you here at the station and make sure you're okay. We need to get a statement from you. But there's no rush. You can take your time and tell us when you're ready."

"Can I call my mom?" Lacy's voice rasped, and she coughed to clear it. She looked at them with pleading eyes.

Stephen exchanged a glance with Mak.

"There's nothing we want more than for you to talk to your family," Mak began with a sad smile. "And we're going to let you do that eventually. But first, we need to hear your story and determine if you're still in danger."

Lacy sucked in air sharply. "Why would I still be in danger?"

"Did you see your kidnapper?" Mak asked.

Lacy nodded. "There were three of them. They have my friends. They're holding them captive. I have to go back. I promised them. I have to help them—" Lacy's eyes got wild as she repeated herself, and she half rose from her chair. It was like her brain was on repeat.

Mak rested a light hand on Lacy's shoulder and lowered her voice even more. She oozed with sympathy. "It's okay, Lacy. You're safe here with us. And we want to go find the other women. But because you've seen the men who took you, we think the best way to save the women is to keep you safe. We can offer you 24/7 protection until we find these guys and lock them away. For now, it's best for you and your family if everyone believes you're still missing."

"Oh," Lacy's eyes filled with tears. "Like witness protection? The men know I got away. It's not a surprise to them that I'm alive and free. Are you sure I can't just call my mom?"

"You may have gotten way, but you can ID every single one of those men and they know it. In the witness protection process, we have no choice but to cut all communications with family and loved ones. It protects them as well as you. The less they know, the less someone can coerce them to talk," Mak assured her with a nod.

"Will they be safe?" Lacy's eyes were wide with fear. "Should they go into protection with me?"

"We usually offer that for immediate dependents and family members whose lives are in danger because they plan to testify against traffickers, terrorists, or organized crime members. Protection should only be temporary," Mak rushed to assure Lacy.

Stephen shot Mak a look. One he was sure Lacy saw. Her eyes were watching all of them in a sharp, focused way. Federal witnesses could be in protection for years on account of the time it took to catch and bring criminals to trial.

"Will the doctor be here soon?" Lacy asked.

"I can't be sure," Sergeant Huntington stated. "We sent for her the minute we picked you up."

"Okay, I'd like to give my statement now," Lacy said with a strong voice.

Stephen felt surprised. He looked at Huntington, who held up a finger and went to turn on her video to record. When Huntington returned, she nodded at Stephen, who began.

He read the date and the time. Then he introduced each officer in the room.

"Can you please state your full name for the record?" Stephen requested.

"Lacy Maureen Donovan," Lacy answered.

"In your own words, please tell us about the day when you were kidnapped."

"I was taken from my own home just over eight days ago—" Lacy's voice cracked, and she worked to clear her throat.

Mak stood and peeked out at Sturgis. She quietly requested water. Sturgis was gone, then back in a flash. Mak thanked him and gave the water to Lacy.

Lacy gave Mak a small smile, twisted the lid off, and guzzled the water.

Stephen felt concerned. She could be dehydrated. Not to mention, who knew when she'd last eaten. Should they really do this interview right now?

"Lacy, when is the last time you ate something?" Stephen asked.

Lacy looked confused. She shook her head. "I don't know."

"Okay, let's get you some food. At this time of night, there might only be fast food. Do you have any requests?" he asked.

Lacy shrugged and looked sheepish. "I'm craving a hamburger and a coke."

Mak was still standing by the door. She leaned out to make another request to Sturgis. Sturgis looked to his boss. Huntington nodded her permission and Sturgis left in search of food.

"We can wait until you eat. There's no hurry for a statement," Stephen stated.

Lacy closed her eyes for minutes. She took ten full, slow deep breaths. They waited patiently. Lacy opened her eyes.

"We do need to hurry. Every second we lose is time my friends are stuck in that earth prison," Lacy stated with urgency.

Mak nodded with understanding.

Huntington leaned forward.

Stephen sat still, his eyes trained on Lacy. "Okay, please tell us your story."

42

LACY

Lacy knew it wasn't going to be easy. She was retelling a story that her brain was already actively trying to block out. But Lacy was a fighter. Her friends were still in captivity and the sooner these cops got her statement, the sooner they would be able to go rescue Lacy's friends, the women she had left behind. So, she would attempt to tell her story in a logical way, by shutting down her emotions.

She took a deep breath and started again. "I was taken from my home. It was a night like every other night. I was talking to my mom on the phone when I walked into my place. My mom is overprotective. She was freaking out because I wouldn't tell her where I was living. I refused to tell her. I'd made a vow to myself that I was going to do it on my own when I moved out. Anyway, I was in the middle of assuring her, yet again, that I would be fine. That's when I walked through the door of my house and looked around. I realized at that moment, I was not fine," Lacy paused and took a drink of water.

They waited quietly for her to continue.

"My place had been turned upside down. Ransacked. It looked like someone had been looking for something. I immediately got off the phone with my mom. I took several steps backward out of the house and ran right into a man. He was a huge guy, standing there in my doorway, blocking my only exit. He grabbed me from behind. I fought, he knocked me out, then carried me to an earth prison—"

"Earth prison?" Mak interrupted gently.

"Yes," Lacy answered.

"Can you describe this earth prison? Do you mean he dragged you somewhere on the same property where your house is?"

"Yes." Lacy swallowed. "Who knew that less than a mile from my tiny home, three women were being held against their will underground?" She shuddered. "The earth prison is like a storm shelter but without real walls. The walls are made up of tightly compacted dirt. The only way in or out was being dropped in or pulled out."

"Do you have the names of the other women who were being held?" Stephen asked. He grabbed a notepad and pencil that had been sitting on the table.

Lacy nodded but then her face fell. "I only know first names."

"Anything you give us helps," Stephen encouraged her.

"Emma, Isa—short for Isabelle, and Lauren," Lacy stated.

"What do they look like?" Stephen asked after writing down their names.

"Like me," Lacy said simply. "Blond, blue or green eyes, thin —only they're too thin. They were dehydrated, emaciated, and frail. I could see their bones through their clothing, which hung on them. Their hair was thinning. They were…" Lacy swallowed hard. "They were dying. They've been there way longer than I was."

Mak covered her mouth. Emotion showed in her eyes.

Huntington shivered though it wasn't cold.

"How many days did you say you were in there?" Stephen asked.

"Eight. I put a tally on the wall each time I saw daylight through the sliver in the earth door."

"What was captivity like?" Mak asked.

"I'd say boring, but I used the time to meditate, practice yoga positions, and talk to the girls. Their stories were sadder than mine. More importantly, they had descriptions of all three men because they'd each been allowed out once. They described their experience, so I knew what to expect. Mentally, I had prepared for the night when they allowed me out," Lacy said. Her voice was peaceful, but her eyes were a storm of emotion.

"That was earlier tonight?" Stephen asked.

Lacy nodded. "What I didn't prepare for was the syringe of fluid shot into my neck that knocked me out before I could act. I woke up in a literal cage that was painted gold. The girls called it *the golden cage*, but I didn't understand why until tonight. I was dressed in this—" She gestured to her body though they couldn't see what she wore under the blanket. "A silky golden dress that barely came to my thighs. Spaghetti straps with a low scoop neckline." Lacy shuddered involuntarily and took a drink of water.

"How did you escape the golden cage?" Mak asked.

"I woke up, but knew I had to pretend I was still unconscious until I figured out where I was and how to get away. I knew it would be my only chance. I could hear the men yelling in another room. I figured out that they were gambling. I had also put together that I, like the rest of the girls, had been photographed to be put up on the black market. Though I didn't know that for sure, that was a hunch. I waited until a man came to drag me out of the cage. I pretended I was still unconscious. When I was far enough out, I kicked him—hard—like my life depended on it. I got up and kicked him again while he was down. I got free. I was out the back door and running toward the woods before anyone else had figured it out."

"Did they see which direction you ran?" Stephen asked.

"Yes, I could hear them yelling behind me when I hit the tree line. But I was too far away for them to catch me. Still, I didn't stop for what seemed like half a mile. Through the woods. That's how I got all these scratches." Again, Lacy indicated to her covered-up body. "Then there was a clearing. I kept running. I could hear a highway, and I thought I'd be free once someone saw me on the road. I just needed to go another short distance through more trees. But then it hit me—"

"What?" Mak asked, leaning forward to absorb every detail.

"Why weren't they following me? They most likely knew this property like the back of their hands. But no one was running after me. So, I stopped to rest against a tree trunk. Then I noticed how climbable the tree looked. I climbed it. I figured I'd stay there and hide if I had to. But when I got up the tree, I saw them."

"You saw the three guys?" Stephen clarified.

Lacy nodded. "Yeah. There were three different cars. The men were standing outside the cars. They were waiting. For me. Positioned right where the property line ended and the highway began. They were parked on the shoulder, far enough away from each other but close enough that no matter where I popped out, one of them would see me and be able to grab me."

"So, what did you do?" Huntington asked.

"I climbed back down, and I ran back the way I came. I knew the direction of the grocery store from my place. Remember, I live on that property. The nearest grocery store was a quarter mile down the road. I ran without looking back. I knew if they got suspicious, they could start driving around and find me pretty easily. But once I saw the lights in the grocery store parking lot, I knew I was safe."

"You must have been running on pure adrenaline by that point." Mak shook her head. "But you made it."

"I managed to make it through the double doors. I think I shouted, *Call nine-one-one!* Then I think I passed out," Lacy said.

Huntington nodded. "You did. You were pretty out of it when we came to get you."

"Lacy, do you think you could describe the men to a sketch artist?" Stephen asked.

Lacy's eyebrows knit together. "I'll do whatever it takes to help you get these guys. But right now, we need to go get the girls. I can tell you the address of my place. I can draw you a map of where I think the earth prison is, but I'm not sure how accurate it will be. I looked for it briefly before I ran to the grocery store, and I couldn't find it. Can you please go find the girls? I promised them I would save us all."

Stephen slid the paper he had been writing on over to Lacy. "Please, write it all down here."

Lacy turned the paper over and took the pencil, her hand shaking.

A knock at the door interrupted them.

Sturgis peeked his head in. He waved the bag at Lacy. "Food's here."

Lacy's eyes got big. "Thank you." She was surprised to find how hungry she was after all that. She tore into the bag and took a giant bite of the burger. Fast food had never tasted so good.

"Sturgis," Stephen caught the man's attention. "Can you print out a Google map for this address?" Stephen tapped on an address Lacy had written down.

"Sure thing." Sturgis eyed the paper like he was memorizing it, then left for a few minutes.

When Sturgis returned with a visual of the property where Lacy had stayed, she felt the urgency of her task, put down her burger, and wrote down more information they needed to go save her friends.

She only hoped it wasn't too late for them.

43

MAK

The doctor arrived and everyone was barred from the conference room, which was now being used as an exam room. Mak was the last to leave the room and saw Lacy drop her blanket to reveal the short, tattered gold dress she wore, along with bruises and the blood from cuts along her arms and legs. Her feet were filthy. The image burned into Mak's brain.

Lacy worked so hard to escape. She didn't let obstacles like a cold, moonless night, tree branches, tangled forest, or bare feet stop her. Lacy was a survivor and Mak would honor her promise. They would find those other missing girls, even if Mak died trying.

"Let's go, Wilton," Mak commanded loudly as she walked back into the station lobby.

"Where?" Wilton looked at Mak with confusion.

"Where do you think?" Mak asked, hearing the way her voice snapped but not caring at the moment. "We have the property address. We need to go rescue those women."

"Hold on," Wilton ran to catch up with her and caught her at the door.

Mak paused but speared him with her eyes. She lowered her

voice. "We don't have time to hold on. Lacy's kidnappers think she's still out there. What do you think was the first thing they did when they figured out Lacy had escaped the property?" Mak didn't wait for an answer to her rhetorical question. "They started making plans to take the other women and run. I guarantee it. We have a small window of time and still might be too late."

"I hear you, and I don't disagree. But play this out. What if they already know exactly where Lacy is?" Wilton looked over his shoulder at Sturgis who still stood guarding the conference room. "Do you think this station is equipped to handle it if those guys broke in here to take her back? Our priority needs to be getting Lacy into protective custody immediately."

"They'd have to be pretty ballsy to knock over a police station—"

"Mak," Wilton's voice conveyed his urgency as he cut her off for once. "This is a small town with the nearest police station for backup at least thirty miles away. The normal rules don't apply here. They could take out this station in two seconds. It's not exactly locked down."

Mak clenched her fists by her sides and glared at Wilton, not wanting to admit his point while agreeing they needed to protect their victim. Not to mention, Lacy would be a witness in a trial at some point.

"Fine. What do you suggest?" Mak asked through gritted teeth.

"Maybe we could do both—protect Lacy *and* go find the women," Wilton puzzled aloud as he stared at her. "I happen to know there's a fire department in this town as well as some volunteer firefighters—"

"But the more people know about Lacy, the more people will talk. We need her identity protected. No one can know she's here," Mak protested.

"Okay," Wilton looked at the front door. "What if we lock

down the station? The firefighters can stay on guard outside with strict instructions that no one goes in or out until we get back—"

"This sounds like a conversation you should be having with me," Sergeant Huntington interrupted from behind them in a low voice. She was standing close enough that Mak jumped a little.

Mak felt her face go red. She and Wilton were so focused on their conversation, they'd forgotten to include a decision-maker. "Sorry, Sergeant. We were brainstorming options. We need to offer Lacy protective custody, but we also need to go check out the location she gave us," Mak began.

"We're afraid to leave Lacy here without backup because that leaves her and your station exposed. As you know, Lacy will be able to ID these guys and take them down." Wilton ran his hand through his unruly curls.

Huntington regarded them with silence. She, too, seemed to be thinking. "I assume your boss is sending someone to take her into witness protection?"

Wilton nodded. "He will. We'll call him and get several marshals on their way to escort her. But it'll take a couple hours to get here. Right now, we need to know Lacy will be safe if we go search the property."

"Our fire chief, Jud Blackwell, is very responsive. He's a bit of a big mouth though… But I think we could get him and his crew here to guard outside the place with no questions asked. My concern is how the two of you think you can rescue three women and take down three kidnappers?" Huntington challenged, narrowing her eyes.

"Those are odds we're going to have to take because we can't ignore the women. They've been there way too long as it is." Mak's eyes must have been shooting fire because both Wilton and Huntington took a step back.

"Mak, let's call Sikes. We really need his feedback on this—"

"You mean his blessing," Mak corrected.

"Well, yeah," Wilton nodded. "I agree with Huntington. This is a pretty big job for two marshals."

"Meanwhile, three kidnappers are loading three missing women into the back of a transport vehicle and driving away, taking all chances of freedom along with them," Mak snapped.

"Tell you what," Huntington said diplomatically. "I'll reach out to Jud. You guys reach out to Sikes. Let's talk in five minutes and nail down a plan. Fair?"

Both Mak and Wilton nodded.

Mak called Sikes and put the phone on speaker.

A minute later, a very groggy Sikes answered his phone. "Don't you two ever sleep?"

"I wish!" Wilton snorted.

"You know we'd only call this late if something was happening, Sikes," Mak cut to the point.

"Right, what's up?" Sikes asked.

"We have a dilemma, sir," Wilton answered. "We have the missing girl, Lacy Donovan. She was held captive with three other girls. She told us their location. We want to go rescue the girls, but we have to keep Lacy safe. She can ID all three of the men who took her."

"The local police think they could lock down the station and guard outside with fire station personnel until we return. But we need a few marshals to escort Lacy to protection," Mak explained.

"Okay, so you need me to send a few marshals. What else do you need from me?" Sikes asked.

"Well, it's a big job. There's two of us, three girls, and three kidnappers," Wilton outlined.

Sikes was quiet for a minute. "Any chance you have the element of surprise?"

Mak sighed. "I don't know about that. It's only a matter of

time before they figure out Lacy has made it to safety. I think they'll try to move the girls."

"Actually," Wilton thought aloud. "If we can get to the girls while they're in transit, we might have a better chance."

Mak shot him a puzzled look.

"I'm just worried about how to physically lift three different women from a hole in the ground," Wilton said. "If the kidnappers are moving them, the heavy lifting might be done for us."

"According to what Lacy said, the women aren't going to be heavy," Mak surmised.

"Is the marshal rover stocked?" Sikes asked. "You have rope, right?"

"Yeah," Wilton said after a second of thought. "Pretty sure we do."

"Okay, you guys. I've already dispatched a few marshals to head your direction while we were talking. You know the drill. Be safe. Do your best to bring the women home but at the end of the night, you two need to prioritize yourselves. You got that?"

"Yes, sir!" Wilton agreed.

Mak hung up the phone. She hated thinking about the details of everything that could go wrong. She knew that's why she often rushed in. To stay ahead of the fear. Fear was immobilizing. The overthinking and not having answers on the front end was not her favorite.

One thing was for sure. Everything was going to be different by the end of this night. She hoped it would be for the better, but she didn't have time to think about that right now.

44

LACY

Lacy knew about the tests doctors did on kidnapping victims. They were the same tests they did on rape and abuse victims. They were humiliating and invasive. As if the horror a victim went through wasn't enough. They had to be poked and prodded post trauma. The only consolation was that the doctor was gentle and kind. But Lacy just wanted it all to be over. Then, it was. The doctor wrapped Lacy back in her blanket and left to process her tests.

Then the lights went out. As if this nightmare couldn't get any worse, they'd literally turned out the lights on the station and went into lockdown. All because of her. She had information to put three dangerous men in prison forever. Lacy closed her eyes and attempted to reach a meditative state. But peace was fleeting and clouded by fear.

A light knock at the door made Lacy jump. Her heart sped in her chest. She knew the truth. Lacy should never have been able to escape. So few girls, if any, ever had.

"Sorry to startle you, Lacy," Sergeant Huntington said quietly. "We are putting the station under lockdown to keep you safe until we have backup agents here. In the meantime, the doctor cleared you to get cleaned up. We have a nice shower in a secure location here in the building. Lock the door behind you. You'll have the place to yourself for as long as you need."

Lacy nodded but couldn't speak past the lump in her throat. A shower sounded like heaven. Her eyes had adjusted to the dark and she could see clothes in Sergeant Huntington's hands.

"I scrounged up some extra clothes we had around the station. We keep a small stash in case—well, situations like this," Sergeant Huntington looked down at her hands. "They won't be a perfect fit. But they're better than what you have on now."

Lacy looked down at the blanket she clung to and thought about the tattered golden dress underneath. She felt her stomach turn. She would never look at the color gold the same way again.

"These will get you through the airport and to the safe house—"

"I can't believe I'm not going home," Lacy sniffled.

"Not yet. But you will. Testifying is very brave. It's the best chance of saving your friends and other women in the future." Sergeant Huntington came into the room.

Lacy wiped a tear.

"I'm sorry. We need to keep you safe and that means no one can know you're alive for now. It's our best defense in putting these guys away and getting you back home." Huntington seemed deep in thought as she offered Lacy her hand. "You do have a choice here. I just assumed you would take the protection they're offering rather than taking your chances out there?"

Lacy hesitated, then nodded. She took Sergeant Huntington's hand and let the policewoman lead her to a bathroom that Lacy thought looked like a safe room. It was walled in with cinderblocks. It was a basic locker room with a bathroom, a sink, a shower, and necessary toiletries.

Sergeant Huntington handed the stack of clothes to Lacy,

complete with a pair of tennis shoes that Lacy judged were at least a size too big. Lacy took them, feeling grateful.

"Thank you," Lacy said.

"Knock three times to let us know when you're coming out so we can look for you. Otherwise, take your time in there. I don't anticipate the agents arriving back here for at least an hour and a half."

"Thank you," Lacy said again. She shut and locked the door behind her. She stepped out of that god-awful gold dress and turned on the shower, adjusting the lever until the water was scalding hot. She closed her eyes and let eight days' worth of grime wash off her.

Then Lacy began to sob. The other women had been there so much longer. What about them? Where was the explanation for why Lacy had escaped but they had not? Guilt flooded Lacy powerfully and her grief wracked her whole body. In fact, she was crying so loud, she'd be surprised if they couldn't hear her over the shower and through the thick aluminum door she was locked behind.

Were the other women, her friends in captivity, still alive? What if she had made things worse for them?

45

WILTON

Stephen and Mak had gone out the back door of the station. Sturgis had been there to lock the door behind them. When the fire trucks showed up, Stephen knew he'd get an interrogation from Jud Blackwell, the fire chief he'd met when he lived in this town, if they didn't sneak out unnoticed. This plan would only work if they kept Lacy Donovan a secret. Stephen jumped in the car with Mak, who rolled quietly out of the parking lot, waiting to turn on her headlights until they were on the road leading away from the station.

Stephen still had so many questions, but Lacy was in with the doctor when they'd left. Questions like, *Were the girls being fed in captivity, or were their captors starving them? If they were selling the girls, why were the three women still there? How long had they been there? What was their story?* But those answers were secondary to this new mission. They needed to prioritize saving the women, and then they could ask questions later. And they needed to save them tonight. Mak was right. The first thing the kidnappers would do would be to move the hostages.

"Hey, Stephen," Mak broke the silence but kept her eyes on

the road as she drove. "I want you to know that I'm real sorry about your brother."

"What?" Stephen asked. His mind had a hard time shifting gears to comprehend her words. "We're about to go into a really dangerous situation, with no real backup, and *that's* what you're thinking about? How do you even know about my brother anyway?"

"I heard you talking about it when you left the message for Alyah earlier. You thought I was sleeping. I was trying to, but I wasn't," Mak admitted with a sigh.

"Well, I'll figure out what happened to him on a different day." Stephen shook his head. "That's not what I want to focus on right now."

"I just want you to know that I care about what's happening in your life. And you can tell me anything. We're partners, you know?" Mak continued quietly.

"Jeez, Mak, you're acting like you've been given a life sentence. You're scaring me a little." Stephen's heart was pounding. Mak wasn't sure about this mission. He could tell. Mak had great instincts, and if she felt something was off, he thought he should listen.

Mak sighed. "It's just that we're in a really dangerous line of work, and anything can happen at any time. Ya know? If this thing goes south, I just want to know we're good."

"Mak, what are your instincts telling you right now?" Stephen ignored her words, feeling a new sense of urgency. "You're not the one who has doubts in these situations. I'm not sure I'm comfortable—"

"There's no time. Get comfortable, Wilton. We're here." Mak turned the lights off on the vehicle and parked just off the road at the edge of the property where the tree line started. It was exactly where Lacy had instructed them to go.

Using the home address Lacy had given them, they were able to print off a Google Earth picture. Lacy had circled the area where she believed she had been held. From that, they determined they would have to hike in about a quarter mile from where Mak had parked. But they both knew circles on maps and traumatic memories were unreliable. They needed to be ready for anything.

They were ready alright. They were prepared anyway. They'd put on bullet-proof vests at the station. Mak and Stephen each had fully loaded Glocks on hip holsters for easy access. Stephen had a flashlight. They both had rope to help the girls out of the hole in the ground.

The complicated part would be finding the trick door in the ground. Stephen reasoned there had to be some physical indication on the ground, like a square where no grass grew, that would point to where the hatch was. Then they would have to look for a handle of some sort that was used to open the earth prison, like a fabricated rock bolted to the latch that was big enough to pull upward.

Mak turned off the overhead light in the vehicle. They both quietly opened their doors, got out, and clicked them shut. For minutes, they stood surveying the land. There was no moon tonight. It was likely how Lacy had successfully escaped. But it didn't work in their favor now.

The property was flat. According to Lacy's description, the woods seemed to serve as a boundary line for the property.

Follow the trees until you see the mansion in the distance—about half a mile to the north, Lacy had instructed. *Then turn toward the mansion and go about ten steps toward the house. It's hard to see but if you really look, there should be an outline of a hatch door. I don't know how they open it.*

Stephen knew nothing about these instructions was specific enough to find what they were looking for. This was an impossible treasure hunt. Only, the treasure would be the lives of three women. He just hoped the women were strong enough to walk because he didn't think he and Mak could carry them. But then, maybe they could, considering Lacy's description of how frail they were.

Mak and Stephen stood side by side as they cautiously took a step into the untamed woods. They walked as quietly as possible through fallen leaves lining the ground. They didn't have an accurate estimate of how far they would have to walk before the forest opened up to the property that would become flat ground.

Stephen ducked to miss a low branch. It missed him, but it caught his jacket and held fast. The stubborn branch yanked Stephen back and he let out a sharp gasp of surprise.

Mak whirled on him. Then she smirked at Stephen as he quickly took off his jacket and disconnected it from the branch. He frowned when he saw a small hole in its place.

They moved forward again. Though it was dark, Stephen resisted the urge to turn on his flashlight. He recalled Lacy's dirty, scratched-up feet. She had run barefoot through these rough, wild woods and he couldn't imagine how painful that must have been.

Finally, they stood at the clearing. They could see the mansion at the front of the property half a mile off.

"Ten steps," Mak whispered. She moved forward, her movement rushed, as was her nature.

"Wait," Stephen hissed. He put his hand on Mak's shoulder to physically stop her movement. He had a bad feeling about this. Something wasn't right.

Mak shook off his hand and gave him a look of disapproval. "There's no time to wait. Let's go!"

Before Stephen could say another word, Mak had taken three quick steps, which put her on the property.

The boom was deafening. A loud explosion echoed through the woods. Stephen had barely registered the sound before everything went quiet. He could only hear the shrill ring of silence.

Everything began to move in slow motion.

He felt the hot, powerful force of the sudden blast. Stephen's body flung backwards. He was flying weightlessly through the air, wondering when he would land. When he hit the ground, he experienced no pain. Confused, he looked around him. He had struck the earth and now lay on a soft cushion of leaves about twenty feet from where he'd been.

He could see Mak. She was still airborne, lifting way higher than Stephen had. Her arms and legs were flailing. She might be screaming, but he still couldn't hear anything. From Stephen's spot on the ground, he looked up just in time to see Mak hit a tree. She hit hard enough that her face registered pain as her back and head smacked into it. She fell to the ground from quite a height.

Though Stephen couldn't hear it, he could imagine the sound her body must have made when it connected with the unforgiving forest floor. Then he tried not to imagine it because instinctively, he knew.

Mak was hurt. Badly.

The flames were sudden and high. They seemed to shoot up out of nowhere. Burning bright and hot, a fire raged close by. Too close for his liking. Stephen's senses processed the tactile feelings of his new surroundings. A series of three more booms occurred, timed half a second apart from the last one. He didn't know how he heard that, but he did. Or maybe it was the rattle of the world around him each time it detonated. Stephen's brain computed quickly.

Remote detonated bombs? Or was it a bomb that had been set to ignite with movement and create a chain reaction? That must have been it. When Mak stepped onto the property, she had ignited the bomb. The light burned his retinas and he had to look away.

Stephen's ears rang, but the aftermath of the explosion was still somehow deafening.

"Mak?" Stephen tried to yell but didn't know if any words came out. He couldn't hear anything but the roar of a fire and white noise in his ears. He was up on his knees now, crawling forward. When he felt steadier, he stood, wobbling to his feet. He caught his balance. Then Stephen was running, or maybe he was just stumbling headfirst. Regardless of how he did it, sheer panic propelled his body through the woods to his partner.

Mak lay on the ground, not moving. The thought entered his brain, *Mak looks lifeless*. Her face was blackened, and he could see burn marks there. She was unconscious. Stephen didn't realize he was holding his breath as he knelt beside her. He put two fingers on the side of Mak's throat, feeling for a pulse. His heart rate quickened when he didn't feel one. Sudden pictures of his partner, Ethan Booker, flashed through his mind and he forcefully rejected them.

"No!" he yelled. "You're not dead, damn it!" He grabbed her wrist and practically lost his balance in relief. Her pulse was faint, but she had one. Mak was alive at the moment. That was all that mattered.

Stephen could feel the heat burning hotter and knew the flames were growing higher. He glanced behind him and could only see a wall of fire approximately thirty-five feet away that seemed to surround the entire square around the property. At least, he assumed that was the case based on what he could see. His brain was temporarily dumb as he strained to process what had happened.

He waited for the fire to move his way. He and Mak were so close to it there in the woods, but the fire didn't travel their direction. In fact, the line of fire almost looked contained. Though it seemed to be demolishing everything within that square. Destructive chaos within an organized plan. That's when it hit him.

Mak and Stephen had walked into a trap.

Lacy's captors had known she'd been rescued and knew the authorities would show up for the other women.

The other women! Stephen forgot to breathe again as he peered through the fire. Had they taken them somewhere else? He didn't know what would happen to them if they were trapped underground during a fire. Surely their oxygen levels would decrease, and they would eventually suffocate. His gut told him the men who'd held these women here were long gone. He just didn't know if it was with or without the victims.

Stephen's gaze fell back on Mak. He needed to get her out of here. But how?

Stephen felt for his cell phone. He still had it zipped into a pocket in his cargo pants. With trembling fingers, he dialed 911, then stopped before hitting *call*. If he called 911, every fire truck in the county would race to the scene, which would leave Lacy unprotected at the station. Stephen couldn't shake that this is exactly what the kidnappers had planned.

Still, Stephen had to call it in.

"Nine-one-one, what's your emergency?" a man answered.

"US Marshal Stephen Wilton, requesting backup. There's been an explosion and my partner is hurt." Stephen rattled off the address and his marshal badge number. "Please send an ambulance immediately and give them my number. We're in the woods. I don't think I should move her, but this fire is getting hot."

"Okay, slow down, sir. You're talking very loudly—"

"What?" Stephen had a hard time hearing the man on account of the fire roaring in the background and the ringing in his ears. "I'm sorry, the explosion… it's loud here."

"Tell me the condition of your partner," the man requested, increasing the volume of his voice.

"She has a pulse, but she's unconscious," Stephen looked at Mak's crumbled body. "The blast blew her back and she hit a tree—"

"Okay, be very careful not to move her," the man commanded. "Do you see blood or any obvious wounds?"

Stephen wanted to kick himself. He hadn't looked. Now he critically scanned her body. "She's lying face up. One leg is bent, and one is straight. No blood there. No sign of—oh no!" Stephen groaned.

"What is it?" the man on the phone asked.

"There's blood. It's coming from under her head," Stephen's pulse sped. Panic clouded his vision for a minute. Or maybe the heat from the fire was disorienting him. Stephen used the back of his sleeve to wipe the sweat rolling down his forehead.

"Earlier you said she hit a tree. Did she hit her head then?" the man asked.

"Yeah, she did," Stephen confirmed.

"Do you have something soft like a shirt? If so, you need to use it to put pressure on the back of her head—"

"But you said not to move her body. What if her neck is broken?" Stephen's words were just tumbling out.

"Assess the angle of her head and her neck. Does it look like it's at a weird angle?" the 911 dispatcher asked.

Stephen scanned Mak's neck. "No."

"Okay, apply pressure to the bleeding by moving her as little as possible," he requested.

"Okay," Stephen put the phone on speaker and dropped it in the leaves. He took off his jacket, then his bullet proof vest. Finally, he removed his shirt, feeling thankful he had on an undershirt. Carefully, he leaned down, gently lifted Mak's head, and place his shirt under her. He let her head lay back down on top of the shirt.

"Got it?" the dispatcher asked.

"Yeah," Stephen answered. "I just don't know how to apply pressure at this angle."

"She's face up?" the man asked.

"Yeah," Stephen confirmed. The air was getting thick, and

Stephen took in a deep breath, desperate for fresh air. Instead, what he breathed in created a coughing spasm.

"Okay, the weight of her head will have to work. You can't move her any more than you have to."

"How much longer until someone is here?" Sweat was now dripping into Stephen's eyes as he watched the fire that raged just the length of a school bus away from them.

"I've dispatched EMS and fire," the man answered. "Can you stay on the phone with me until someone gets there?"

Stephen felt panic. "No, I'm sorry. I need to alert others, but you have my call back number."

"Okay, hang tight. They'll be there soon."

Stephen hung up and dialed the station.

"Huntington," came the answer.

"It's Wilton—"

"Thank God. Maybe you can explain why all the fire trucks are pulling out?" she barked.

"There was an explosion here at the property. We walked into a trap. I had to call it in. Mak's hurt. She's unconscious. Nine-one-one dispatched everyone. So listen, my hunch is the kidnappers are long gone. Unless I'm wrong and this was all part of the plan to get Lacy back. Hunker down. As soon as they load up Mak, I'll be there. I assume the relief marshals are still an hour out."

"Got it." Huntington hung up.

Next, Stephen dialed Sikes.

"What's up?" Sikes answered, sounding alert.

"I've got a problem, sir," Stephen started. "It's Mak. She's hurt. Alive but unconscious."

"What the hell happened?" Sikes snapped. His voice sounded anxious.

"We walked into a trap. The minute she stepped onto the property, there was an explosion, followed by three more. It blew in a controlled sort of way. Like they knew we were coming and wanted to burn away any shred of evidence and maybe blow us up in the process. The explosion threw Mak backward into a tree. Her head's bleeding and she's unconscious. EMS is on the way. How far out are the relief marshals?"

"Give me a minute," Sikes said. The line went quiet and Stephen knew Sikes switched over to another line. Then he was back. "Forty-five minutes. Can you hang tight?"

Stephen sure hoped he could. "Well, the fire department has just been dispatched to come here and put out this fire, leaving the station, where Lacy is, exposed." Stephen wiped sweat from his brow. That fire was hot, and he felt lightheaded.

Then Stephen heard rescue sirens. Relief flooded through him.

"Is that an ambulance I hear?" Sikes asked.

"Yeah, small town. It doesn't take long to get here, thank God! Gotta go, sir. EMS is pulling in. I need to guide them to Mak."

46

WILTON

Stephen watched, feeling helpless and in a daze as EMS carefully placed Mak on a stretcher. He walked beside Mak's unconscious body all the way to the ambulance that was now parked on the road in front of the US Marshal vehicle they'd abandoned earlier.

He wanted to scream at her. To shout at Mak, *Wake up!* But it wouldn't have helped. Nothing he could do would fix this. Fix her.

"Well, I'll be—" a loud, jovial voice sounded behind Stephen as he watched EMS load Mak into the back of the ambulance. "There's a man I thought I'd never see again!"

Stephen turned slowly. "Jud Blackwell," he said through gritted teeth, observing the large man wearing a ball cap over his balding head. Stephen made himself offer his hand. He didn't have time for this. Jud Blackwell was the fire chief and town's loudest gossip. But he was also the man who'd found Stephen dying from a bullet wound at the *Mynart Murder House,* the nickname of the place where he'd once lived. All that was a former life. It all happened years ago when Stephen was still a detective.

Jud grabbed Stephen's hand and pumped it a couple times. "Damn shame what's happened here," Jud shook his head.

"Shouldn't you be helping fight this fire?" Stephen wondered. He suddenly felt tired. The double obligations he felt to follow Mak to the emergency room and get to the station to help protect Lacy suddenly built an urgency in him. There was no time to sit and chat.

Jud let out a belly laugh. "My guys have it under control." He took off his ball cap and rubbed his bald head a few times before putting the cap back on. "Don't get me wrong, it'll be morning before we get this thing to smoke and ash but they're hitting it from every side. I just don't know how I'm gonna tell Mr. Gerritt his place went up in flames tonight." Jud leaned forward. "I'm being optimistic, of course. It's too soon to tell if anyone was inside."

"Mr. Gerritt?" Stephen repeated, the horror of this realization dawning. "As in Anthony Gerritt? Is that who owns this property?"

"Yes, sir. Surprised you didn't know that, Wilton. You've still got family in the area... Mr. Gerritt's a right, good business-man," Jud stated.

"What?" Stephen couldn't believe his ears. Panic formed in Stephen's gut. Why hadn't he put it together? Of course, it was no coincidence that Anthony Gerritt showed up in this town and women started going missing.

"Yep. He came in here little over a month—or was it two?—and started setting up shop. He's already revitalizing the economy around here—"

"I gotta go, Jud," Stephen interrupted. Stephen had been watching as an EMT worked on Mak before he shut the ambulance doors. "But I do need your number. Can you put it in?" Stephen unlocked his phone and thrust it at Jud.

"Why, sure!" Jud grabbed Stephen's phone and put in his

number. He handed it back, put his hands in his pockets, and rocked on his heels as if he had all the time in the world.

The EMS vehicle turned on. Stephen jogged toward his vehicle.

"Nice car! You fancy US Marshal!" Jud called. "It's a step up from detective. Congrats, man."

Stephen waved but got in the car.

Keys! His stomach lurched. *Mak had the keys.* He got out of the car and flagged down the ambulance before they could drive off. The EMT driver rolled down the window.

"Partner's got my keys," Stephen explained. He followed the EMT who got out of the driver's seat and let Stephen into the back. *Please let me find the keys.*

He jumped into the back, feeling overwhelming dread as he climbed to Mak's side. Her breathing was shallow. He carefully searched her pockets. *Nothing.* He looked around frantically. Time was ticking and Mak wasn't waking up any time soon. He turned to the EMT who was watching him.

"She was wearing a vest. Did you take it off her? Maybe the keys are there?" Stephen asked.

The EMT nodded and pointed to the extra clothing they had taken off Mak. The vest was there. Stephen searched. Relief flooded him when he found them.

His eyes fell on Mak again and he felt rage and hopelessness roll into one. He leaned over and grasped her shirt in his two fists. He didn't bother lowering his voice. Mak was in there. She was still alive. Stephen knew something about being in a coma. He knew she would hear him.

"You fight, Mak! You hear me. You're a fighter. You wake the hell up. Don't just lay there doing nothing. Get up! Fight! Fight! Fight!"

"Sir?" the voice of the EMT came from behind him as if in a warning.

Stephen let go of Mak's shirt and straightened. It was then

that he realized he was crying. Desperation, exhaustion, and fear all rolled down his cheeks. He hopped out of the ambulance and jogged to his car.

As he started the car and followed the ambulance away from the fire, the realization dawned on him. He was still alive. Along with that thought came the reality of how close he'd come to dying. Guilt wracked him, and for a minute, he could not breathe. He had his life and his partner was fighting for hers.

Stephen ground his teeth. He had to make it worth it. He had been spared.

"I'm gonna get this bastard!" He hit the steering wheel with his hand.

47

WILTON

Stephen was driving behind the ambulance. That feeling of uselessness overwhelmed him again. His brain was on hyperdrive with so much unprocessed information. He started making phone calls.

"Jud, it's Wilton. Listen, I forgot something. I need to give you a very important task. Top secret. Can you keep a secret?" Stephen knew even as he asked that the answer was no. But this was his best chance of getting an answer about the missing women.

"Hell, yeah. They didn't name me Chief for nothin', ya know," Jud bragged.

"Okay, listen to me. I need you and your guys to look for a trap door on the property. It's going to look like the rest of the property—like the ground. It's real hidden. I assume you'll find a big rock or something that will help you lift it. Call me when you find it and let me know if there's anything inside," Stephen commanded.

"Got it. Trap door in the ground. But what's inside, son?" Jud asked.

"You'll either see nothing or you'll know immediately what

you're looking for," Stephen answered evasively. "But once that fire is out, don't let your guys go home until you find that hatch. You hear me?" Stephen asked. He gave Jud the instructions that Lacy had given them earlier in the night on where the earth prison was located.

"Okay," Jud sounded unsure. "We'll look."

"Great, thanks!" Stephen hung up. Next, he called Sikes to fill him in.

"Listen you've got two marshals incoming. Twenty minutes. Can you hold the fort until then?" Sikes asked.

"Sure hope so," Stephen said, knowing he had no idea what state he'd find the station in once he got there. "I'm escorting the ambulance to make sure Mak gets inside. Did you call John to let him know?"

"Yeah," Sikes said with a serious tone. "He's on his way there."

Stephen nodded. "I'll poke in the hospital to make sure no unwanted visitors sneak back to Mak's room in the meantime. Then I'll head back to the station. I'll be there when the guys get there. Who are you sending?"

"Jonas Petry and Mike Bacon," Sikes reported.

"Good choices. Listen, sir, I have news," Stephen said with urgency.

"I'm listening," Sikes said.

"The property we attempted to search tonight belongs to Anthony Gerritt."

The line went silent for a second. "How do you know?"

"The fire chief is an old acquaintance of mine and the town gossip. He told me," Stephen answered.

"Okay, you protect Lacy Donovan at all costs. If he's one of the men who took her, her testimony can put him behind bars," Sikes reminded Stephen with a hint of excitement.

"And if he gets to her first, it will cost her life," Stephen commented. He hung up with promises to keep Sikes informed.

Stephen pulled into the hospital and jumped out of his car. He approached the check-in desk with his badge already pulled.

"Can I please talk to your shift manager?" Stephen requested.

The woman nodded briskly. "That's me, sir."

"Okay, is there somewhere we can talk?" Stephen indicated to the room just behind the desk.

The woman seemed inconvenienced, but stopped what she was doing and followed him.

"Do you have security in this hospital?" Stephen asked her after she shut the door.

"We have a night guard but that's it, sir. We're a small hospital," she answered.

"Okay, listen carefully. My partner came in with EMS. Her name is Mak Cunningham. She's unconscious. I need that guard to protect her. No unauthorized person in or out of her room except her husband, John Cunningham. Do you understand?" Stephen felt out of breath but really, he was just breathless over the possibility of leaving Mak here by herself.

"Sir, we have a strict policy not to let anyone but family in any room," she sounded annoyed and looked a little bored. "But if you will fill out this form and just write down her name and her husband's name and phone number, he can take it from there."

"Okay," Stephen took the clipboard and started scrawling the information he knew. He did have John's number because Mak had thought it important that Stephen be able to get in touch with John—for occasions such as this one.

The information on the paper Stephen had written faded from his focus. If Anthony Gerritt could find his family, he could find Mak's. He thrust the clipboard at the shift manager and jogged out the door.

Stephen dialed John's number. "Come on, pick up…" he muttered.

"Wilton?" John answered. He sounded serious but put together. "How bad is she?"

Stephen paused. "I'm not gonna lie, man. That blast threw her hard into a tree. She hit her head. I did what I could to stop her bleeding. Sikes told you she's unconscious?"

"Yeah," John answered quietly.

"John, I need to ask you a question," Stephen abruptly turned the topic.

"Yeah?" John answered.

"Where's Harper right now? Is she with you?" Stephen asked.

"No. My mom came to stay the night, so I didn't have to get Harper up," John responded.

"I need you to listen to me. Your mom needs to take Harper and stay somewhere no one would think to look. A hotel, VRBO, or a distant friend's house. Somewhere else—"

"What are you not telling me, Stephen?" John asked directly.

"You know there's only so much I can say," Stephen hedged.

"Tell me what I need to know to keep us safe," John said.

"The guy we've been looking for has a knack for finding out information about our lives and our families. I sent mine out of town earlier tonight. You need to do the same with yours," Stephen warned.

"Got it," John said. "I gotta go."

Stephen reached the police station and called Huntington while tapping on the back door. She had listened to his instructions. The police station looked like a ghost town.

"Hey, Stephen," Huntington answered. "That you at the back door?"

"Yeah, let me in," Stephen urged. He walked through the door after it opened a crack. Relief filled him as he walked in and saw Lacy sitting on the floor, unharmed, her legs in lotus position.

Stephen turned around to scan his surroundings before he

went further into the station. It was standard for him to check his surroundings, but he was on extra high alert now.

The night was dark and moonless. Which might be why he missed the large, black Denali truck with tinted windows sitting just off the road in the shadows behind the station, watching Stephen's every move and tracking what was happening just beyond the doors of that dark police station.

48

MAK

Mak was drifting in a space of nothingness. Where was she? She searched her brain, her thoughts, her memories. The words played over and over again in her mind like a mantra or a heavy metal rock song.

Fight, fight, fight... Who was she supposed to fight? Whoever it was, it seemed important—urgent even.

She tried to move her body, but she felt a white-hot flash of pain. She moaned a little but let her mind drift away again. Mak was so tired. She thought it had been a while since she'd slept. It felt nice to relax. A gentle lulling of slight movement rocked her back to sleep.

Fight, fight, fight... the words made her try to fight sleep. Maybe she could sleep for now and fight later. The movement stopped and she could hear a low hum of voices. She could feel the energy change. She felt gentle hands push and prod.

Mak moaned again. With each touch, she felt sharp pain flood through her. A sudden explosion reenacted in her brain. One minute she'd been searching the ground, stepping carefully. So close to finding the missing women. The next, she heard an explosion. Heat ignited and lapped at her body. She'd lifted off the ground and felt herself flying uncontrollably through the air. Then she'd hit something. Hard. Blinding agony exploded through her body. She didn't remember anything after that.

She was moving again, jolting with each start and stop. The discomfort was so great, she wished she would sleep again. But this pesky mantra wouldn't leave her alone.

Fight, fight, fight!

49

WILTON

Jonas Petry and Mike Bacon were damn good US Marshals who had served beside Stephen the entire time he'd been a marshal. In fact, Jonas had been instrumental in protecting the mother of the woman who had been kidnapped in the last case they solved.

Stephen sagged with relief when they arrived. He'd quickly let them in to the station to introduce them to Lacy while giving them a brief update on the situation. They'd all agreed they would transfer Lacy to Kansas City and fly her out on a US Marshal jet to a secure location.

Stephen couldn't shake the feeling that something was amiss. There had been no play to break in and recapture Lacy. They were now getting ready to drive back with no stops along the way. As Stephen helped escort Lacy securely into the back seat of the US Marshal SUV, he realized what was making him feel uneasy.

"It's been too easy," he muttered. He tapped on the window and Jonas rolled his passenger side down.

"What's up, Wilton?" Jonas asked.

"Keep sharp," Stephen warned him and Mike. "This was too easy. Assume you'll have trouble before you get her on a plane."

"Wilton, we've got this. We've been doing it for years. These are bullet proof windows. We're going straight to the airport where there are cameras everywhere. Gerritt is on a *No-Fly List*. Now, let's get going before you give him a chance to ambush us here," Mike stated directly.

Stephen nodded and walked back to his SUV. He got in, started the car, and followed them out of town. Though he looked around, Stephen didn't notice the black Denali pull out off the street where it sat a block away because the man driving it kept his lights off. And when the truck found it's place behind Stephen, it followed from a distance far enough away that it went unnoticed—even by Stephen's hypervigilant eyes.

Stephen's phone rang. It was Mak's husband. "Hey, John. Did you make it to Mak yet?"

"I was about an hour away when the hospital contacted me. Consent to treat and all that..." John answered.

"Right," Stephen answered. "Do they know anything yet?" His gut was churning. He'd already lost one partner and he wasn't ready to lose another.

"Mak has a nasty gash on the back of her head which they stitched up. She lost a lot of blood but when they did a CT scan, they were pleasantly surprised to only find mild traumatic brain injury. The swelling is minimal. They were most worried about the blood loss," John's voice was matter of fact.

Stephen could hear the *but* coming. "Well, this sounds positive so far," Stephen tried to stay optimistic.

John's pause said everything. "She has what looks like some fractured vertebrae. She needs surgery, but they don't have anyone here who's specialized to do that. They plan to airlift her to Kansas City. So, I've turned around and will meet her back at Kansas City Medical Hospital."

"Fractured vertebrae?" Stephen whispered. "How bad?" He

could only imagine how long it would be before Mak could return to duty.

"They called it a burst fracture. They can see some bone fractures and they need to realign everything. She'll likely need surgery to put her back together. We won't know the extent until she gets in with a specialist," John said.

"But is it safe to fly in her condition?" Stephen asked.

"Yes. They can give her something for the pain to make her feel comfortable until the surgery, but they say when she wakes up, she's going to be in a lot of pain," John said.

"Man," Stephen sighed, feeling empathy for his partner but intense relief that she was going to be okay, even if it looked like a long recovery. "How're you doing? You okay?"

John sighed. "Not my favorite night. But Mak and I know this is always a possibility. We plan for it. We have this *live every day as if it's our last* philosophy. I think I'll feel better when I have all the facts. I might be a little numb right now. Running on exhaustion."

"I get it," Stephen said. He tried to calculate when he'd last slept. He knew it was just under twenty-four hours at this point. "Let me know when you have updates. I'll be there as soon as I get back in town."

Stephen hung up the phone and noted that it was well after four in the morning. He knew she wouldn't pick up the phone, but he would also bet she put her phone on silent when she slept. As he suspected, Alyah's phone went right to voicemail.

"Hey, it's me," Stephen began.

He was watching the US Marshal SUV in front of him. Traffic was light at this hour, and he could see no concerns so far.

"Mak got hurt tonight. I can't go into detail with the operation, of course. But she's pretty bad off. I—" Stephen's voice broke. He restarted. "I got lucky. She was in front of me. You know Mak, always charging right in. There was an explosion. It threw her into a tree. She's being airlifted to Kansas City Medical Hospital to see a specialist. I know it's not my fault. I know I'm in a dangerous line of work. But I feel—"

Stephen stopped and searched his emotions. He felt a dark, ominous feeling in the pit of his stomach. He was afraid that Mak wouldn't make it back to fight crime with him. There was a nagging sense of dissatisfaction that they hadn't found the girls or taken down Anthony Gerritt yet. It hadn't been worth it.

"Guilty," Stephen landed on the word that described the emotion at the forefront of his mind. "I feel like *why Mak and not me?* Like now I have this building anger, this vengeance, and pressure to take this guy down."

Stephen's eyes searched the horizon. He looked in his review mirrors. All appeared fine.

"Anyway," he said into the phone. "In case you and Mak were close… I thought you should know she's been hurt. I guess that's all I can say right now."

Stephen hung up the phone. He ground his teeth in anger and frustration. He had an hour and a half to think about how he was going to find Anthony Gerritt and make him pay for what he'd done to his partner.

50

LACY

Lacy sat in the back of the US Marshal SUV. She was shaking uncontrollably. Not because she was cold. Quite the opposite. She assumed it was nerves. Regardless of the reason, Lacy couldn't seem to get her body under control. She knew she was probably the only one who could hear her teeth chattering, but she tried to clench them together in effort to make less noise. She felt embarrassed over her lack of control.

Get it together, Lacy! she chastised herself.

Then she realized what this reaction was. Fear. Lacy was afraid. No, she was terrified. If she could be plucked from her own home in the middle of the evening, what could happen to her in public? Especially with three evil men actively looking for her?

She glanced at the men driving the vehicle. She wished she had requested to ride with Marshal Stephen Wilton. There was something about his mannerism that made her feel more comfortable. In fact, she probably would have been talking to him and asking him the questions that were rolling around in her brain and triggering her fear. Would Wilton be coming with them to the safe house? Or was she just going to have to get used to these new quiet and somewhat stiff agents? Agents who at this moment, didn't even know her full story.

An audible sigh escaped her lips, much to her embarrassment.

"You doin' okay back there?" The man who was sitting in the passenger seat asked. She thought his name was Jonas.

"Yeah," her voice cracked a little and she cleared it. "Yeah," she repeated, trying to sound more convincing.

"Okay, we're pulling into the airport. We'll be escorting you and will stay on either side of you the entire time. We were able to connect one of the men who kidnapped you. If we're correct, we know he's on a *No-Fly List*. With cameras all over this airport, we believe we'll be safe. Then we'll walk you through a sky bridge to the jet. We're walking you through the airport because we don't think it's safe to pull straight up to the jet. The quicker we get you inside, the quicker we have extra security. You with me?"

"Yeah," Lacy said again. It seemed to be the only word in her vocabulary right now. She didn't ask him the question that flooded her mind. What if the man tried to shoot her before she walked into the airport?

Lacy tensed when they came to a stop. US Marshal Jonas opened the back door and offered her his hand.

"Watch your step," he gently guided her. The other man filed in on her other side. Lacy didn't remember this agent's first name but remembered that his last name was Bacon. She didn't think she could forget that name.

They were both tall guys. Much bigger than Lacy. Jonas was tall but slim with a muscular build and Bacon was taller than Jonas and much stockier. The way they flanked her sides made Lacy feel protected. They each gently grabbed one arm on either side of Lacy and propelled her forward at a quick pace. Lacy let them lead her, understanding the urgency.

Marshal Stephen Wilton caught up with them in the parking

lot and brought up Lacy's back. She was surrounded by a team of security right now.

They walked into the airport and Lacy gasped inwardly. At least she'd kept her anxiety inside this time. The bright lights burned her retinas. The lines to the ticket counter teemed with people. She felt surprised by that.

"Are there usually this many people so early in the morning?" Lacy asked, clearing her voice.

Jonas looked around and dipped his head down. "First flight of the day. People catch this one to get to meetings in the same afternoon. Or they're flying internationally and have to be here a few hours before their flight leaves."

There was a quiet hum of voices and an occasional burst of laughter somewhere in line echoing in Lacy's brain. There was too much to see. Too many places to look. Something like attention deficit disorder seemed to hijack her brain. She started to panic. Before she could melt down, she felt a hand in the middle of her back, and she felt calm again.

Lacy looked up.

It was Jonas. "Hey, it'll be okay. Look, Bacon is working on getting us through lines quickly." Jonas pointed as Bacon located a security officer and spoke to him for a few minutes. Bacon was back at their side seconds later.

"Let's go," Bacon said.

"I don't have ID," Lacy rushed to remind them.

"It's okay," Jonas answered her. "We've got this covered."

Lacy looked up at Marshal Wilton. He seemed calm, bored even, but his eyes roamed the airport. He was on lookout. He seemed to sense Lacy watching him and let his eyes fall on hers.

"Are you coming with us?" Lacy asked.

Wilton shook his head. "No. But these guys are the best in the business. They'll take a bullet for you."

"Let's hope they don't have to," Lacy shivered.

"Agreed," Wilton really looked at her now. "Sorry, that

wasn't as reassuring as I meant it to be. But I promise, you're in good hands. Safe hands."

"What about the female cop?" Lacy asked.

A mix of emotions passed over Wilton's face—hesitation, uncertainty, fear, but settled on sadness. "Right. Of course you don't know what happened."

Dread filled Lacy's heart before he said the words. Somehow, she knew it had all gone wrong.

"I suppose it's okay to tell you. There was an explosion when she stepped onto the property. Everything went up in flames. Mak—Marshal Cunningham—was hurt. She's alive but she's gonna need a lot of work," Wilton's jaw clenched.

Lacy gasped. "And my friends?"

Wilton's eyes flitted to hers and then away. "We couldn't get close enough to find the earth prison. I'm sorry. We aren't sure if the women were left behind. The fire chief has strict instructions to find the hole in the ground and communicate back to us once they put out the fire."

Tears filled Lacy's eyes. "Then it was all for nothing?"

"Hey," Wilton said. They'd stopped moving and were standing at the TSA Pre-Check counter. "You saved yourself. You gave us the best possible lead for finding your friends. And maybe more than your friends. What you did was courageous. You are a hero."

Lacy brushed a tear away. "Okay." She turned to the other agents and paused as they flashed badges and spoke in low voices to the TSA agent. The agent scanned Lacy and nodded. He allowed them to keep walking.

They walked further until Bacon steered them to a hallway Lacy wouldn't have noticed had she been traveling by herself. He scanned his badge and waited until the door clicked open. In the room was a small woman. She wore a shirt with a US Marshal emblem on it.

"Hello," the woman greeted in a calm, quiet voice. "I'm Carol. I'll be your pilot tonight."

"Hello," Lacy said.

There was one other person in the room. Lacy's eyes went to him in question. He looked tired, his hair was mussed, and he was going through the art supplies he had with him. He pulled out three canvases and black charcoal.

"Lacy, this is Lance. Lance is a sketch artist. I know you're tired. And I'm so sorry, but we find that the longer victims wait to talk about the bad guys, the more chance their memory has to fade or their mind starts protectively blocking it out. Can you give this man a description of the three men who took you?" Jonah asked kindly.

He made it sound like Lacy had a choice. Regardless, Lacy wanted to do this. She needed to do this. Once she dumped it out of her brain, maybe she could forget. She nodded and bravely sat at the chair the artist indicated for her.

Lance's voice was meditative as he coached her to close her eyes and remember back. He acknowledged it would be hard but told her he believed she could do hard things. He asked questions and she answered.

Within the hour, the sketch artist had created an accurate picture of all three men. They were such a startling likeness to the men, Lacy gasped, brought her hands to her mouth, and started to cry.

"That's them," she sobbed silently. She was so ready for this nightmare to be over.

"Thank you, Lacy," Jonas moved in and placed a supportive hand on her shoulder. "You did good. Now, let's get you on this plane."

"But wait," Lacy turned to Wilton, who was getting ready to leave, her eyes peering intensely into his. "Are you really not coming? I'm going to be living alone with these guys?"

Stephen gave her a smile of encouragement and lowered his

voice. "These guys are good, trustworthy men who have been doing this job longer than I have. You'll have your own space—most likely a bedroom and bathroom suite. You won't even need to come out of the room if you don't want to. If you do want to, once they determine the area is safe, we can get you a new identity and you can live a semi-normal life until the trial. Okay?"

Lacy nodded. She weighed his words. It didn't seem too bad.

"This is where I leave you, Lacy," Wilton said, offering her a handshake. "You're in good hands."

Lacy shook his hand and watched as the sketch artist disappeared from the room with Marshal Wilton.

The three of them, Lacy, Jonas, and Bacon, walked down a long sky bridge to a small jet with seats like a commercial airline.

"Have a seat wherever you like," Carol, the pilot, said with a calm smile.

Lacy randomly chose a seat. "How long is the flight?"

Bacon sat in the seat in front of Lacy.

Jonas sat across the aisle from her. "Approximately four and a half hours."

"Where are we going?" she asked.

"It's better if you don't know yet," Jonas answered.

"Okay," Lacy swallowed the lump in her throat and tried not to think about how isolated and alone she felt.

Jonas seemed to recognize her anxiety. "I know it doesn't mean much right now, but this will be over soon. With you, we win."

"How?" Lacy asked.

"The sketch artist renderings. You gave physical descriptions of the men. We take that and use it to arrest the men. From there, it's a matter of court dates. Your testimony will put them all behind bars for life."

"I'll have to testify?" Lacy whispered, fear in her heart.

"Yes, but not in front of them. We can arrange for you to ID them and then tell your testimony in judge's chambers. But for now, let's get you in a safe place. We can worry about the rest later."

Lacy nodded and tried to smile. Jonas was working hard to reassure her. He had a nice smile and compassionate brown eyes.

Lacy looked away from him and out the window. It was still dark out, but Lacy knew the light of day would seep through the moonless night any minute. She shuddered, feeling the evil that was lurking out there, ready to finish the job they had started.

What Lacy didn't know was that the black Denali that had followed them from the property where she had escaped now sat waiting for Marshal Wilton.

Was it only a matter of time before Lacy was recaptured?

51

MAK

Mak was prepped and ready for surgery. They had just given her medicine intended to take her under. She fought against the blanket of unconsciousness she'd been under since the fire.

Her eyes fluttered open. They immediately fell on her husband. John stood over her bed, commanding and tall, his hand tucked firmly in hers. She searched his eyes for fear or worry but there was none. John gazed at her with a peaceful look on his face.

"Hi," he smiled when he noticed her eyes on him.

"Hey," she croaked. She cleared her voice. Her eyes flitted around at what she could see from where she lay. "I'm alive?"

John chuckled. "Yeah. But you had me pretty nervous."

"You don't get nervous," Mak licked her lips. "Harper. Is she—"

"She's safe," John assured her. "Wilton called me. Told me what happened. He said Harper wasn't safe at home. Mom took her to a hotel. She'll stay there until I give her the okay."

Mak looked relieved. "Where am I?" Mak asked.

"They're about to wheel you into surgery. The nurse just stepped out."

"Okay." Mak blinked a few times. "What's wrong with me?"

"Mild grade brain trauma. Broken vertebrae. Listen, Mak, they gave you drugs to put you under. The nurse will be back in just a minute to make sure the anesthesia has kicked in. You're off to surgery soon so we don't have much time."

"Brain trauma?" Mak asked.

"The blast threw you back into a tree. You hit your head and spine, then you fell to the ground. That, you'll bounce back from."

"And my back?" Mak asked.

"The doctor says the fact that you have reflexes in your legs and arms and can move your head without obvious pain are very good signs. But they also said there are possible complications that can occur from this surgery that could affect your spine, which could result in nerve damage."

Mak was silent, contemplating her mortality for minutes. Then she spoke again. "I always knew that I could get hurt. But this is the first time I have. I didn't realize—" Mak's voice broke, and a single tear escaped down her face.

John smiled softly. "You thought you were superhuman, didn't you?"

"Well, no," Mak looked confused. "I guess I thought I was just damn good at my job. That if I was really good at it, nothing could touch me. I never meant to—wanted to put you and Harper in danger."

"Hey, hey." John wiped the tears that were now coursing down Mak's face. "I knew this could happen, but the alternative —living a life without you in it—wasn't an option. I considered all that before I proposed to you. You're going to be fine. You're going to get through this surgery, do physical therapy, and you'll be back to normal in no time. But I need you to stay strong. Here," John pointed to Mak's head. "Fight. Recover and decide what you want to do from there."

"We didn't even save them," Mak cried. She took two gasping breaths. "Everything blew up before I could."

"I understand, Makayla. But right now, I need you to focus on you. Remember the *Mind, Body, and Soul Guy* podcast?"

Mak nodded.

"You are the most important thing to think about right now. Focus on you. You can't help anyone until you help yourself. Okay?"

Mak nodded again, taking deep soothing breaths.

"I'll be here when you get out. It will all go fine." John assured her. He squeezed Mak's hand.

Mak turned her head away from John. She remembered everything now. The memory of the blast flooded back to her. Wilton had tried to warn her. He told her something felt off. She'd stubbornly shaken his hand off her shoulder and marched right into a war field that had been rigged to take her life.

Deep down, she knew that this was all her fault. Her injuries, the girls trapped underground and unsaved while the fire raged overhead. Not to mention, would Wilton trust her as a partner ever again?

After all, Mak had led him right into danger.

52

WILTON

When Stephen got into his vehicle, he sat and stared at nothing for a solid five minutes. Fatigue was setting in. Stephen had walked out with the sketch artist and knew the sketch artist was going straight to the Kansas City Metro PD where they would immediately run the photos through their databases and let the marshals know what they found. The sun was starting to rise over the horizon. He knew the jet with Lacy was getting ready to take off. She was safe. Stephen was free to go.

He pulled out his phone and checked his text messages. He had missed a few while he was with Lacy.

John: *Mak is being prepped for surgery. I'll keep you posted.*

Jud: *Found the hatch. Nothing inside. What were you looking for?*

Alyah: *Ohmigod. Stephen, are you alright?*

Stephen scrolled through his missed calls to see that every one of them had tried to call him first. They must have left the text messages when he didn't pick up. He would call them back. But for now, he simply sat in his car and watched the sun rise.

At the moment, everything was in place. At least, as much as it could be in the aftermath of an explosive night. Lacy was safe. If the women weren't in the hatch, it meant they hadn't suffocated underground. Mak was in surgery, but she was alive. And Alyah was still talking to him.

So why did he feel like something was wrong? He was missing something. He went over all the facts again. His brain was so tired. How long had he been awake now? His eyes burned as the sun found its way brightly into the morning sky.

He shook his head. There was nothing more for him to do. He found a pair of sunglasses and put them on. He turned on his vehicle, put it in drive, and steered toward the exit.

He glanced in his review mirror and saw a large, black Denali truck with dark tinted windows behind him.

"Illegally tinted windows," he smirked, remembering his time as a cop and then later as a detective, then shook his head. "Not my problem anymore."

He stopped at the parking booth, reached over, and fed the ticket he'd received when he got there last night. Or was it this morning? The kiosk took his ticket and popped a total on the screen.

As Stephen pulled out his company credit card to pay, he caught movement out of the corner of his eye. The Denali's door opened. Stephen paused with his credit card hanging in mid-air. He waited like that for a few seconds. Suspended in time, watching to see what would happen next.

Then the car door slammed shut.

"Weird," Stephen murmured, feeling relieved and silly for his instant concern. He shoved his credit card in the ticket taker. He grabbed it when it spit back out. Slowly, Stephen drove out of the airport and accelerated his car onto the highway.

He didn't know where he was going exactly. Only that he

wasn't going home. He drove on autopilot to the office. He checked the time. It was 6:48 a.m. What were the chances Sikes would be in?

The chances were pretty good. Sikes met Stephen at the door with a hot cup of coffee. Black, just like Stephen liked it. No one else had made it in yet. He lifted his eyes to question why Sikes was here but Sikes spoke first.

"Saw you pull into the parking lot," he said. "Come sit down. You look like hell."

"Gee, thanks," Stephen smiled despite himself.

"No, really. When's the last time you slept?" Sikes asked. They settled in the cushy chairs in the conference room.

There was something majestic about this room. Stephen always felt important in here. It was a big room. Big enough to accommodate ten to twelve people. Stuffed, black leather chairs on rollers sat around the table. The US Marshal emblem was etched into the middle of the long, rectangular, mahogany table. It was an important room where they conducted critical business.

Stephen swallowed the lump in his throat as his emotions bounced all over the place. From relief to sadness to fear—it all must have shown on his face. As Stephen felt his body weight sink into the comfortable chair, he felt one thing override it all. Fatigue. He was so tired.

"Wilton?" Sikes snapped his fingers across the table from him. "You never answered me. You with me? When is the last time you slept?"

"I actually don't know. It was before Mak and I left—"

"Holy Lord. You need to get some rest," Sikes stated. He looked as if he was ending this conversation as he half rose.

"No, wait," Stephen said. "They found the hatch, but the women weren't there."

Sikes nodded. "I'd say *that's a shame*, but I think we both know they wouldn't have survived with that fire raging overhead."

"Yeah," Stephen said. "We didn't rescue the girls. We didn't get Anthony Gerritt. My partner is in surgery as we speak."

Sikes sighed loudly and sat back down in his chair. He put his feet up on the conference room table. "You of all people should know that cases don't always get tied up with a neat little bow. Hell, I had to send you two back to New York a second time to solve the last big one you worked."

"But it got solved," Stephen stated.

"This one will too. But it won't get any further until you go home and get some shut eye. You're no good to anyone like this. This," Sikes hands made an up and down movement implying Stephen's whole body. "This is how mistakes get made."

Stephen said nothing. He knew Sikes was right. He didn't ask the question he really wanted to ask. *Why Mak, not me?* It wasn't an unfamiliar feeling. He'd felt the same thing when his first partner, Ethan Booker, had been shot simply because he was the first one to walk out the door. Survivor's guilt mingled with anger and resentment. He'd get Anthony Gerritt. He'd get him for Mak. If it was the last thing he did.

"Go home. Get some sleep. Come back when you're rested. We'll figure out where to go from here. Together. We're a team, Wilton. I've got your back," Sikes said as he rose to his feet.

Stephen did the same thing. Not because he was ready for this meeting to be over, but because he was too tired to figure out how else to respond. He left the building.

Stephen got in his Tahoe and turned on the car. He squinted at the burst of sunlight that broke through the clouds. His eyes began to water. He groped around his center console until he found a pair of sunglasses. As he zoned out, staring at the few cars parked around him, he acknowledged his exhaustion.

As Stephen drove out of the parking lot, he didn't take Sikes' advice—or had it been a direct command?—to drive home. Instead, he found himself driving in the direction of the hospital. Without meaning to, he'd left during rush hour traffic. Stephen fought the slow, steady stream of morning commuters. He was too tired to care that they were in his way.

When Stephen walked into the hospital, he hesitated, not quite ready to take off his sunglasses on account of the floor to ceiling windows that allowed large doses of sunlight to flood in. But he hated when people wore sunglasses inside. It made him think they were hiding something.

Fighting sleepiness, Stephen went straight to a coffee kiosk inside the cafeteria and waited patiently in line for his turn. He ordered two coffees and stepped to the side, watching as several baristas scurried to make orders. When they called his name, Stephen smiled kindly and thanked the woman who set down the warm cups.

From there, Stephen found the elevators to take him to the ICU floor and pushed the up button with a pinky he could spare without spilling the drinks. He stepped onto the elevator, then off at the intended floor. As he stepped off, he was struck by the thick silence, punctuated by random beeps and nurses speaking in low voices. Here, patients were fighting for their lives.

Stephen gulped as he spotted the waiting room. He could see John, through the half-glass wall, sitting on a stiff-looking couch in the room with his head rested in his hands. Stephen moved that direction. As he entered, he was struck by how drab and dark the room seemed despite the sun that filtered in. The lights were off, which was fine. The matching plastic-looking stuffed chairs lined in a row around the room and were a muted greenish blue with a brown diamond-shape design on them. There was a TV mounted up in the corner, but it was turned off. A rack of magazines and books with a nice selection sat against a wall under the TV.

Stephen could appreciate the attempt to make a waiting room homey but, like every other hospital room he'd been in, the intention fell far short.

"Hey man," Stephen said as he walked in.

John looked up at Stephen. John's eyes looked as bloodshot as Stephen's felt.

"Hey, thanks for coming," John said as he accepted the coffee.

"How are you doing?" Stephen asked.

"Been better." John tried to smile but it came out a grimace.

"Yeah, me too," Stephen said.

Stephen's phone rang suddenly, startling his brain alert. It was Paige's phone. He was sure it was Anna.

"Sorry, it's my daughter. I should get this," Stephen said.

"Of course," John nodded.

"Hey, Anna! How are you?" Stephen said as he left the room and went to the hallway. He kept his voice upbeat and chipper though his energy was dragging.

"Daddy!" Anna squealed. "I miss you!"

"I miss you, too, kiddo. How's Canada?" he asked.

"It's cold!" Anna said. He could hear the pout in her voice.

"Yes. I remember. Canada *is* cold." He smiled despite the fact that he was standing in a hospital waiting for his partner to make it out of surgery.

"Brrr," Anna said, chattering her teeth for emphasis.

"How are the grandparents?" Stephen asked.

"Good! Nice. They had snacks, like cheese and crackers, and little box cakes when we got here," Anna said.

"Box cakes?" Stephen asked.

"Yeah, you know the little cakes in a box? Only the ones here don't look the same. I thought they would taste like weird Canada food but they're just like ours," Anna said the words quickly.

"Anna!" Stephen said, trying to reprimand her in case

anyone overheard her and thought she was saying something unkind or rude about Canada.

"What? The box was weird. Canada is weird. Like different—"

"Okay," Stephen relented then changed the subject. "How was your flight?"

"It was awesome!" Anna said excitedly. "I love flying!"

"I'm not surprised," Stephen said.

"Where are you?" Anna asked suddenly.

Stephen was not about to tell her he was in a hospital because his partner got hurt. "I'm at work."

"Ew, that sounds boring!" Anna said. Stephen pictured her wrinkling up her nose when she said it.

"Far from it," Stephen said. He heard James call Anna's name.

"Oh, I've gotta go. James made M&M pancakes!" Anna told him. "Bye, daddy!"

"Bye, silly girl," Stephen hung up the phone. He went back in the waiting room to find John standing.

"They're wheeling her out of surgery," John said.

"Already?" Stephen asked.

John chuckled. "You just got here. I've been here for hours. Come on, we'll check with the nurse's station to see what room she's in."

"Great," Stephen fell in step behind John.

After a quick conversation, John and Stephen found themselves in the room with an unconscious Mak. They met the doctor at the door.

"Perfect timing!" The doctor was clearly a morning person. He consulted a clipboard. "She did great in surgery. Everything went well. As you know, she had a burst fracture. It was at L1 and here's the good news. We originally thought the break was in two places. It was in one. We went in, reset the break, and had to put in a few rods and screws to hold everything in place.

But it should heal up nicely and she will be good as new in no time."

"When you say *no time*, do you mean days, months, years…?" Stephen asked with concern for his unconscious partner. She looked so frail and white lying under that sheet on the hospital bed.

The doctor laughed. "Well, that's up to her. As long as she does the work, goes to physical therapy and does her exercises like a good girl, there's no reason why she won't be able to report back to duty in three to six months. Maybe. It'll depend on how quick she heals."

"Well, she'll hate to hear that," John said cheerfully as he shook the doctor's hand.

The doctor chuckled and left the room. It was a large room with two beds. John sat in the chair in the corner.

"May I?" Stephen asked as he sat on the second bed in the room.

"Absolutely. I requested a private room, but this is what they had available. They won't be bringing anyone in here today."

"Thanks," Stephen said. He tried to get comfortable sitting up. When he couldn't, he gave up and laid back, adjusting the bed and pillows so he could sit up and talk to John. "Did you tell Harper what happened?"

"Are you kidding?" John answered with a grin. "That daughter of mine is one step away from a dramatic meltdown every minute of her life. I didn't want to tell her anything until it was absolutely necessary."

Stephen nodded. "Makes sense. Anna asked me where I was, and I used the cop-out. Told her I was at work."

"I really do try to answer all of Harper's questions with honesty and remember if she's old enough to ask, she's old enough to hear the answers. But in this case, I thought I'd get all the facts first."

"Yeah, that's wise," Stephen said.

Then a comfortable silence fell, then stretched, and Stephen's eyes got heavy. Before he could say another word, he had retreated behind his eyelids.

A slight snore escaped Stephen as he fell instantly fast asleep.

53

WILTON

Stephen was dreaming. In his dream, everything was piling up on him. Blurry images of women's faces haunted him. He knew who they were. They were the women who he hadn't saved. Here, Mak was missing. No matter how long he looked and where, he couldn't find her. Then there was a dark presence looming over him. Waiting for Stephen to make a mistake so he could end Stephen's life.

Stephen gasped awake to find a different reality. As he came to, he became aware of two things. One, there were several people talking and laughing all around him. Two, he was not in his bed or in his own home. He cautiously opened his eyes and absorbed the atmosphere. It was like a party in... a hospital room?

"Hey, there you are, sleepyhead!" Mak cried loudly.

Stephen lifted his head and looked at his partner, whose bed next to him was angled up. She had a wide, dopey grin on her face. Her forehead and cheek sported black charred burn marks. They'd been cleaned up and looked like they would heal up nicely.

"I was starting to wonder if you were ever going to wake up!" she said. "Ladies and gentlemen, he's alive!"

Is she drunk? Stephen wondered as he took in the tubes and monitors hooked up to her. No, she was quite comfortable on something like morphine, he decided.

The room of people started clapping. That's when Stephen looked around. John still sat in the chair in the corner where Stephen had seen him last. Rob Sikes was leaning against the wall. A man Stephen had never seen before sat in a chair next to Mak's bed. He looked a little like Mak. Could he be Mak's infamous street-racing dad? A couple guys from the office who were looking a little uncomfortable kept glancing at the clock. And—

Wait! Stephen's eyes paused on the lone figure leaning against the doorframe. He stared rudely. Was he still dreaming? Alyah stood there. Her long, dark brown hair waved down her back. Her piercing green eyes rested on him, an amused expression on her face. Her red, heart-shaped lips held the hint of a smile. She wore a stylish leather jacket that accented her waist with a red crinkly camisole under it. A pair of black skinny jeans hugged her curvy hips and thin legs. Her petite frame was made only a few inches taller in the dark brown suede ankle boots on her feet.

Commotion interrupted Stephen from saying anything.

"Pay up!" Sikes said loudly and money started flying around the room. Even Alyah pulled out a ten-dollar bill with a quick, apologetic smile in Stephen's direction.

"What's going on?" Stephen threw off the sheet that covered him and swung his feet to the ground. He stood up and walked over to Mak's bedside.

"They had bets going on how long you'd sleep," Mak giggled.

"I see," Stephen said, trying to push down his embarrassment. "How long did I sleep?" He looked out the window to see the sun was bright overhead. He had no idea what time it was.

"Six hours and forty-five minutes," Sikes announced loudly.

Stephen's eyes bulged. Had he really slept that long with all these people in the room?

"This is my dad," Mak abruptly changed the subject and pointed to the man who was now standing beside her bed. "Stephen, meet Larry the Epic. Larry, meet Stephen the stiff…" Mak laughed hysterically.

"Hey," Stephen couldn't help but grin as he reached across Mak's bed to shake her dad's hand.

"Stephen the serious…" Mak was still grinning.

"I'm really glad to see you didn't lose your sense of humor in surgery," Stephen said wryly. He glanced up to see John grinning at his wife. Stephen shook his head, realizing he was going to get no help there.

"No really. This guy," Mak announced to the whole room as she pointed her thumb at Stephen. "Never loses control. Always got it together. Man, would I love to see you lose control sometime, Stephen. That'd be the day!"

There were snickers around the room. It appeared, even in her doped-up state, Mak didn't hold back her truth.

"Did you see that you have a visitor?" Mak got mock serious and tried to stage a whisper, but it came out just as loud as her normal voice.

"Oh, I think all these visitors are for you," Stephen answered, but his eyes were on Alyah's again in question.

Alyah raised an eyebrow.

"She's here for you. Worried about *you*. She looooovvveees you." Mak made kissing noises.

Alyah's eyes widened and her face turned pink.

"Okay, okay," Stephen stopped her and routed the conversation back to Mak. "Hey, are you gonna be okay?" He wasn't sure if he should leave yet, but he also felt pulled to see Alyah.

"I feel great!" Mak threw up her hands and smiled that dopey smile again.

He hated to think how she would feel when the drugs wore off.

"I'm gonna be good as new in no time," Mak reached up and tweaked Stephen's nose.

"Good to hear." If there was one thing Stephen knew, it was that Mak was a fighter. She would do all the necessary physical therapy and exercises it took to get her back to work as soon as possible.

"Come here," Mak motioned with her hand.

Stephen leaned in.

"Alyah's here," Mak whispered. This time, it really was low enough for only Stephen to hear it.

"Right," Stephen smirked.

"Don't forget the *Mind, Body, and Soul Guy*, Stephen." Mak wagged a finger at him. "You need to take care of yourself."

"Okay," Stephen agreed.

"I mean you need to go take a shower and take her to dinner," Mak whispered again.

Stephen was pretty sure he'd showered and changed last night, but time was slipping away from him so he couldn't be sure. He sniffed his shirt. It smelled like fire. Keeping the quiet volume of his voice, he asked, "Am I that bad?"

"Yes, Stephen. You are. Now go take Alyah home. Live like you don't have tomorrow," Mak whispered back.

"Thanks, Mak. Get better soon."

"That's what partners are for!" Mak sang cheerfully as Stephen moved away from her bedside.

Stephen greeted everyone as he made his way through the room, careful to keep his distance in case he really was *that bad*.

Then he found himself in front of Alyah.

"Hi," he said. The chaos of the room faded around him. He saw only her.

"Hi," she said back with a shy smile.

"You're here." His eyes searched her face.

She shrugged lightly. "I came as soon as I could get a flight. I was worried... about Mak."

"Ah," Stephen said. "It looks like Mak is going to be okay."

"And you?" Her pretty green eyes held concern.

"Well, I need a shower. I need to eat. Could probably use some more sleep at some point," Stephen stated.

Was it his imagination or did Alyah move a little closer?

"I could help you with those things," Alyah whispered suggestively. She ran her long, red, manicured fingernails up and down his forearms.

"Can you follow me home? Let me get cleaned up and change?" Stephen asked.

"Absolutely," Alyah smiled.

They said *goodbye* to everyone in the room. Stephen grabbed her hand, and they walked out into the bright afternoon together.

She followed him home. Her lips were on his before he had his front door open. As she followed him into the house, Stephen's eyes scanned the road before he shut the door. His brain poked at him as a black Denali truck with tinted windows drove by.

But Alyah demanded his attention. All of it. Stephen closed and locked the door. Then he relaxed into her touch. She was already taking his clothes off.

"Alyah, honey," Stephen hated to interrupt her progress. "I need a shower."

"Right," Alyah said, clearly not caring.

Stephen stripped out of his clothes and dropped the jacket off her shoulders.

"You wanna join?" he asked as he went to turn on the shower.

Wordlessly, in agreement, Alyah followed him.

He turned around to find her taking off her shoes and unbuckling her jeans. Stephen took over, gently dropping her jeans to the floor. His gaze roamed over her lacy red bra and panty set.

It was so reminiscent of the first time they were together. Like they were reliving their last experience. Like a redo.

Stephen picked her up and she wrapped her legs around him. He stepped into the shower and closed the shower curtain.

54

WILTON

The restaurant held a dark, romantic glow. The main lighting came from candles on the tables which created the soft, romantic mood the restaurant was known for. Classical music played in the background. The smells of seasoned steak and baked potato wafted from the table next to them.

Alyah looked up from her menu and caught Stephen's eye. "Stephen, this place is amazing. How did you get a reservation so last minute?"

Stephen winked. "I know the owner."

"I see," Alyah smiled as she sipped her wine.

They ordered when the waiter came to the table. They watched him move away to turn the order in to the kitchen.

"So, you know what's going on with me," Stephen paused thinking of the vulnerable messages he'd been leaving her. He hadn't realized how hard it would be to look her in the eye knowing the things she now knew about him. "How are things going with you in DC?"

"Good but hard," Alyah admitted.

"Hard how?" Stephen asked. He hoped she would tell him she was lonely there and regretted her decision to leave.

"I'm a country girl who's suddenly found herself in the big city. Bigger than Kansas City... I mean *big minded*. DC is full of politicians—governors, wives, businessmen and women. They dress different, talk different, have fancy manners. I think I'm pretty cultured—"

"Classy," Stephen interrupted, taking her hand in his.

"Thank you. I just feel like I've been dropped into a different world." Alyah's face flushed. Stephen wondered if she had surprised herself with her own honesty.

"But you're overcoming and succeeding despite that?" Stephen was torn. He wanted good things for her, but if he was honest, he hoped she'd say *no*.

She nodded and regarded him as if she wasn't sure how much to say. "It's odd to talk about this," she hesitated. "It will seem like bragging."

"But?" Stephen encouraged her.

"I don't know. I just dropped right into the position with total ease. The job itself isn't any different than the job was here. But the cases are bigger and have higher stakes. So far, I've been winning cases and in the short time I've been there... I don't know. I guess I'm making a name for myself."

Stephen squeezed her hand, his smile frozen in place. "So this isn't going to be a conversation about you coming back?"

Alyah smiled sadly. "I really love my job, Stephen."

"Of course. I'm happy for you. But I'm wondering why you came," he admitted.

"Does there have to be a reason?" she asked flirtatiously, massaging the hand that held hers.

"Yes. You came a long way. We're in the middle of a case. We're not exactly out of the woods here. Only, now we're down by a man—or woman... and this guy we're after is dangerous."

"Dangerous how?" Alyah's eyes widened as a look of concern clouded her pretty features.

"Well, you know there's only so much I can share. But I can

tell you this guy knows exactly who we are. It's like he's done his research and tries to worm into our loved one's lives—"

"In what way?" Alyah asked. She pulled her hands away and her back stiffened.

"He knew exactly who Mak was the day we got to town. We were undercover, but he knew we were marshals. He went out of his way to sponsor her dad's race car for a big, televised race—"

"So many questions," Alyah interrupted. "What do you mean? Mak's dad is a street racer? The guy I met in the hospital room?"

Stephen smiled. "Yeah, she used to race too. In fact, she showed up to an event last week and ran smack into our bad guy."

"With her car?" Alyah gasped.

"I wish," Stephen smiled. "No, he was there at the race."

"What? Really? Do you think he knew Mak would be there?" Alyah asked, leaning forward. There was fear in her eyes.

"Considering that her dad's car caught on fire when Mak took it down the track that day, I'd say he was playing games and sending her warnings the whole time." Stephen shook his head. "I admit, it sounded crazy. It was debatable if this guy was messing with her intentionally. Until I learned he'd also offered a construction job to one of my family members who lives in the area not too long after that. It's like reverse stalking. He's finding ways to hook into our families. To make himself important to them. Put himself in a place that makes them feel like they owe him."

"What did you do about it?" Alyah asked with a soft voice.

"I flew my daughter and the family to Canada to get them out of his line of target. I really don't trust this guy," Stephen finished. "I didn't want my family in danger."

"Am I safe here with you?" Alyah asked suddenly.

Stephen leaned forward. "I would die for you rather than let anyone hurt you."

"Okay," Alyah nodded, holding his eyes. "I believe you."

The food arrived and they were quiet for a bit.

"When you say the stakes are higher on your cases...?" Stephen asked with curiosity.

"These are politicians, Stephen. They're accused of egregious wrongs. If they're guilty, it's career-ending, and possibly life in prison. And they'll take down a lot of people with them. There are accusations that judges are in pockets of powerful millionaires. It's my job to determine who's telling the truth. I can't afford to be wrong." Alyah speared a piece of steak, put it in her mouth, and chewed.

"Sounds like you might be in a dangerous place too," Stephen answered. His gut was churning that she was out there so far away, all alone with no one to protect her.

"Oh, I don't know about that," Alyah shrugged.

After they'd finished their food and were waiting on the ticket, Alyah looked at Stephen with soft eyes. "About your brother..." Alyah started. "Stephen, that's terrible."

Stephen struggled with what to say. "Well, I don't know what actually happened. I mean, I know that he was killed, but I don't know who killed him. And the *not knowing* is the hardest part. Before, we had a resolution. We had a confession from a murderer who went to juvie. It made it easier to shut the door on a really terrible situation. But now..." Stephen shook his head.

"Does it change anything for you?" Alyah asked.

"Well, yeah. We believed that Greg was a bully and one day his mouthing off got him killed. I recently reconnected with an old friend, a girlfriend of his, and she mentioned that she never thought of Greg as a bully. If someone else killed him, there could be a different explanation for the *why*. Might change my whole perception of who my brother really was," Stephen admitted. He rubbed the back of his neck, knowing it had gone beet red.

"Have you mentioned any of this to your parents?" she asked.

"No." Stephen shook his head. "I went to see them, but I just didn't have the heart. I want answers first."

"I understand," Alyah admitted. "Have you discovered anything new? Are you investigating on the side, when you aren't on a case?"

"Nothing new. Got my ass kicked when I tried." Stephen pointed to his jaw where there was a faint, yellow outline of a bruise still visible. "I went back to the guy who gave me the lead. Apparently, he didn't like me showing up at his house. He wanted to stay anonymous, I guess." Stephen flinched at the memory.

"Makes you wonder what the heck is going on," Alyah sympathized.

"Since I've been on this case, I haven't had any more time. I ran the picture through facial recognition software and got no hits. I went back home and started nosing around. Then I started this case. There just hasn't been time," Stephen admitted.

Alyah reached for his hand. "I'm sure you'll get closure. Eventually."

Stephen stared into her compassionate eyes, remembering the closure she had been looking for when her sister was murdered. They had that in common, he supposed.

"Thank you," Stephen said. "All in time, I guess."

As they left the restaurant, Stephen was tucking Alyah into his vehicle when he looked up and froze. It was the puzzle piece that had been tugging at his mind. He shut the car door and stared hard. A black Denali drove by on the road right at that moment.

Stephen walked over to his driver side and got in. He immediately locked his door.

"New plan," Stephen announced. He had intended to take Alyah home with him. That wouldn't work now.

"What's happened?" Alyah asked.

"Maybe nothing. Did you book a hotel room?" Stephen asked.

Alyah nodded. "Of course."

"Let's go there for the night," Stephen decided.

"Okay," Alyah agreed quietly as she stared out the window.

Stephen set his jaw. This was the third time he'd seen that Denali today. It was too big of a coincidence to ignore. What he told Alyah at dinner was the truth. He would die for her if it came down to it.

He just hoped he wouldn't have to kill anyone tonight.

55

WILTON

Stephen stirred, feeling fully awake but not knowing why. It was dark in the room. He spied the time on the alarm clock. It was just past midnight. Then the past hours downloaded into his brain. He groaned softly. He rolled over, looking for Alyah.

Alyah sat on the side of the bed, looking out the big bay window whose curtains were pushed to the side to reveal the landscape of Kansas City. The view from the fifth floor revealed the city lights, along with a small sliver of moon, which cast a beautiful glow on the trees outside. The stars twinkled brightly in the sky. He could make out her silhouette, the curve of her shoulders, the muscular definition of her back, and the graceful way her spine arched.

He couldn't help himself. He got up, swung his legs to either side of her, and pulled her into him, hugging her tightly. His fingers traced down her flat stomach and settled there, wrapping his arms tightly around her. He rested his chin on top of her head, breathing in her shampoo. The familiar scent of orchids took him back to when they first met.

Alyah shuddered. She leaned her head back against his chest

and snuggled her backside into him, melding into his body. It felt like she belonged there.

Stephen was surprised by the way her body responded to his. He said nothing. He just waited. There was a reason she was up.

"I lied to you, Stephen," she began. Her musical voice, along with her words, played with his heart. Lulled him into denial. She could never lie to him.

Still, Stephen's heart beat quickly in his chest, and he forced himself to sound calm. "How so?"

"I told you the reason I left was the job, and I would always wonder what would have happened if I didn't take it. There was more to it," Alyah admitted.

Stephen kissed the top of her head supportively to encourage her to continue.

"You were right to question me back in the parking lot before I left. Your instinct was correct. I *was* running away. I was scared. I'm not the type to let someone in—to sleep with a man so quickly. I'd shocked myself. But I didn't feel regret. Instead, I had all these feelings I don't normally have. I decided I needed to talk to you to sort through it. So, I went to see you. When I showed up in your office, I heard enough through that open conference room discussion to know two things."

She held up one finger. "One, you weren't happy with the way the case had ended so you were advocating to go back to New York." She held up two fingers. "Two, you had hooked up with someone there. I panicked. The other women bothered me, sure. But it was more than that. Something that took precedent. I was worried about *you* going back into a dangerous situation. It was right there that I decided there was no way we could work in such close proximity and be in a relationship. My feelings for you were already…" Alyah tried to find the right words. "Way too strong."

Stephen was stunned silent for a minute. "I had no idea. We

could have—" Stephen stopped talking abruptly then reworded. "We can work through that."

Alyah sighed. "I wish we could, Stephen. You don't understand what your messages do to my heart. Then, when I heard about what happened to Mak—" Alyah's voice broke, and a tear fell onto his arm. "I knew it could be you next time. I'm not strong enough to handle that. That's why I left. I can't stand the idea of becoming a widow at a young age. But this is who you are. I would never—could never—ask you to change what you do for me."

"We can work that out," Stephen said again. *Could they though?* he wondered. He would no more give up his job than he would ask her to give up hers.

"I'm leaving in the morning, Stephen," Alyah told him.

Stephen's heart plummeted. "Please, don't."

"I have an important case I'm working on—"

"But we both know that's not why you're leaving," Stephen said. He moved his hand to her side. His thumb moved in circles, massaging her hip. If she was leaving, he wanted to give her one more lasting memory of them together tonight.

"No," she agreed. She turned, switching her position so that her body was straddling his. She looked up at him.

Stephen could see the conflict in her eyes as he stared into them. He kissed her. Gently at first, then with all the feeling he had been holding back. He pulled away slightly.

Alyah pulled him back to her.

"Let's make the most of the time we have left," Stephen suggested. He hooked her under the arms and pulled her back into bed with him. Alyah was on top. He saw her smile. Only, it wasn't a smile that lit up her face. It was sad. He twined his hand in her hair and pulled her face down to meet his.

"I'm sorry this is the way it has to be, Stephen," Alyah whispered. Her lips were so close to his, they tickled him when she spoke. Then she kissed him until he forgot she was leaving. All they had was tonight, right?

In the early morning hours, Stephen finally fell asleep. When he woke, Alyah was packed up. For a minute, Stephen stared at her and tried to think of words that would keep her from leaving, knowing all the while that she was safer if she was far away. He got up and put his clothes on. He brushed his teeth and splashed water on his face.

He took Alyah to the airport.

Just outside of the pre-check line, Stephen stopped and pulled Alyah close. He gave her a long, lingering kiss.

"Let's not say goodbye," he requested.

Alyah shook her head with tears in her eyes. "I'm sorry, Stephen. This is how it ends for us. You are *so* special to me. But my heart can't handle watching you and worrying about you each time you leave for a new case."

"We can work it out," Stephen tried again. "I could go see you in DC. You could come here."

"I know you're listening, but you aren't accepting what I'm saying. This is it for us. We will never work. Distance didn't ease my fears. They're stronger than ever." Tears now streamed unchecked down Alyah's face. "You deserve someone tougher than me. Someone who loves you unconditionally. Go find that person. Be happy."

Alyah's words tore Stephen's heart in two. He finally believed her. This was really it. He'd had such hope when she showed up. But he'd only confirmed her worst fears while she'd been here. Worse than that, he couldn't promise he could always keep her safe. His mind drifted to Mak. This case had proven that so far.

Alyah leaned in one more time, stood on her tiptoes, and kissed Stephen on the cheek. "Goodbye, Stephen."

Then she turned away, leaving his body cold and taking with

her his chance for happiness. Stephen wondered if he'd ever be the same.

56

WILTON

Stephen didn't linger at the airport. Something in him had snapped when she said *goodbye*. He knew she meant it. Now he had to be tough and let her go. He would need time and distance to do that. He would give her that.

As he drove into his driveway, he pulled up next to his mailbox. He had to use both hands to grab the large stack of mail. He accelerated forward lightly, stopping just outside his house. He got out of the car and opened his front door. He tried not to remember that Alyah had been with him the last time he'd been here.

He threw the pile of mail on the couch. He kicked off his shoes at the door. He went straight for his shower and turned it on, trying not to think about the last time he'd taken a shower here. Memories of his time with Alyah were already haunting him. He moved on autopilot, showering, drying off, placing his dirty clothes in the hamper, and putting on clean ones.

He grabbed his shoes from where he'd discarded them at the door. He looked around at the living room that showed dust as the morning light streamed through the window curtain that was opened just a crack. He was never here long enough to care if his place was dusty. But he supposed he'd clean it soon.

Shoes back on, Stephen tackled the mail.

"Adulting," he grumbled with a shake of his head. He opened the mail and put it in three neat piles—junk, bills, and magazines. Then he tackled his bills. There was one odd manila envelope sitting off to the side. Stephen flipped it over. It was unmarked. He immediately lifted his hands and swore to himself.

He stared suspiciously, remembering stories of the Unabomber sending bombs in boxes through the mail. Stephen got up, washed his hands, and called 911. He debated putting on a pair of gloves to pick up the package. But he'd been trained better than that.

"Nine-one-one, what's your emergency?" a dispatcher answered.

Stephen left the package lying on the flat surface and walked outside his house. "I need to report a suspicious package. I'm a US Marshal and I received an unmarked envelope in my mailbox." He rattled off his badge number.

"Okay, sir, did you touch it?" the dispatcher asked.

"Yes, and then I washed my hands," Stephen hated this formality. It was probably nothing, but he couldn't take that chance. Not when he was being followed.

"Okay, where is the package now?"

"In my home. I'm standing outside," Stephen answered.

"Good. Dispatching a unit and Postmaster to your address now." The dispatcher confirmed Stephen's address.

Forty-five minutes later, they gave Stephen the "all clear." They declared the package safe. They'd managed to lift a print off the envelope, which they would run, but there was no guarantee the print wouldn't be Stephen's since he had handled it.

"It's pictures." The postmaster handed the envelope to

Stephen. "Don't feel stupid just because it came up negative for a bomb. You did the right thing."

Stephen barely acknowledged the man's words as he waved and left. Stephen's attention was glued to the pictures he was pulling out of the envelope. There were four eight-by-eleven-inch glossy photos. Stephen's breath caught in his chest.

The first one was of an ambulance unloading an unconscious Mak Cunningham, lying on a stretcher in front of the emergency room at the hospital back in Brighton, where she'd been hurt. The second one was of Stephen, Bacon, and Jonas flanking Lacy Donovan as they walked her into the airport. The third picture was of Stephen and Alyah Smith leaving the restaurant after dinner, and the fourth picture was back at the airport as Stephen led Alyah through the parking lot holding her hand.

Panic, then anger, then rage shot adrenaline straight through Stephen. He stormed out of his house, locked his front door, and got in his Tahoe. He drove to work, barely jamming his car in park before jumping out.

Sikes met Stephen at the door again, this time without coffee.

Sikes pointed to the envelope in Stephen's hand. "What's this?"

"Showed up in my mailbox, unmarked. On the off chance that there was a bomb inside, I called it in. Not a bomb. Total waste of time and resources. But. They might have lifted a print off it," Stephen said.

"Well, that's good," Sikes said. "You look at it?"

"Yeah, I've got a stalker," Stephen responded angrily. This is the exact reason why Alyah had run away. He knew now that it was justified. He was glad she'd put hundreds of miles between them. She was right to feel unsafe. He started laying out the pictures.

Sikes whistled.

"It's Gerritt. It's gotta be," Stephen said through clenched teeth. "From what we've seen so far, it's got his MO all over it. The guy seems to learn all about us, tries to infiltrate himself into our loved one's lives, then if we don't give him enough attention or credit, he finds a way to show all the information he knows about us. Grand standing narcissist if I've ever seen one. And there's more," Stephen announced.

"Yeah, I've got some news too. Go on," Sikes nodded.

"I've had a black Denali truck following me since I left the airport yesterday morning. Bet if you look in the system, Anthony Gerritt owns that make and model," Stephen said.

"Could be," Sikes agreed. "We'll look. In the meantime, we were able to run facial recognition software and located all three men Lacy Donovan saw. One was Anthony Gerritt. But the other two are men who only have infractions on their records. Their names are Boyd Allister and Mickey Upton."

"So, we have what we need to put these guys away, right?" Stephen asked. All he could think about was Alyah. He'd get on a plane and go sit outside her place every night as a bodyguard if that's what it took to keep her protected now that Anthony Gerritt had her picture. Then Stephen deflated. He didn't have a right to do that. Alyah was done with him, and this situation only illustrated why that was necessary.

As if reading his mind, Sikes tapped on the photo of Alyah and asked, "Have you warned her yet?"

Stephen shook his head and sank into a seat. He put his head in his hands. "She's probably still on the plane."

"That was a quick trip," Sikes said with a knowing expression.

"She's busy. She had to get back," Stephen answered.

"Uh-huh," Sikes clearly wasn't buying his story.

"Fine. We were sort of seeing each other and now we're not," Stephen informed him.

"Another *Love 'Em and Leave 'Em* victim—"

"Don't," Stephen snapped. "Just don't." He was so tired of

that stupid nickname. Stephen had no problem getting a girl, he just couldn't make her stay. On top of that, his reputation as a ladies' man at the office had gotten out of control. The guy who burns through women. It wasn't true and he hated that people believed it.

"You need to give her a heads up. If you don't, I will," Sikes responded. "What's it gonna be?"

"I'll warn her," Stephen took the task. "It's the least I can do since I'm the one who put her in danger in the first place."

"Did you ask her to come?" Sikes challenged.

"No, I had no clue she would," Stephen responded.

"Then I think she put herself in danger," Sikes stated.

Stephen nodded slowly. But Sikes had no idea that it was the very reason why she'd left when she had.

Sikes' cell phone buzzed on the table. He checked the text message and looked up at Stephen.

"The print they lifted off your package belongs to Anthony Gerritt," Sikes stated solemnly.

Knowing this had been hand-delivered mail, Stephen came to a horrible conclusion that didn't surprise him.

So, Anthony Gerritt knows where I live.

A quick search confirmed that Anthony Gerritt did, in fact, own a black Denali truck. All the pieces were coming together. But they were painting a terrible picture.

57

WILTON

Stephen was sleeping hard. For once, he had no trouble falling to sleep. It had been a long day of meetings and research at the office. They couldn't seem to decide on a clear next step. The tables had turned on all of them. Instead of tracking down Anthony Gerritt, Gerritt was stalking him.

There was something unnerving knowing that the very criminal Stephen sought to apprehend was learning more and more about his nemesis every minute of every day that Stephen failed to find him.

Though he slept deeply, his dreams were tortured. Nightmares of hot flames and explosions. His logical, awake self would have rationalized this as a reaction to the explosion he and Mak had survived. And maybe that's why he continued to sleep. He wrestled in his blankets, which seemed to wrap around him and suffocate him.

Then a high-pitched alarm sounded. Stephen's brain picked at his subconscious. The night they went to rescue the women, there had been no alarm in response to the blast. Only deafening silence and white noise. He fought through the dark fogginess of his unconscious state until he lay in his bed, slowly waking. As the dream faded, the sound only got louder. Stephen lie there trying to make sense of the sound.

What is that? he wondered.

When the answer came to him, he reacted quickly. Suddenly wide awake, he threw off the covers and jumped out of bed. He could hear the fire alarm wailing loudly in his house. Stephen wasn't dreaming anymore.

He started coughing and panic filled his brain. A ghostly mist hovered above his face. He held up his hand and couldn't see his fingers. The acrid smell of something burning scorched his nostrils. Then there was the noise. Beyond the sound of the shrill alarm still screeching, there was a dull roar and crackle. It took Stephen's mind far away to a time when a criminal had locked him in a shed and set it on fire. And that's what he hadn't been able to comprehend.

His house was on fire!

He dropped to the floor where the air was less smoky. From that position, his brain cleared a little. He stopped reacting and started coming up with a plan.

"Gun, phone, pants, shirt," Stephen said as he located the items in seconds, feeling thankful that he hadn't picked up after himself before he fell into bed that night. He quickly shimmied his pants on, which was no small task since he was still lying on the floor. Pants in place, he threw a shirt over his head. Then he army crawled out of the room. He made it to the door and grabbed his shoes, which he'd left on his welcome mat. He shuffled the shoes under one arm and reached out to open the front door.

"Ow!" he hissed. The metal doorknob was blazing hot. He took his shirt off and wrapped it around the handle and turned. The door creaked and opened with some difficulty. The heat must have caused the door to expand in its frame. But when a sudden blast of fresh air filled Stephen's lungs, he sprang outside and ran toward his mailbox.

When he felt he was far enough away, Stephen called 911, painfully aware that this was the second time in less than twenty-four hours. He turned, looking back at the house while the phone rang. Stephen watched, feeling shocked, as yellow and orange flames lit up the still-dark sky. His mind barely registered the time on his phone. It was after four in the morning.

"Nine-one-one, what's your emergency?" the voice answered.

"My house is on fire—"

"What's the address, sir?"

Stephen forgot he was on the phone when he saw it. Was his mind playing tricks on him? He took a few steps down his sidewalk as he processed what his brain was telling him. Parked down the street, not exactly hidden, was the black Denali. The same truck he'd seen with the same tinted windows, following him around.

Anthony Gerritt is really sitting down the street from my house that's now engulfed in flames, watching the aftermath? Stephen was momentarily dumbfounded. How could a criminal be that stupid? Then the answer came to him. *Anthony Gerritt didn't plan for me to make it out.*

"Unbelievable!" Stephen forgot to curse as he simply reacted, anger and adrenaline pumping through his veins.

He shoved his sneakers on his feet, and he took off running at full speed.

Full fury surged through Stephen. Pure rage took over any prior training. There was no plan. No stopping to think things through. No control. He approached with no pretense of hiding and duping the criminal into leaving his vehicle. He tried to open the truck door and found it locked.

Before he could rationally think through the repercussions of his actions, Stephen did something he'd never done before. He threw a fist at the window. Though he'd hit it hard, he did not damage the window, but now his fist pulsed with pain. He refused to be intimidated, threatened, and now, smoked-out of his own home, any longer.

The hit to the window had its intended effect because the tinted window slowly lowered. A sleepy-looking Anthony Gerritt peered down at Stephen from his lifted truck.

With arrogance all over his face, Gerritt smirked. "Can I help you?" he asked lazily.

Stephen pulled his gun. "Get out of the truck. Now!" he yelled loudly.

Doubt flickered in Gerritt's eyes. He raised his hands. "Okay, I'm going to open the door now."

"No! Keep your hands where I can see them. Unlock the door. I'll open it."

Gerritt held up a key fob and hit the unlock button. "I'll cooperate."

Stephen opened the truck door and reached in, hooking Gerritt around the shoulder. He pulled him out of the seat and flung him to the ground, which was quite a ways down. Gerritt fell ungracefully.

Stephen put his sneaker against Gerritt's throat, cutting off his air supply. Gerritt gasped for breath.

Stephen put his gun in its holster and noticed his phone was still lit up. They'd asked him where the fire was. Stephen got back on the phone, rattled off the address, and hung up. He put his phone in his back pocket.

Stephen released his foot and jumped on Gerritt, pinning him down with his body. Stephen punched Gerritt in the face as Gerritt was trying to catch his breath. Only, Stephen didn't stop. He punched Gerritt three more times.

Blood slicked over Gerritt's face, streaming out of his now crooked-looking nose.

Stephen drew his arm back for another punch but stopped

his hand mid-air. Anger and panic were warring for his immediate attention.

"You think you can stalk a US Marshal? That you can intimidate a law enforcement officer? Do you think you're above the law? You narcissistic piece of—"

Stephen stopped talking mid-sentence as Gerritt's face slowly broke into a grin. Blood marred his teeth, and his eyes were as black as coal.

"You're gonna want to watch what you do and say next," Gerritt said in a low, gravelly voice.

"The hell I will," Stephen punched him again, hoping to strip the arrogance right off Gerritt's face.

"You kill me and your only lead on your brother dies with me," Gerritt said.

Stephen paused, his fist pulled back, ready to strike again. "What?"

"Your brother. I know more about your brother than you do." Gerritt smiled again. "I'll cooperate."

"You mean to say, you know who killed my brother?" Stephen was breathing hard from all the energy he'd exerted.

"I'll tell you what I know. But you have to take me in to get my testimony."

"Why?" Stephen asked. "Why not tell me right here, right now?"

"Let's just say, I like my odds with the real cops a little better right now," Gerritt said, his head tilting toward Stephen's frozen fist.

Stephen uttered a curse word as he pulled out his phone and called Sikes.

Sikes answered on the third ring.

"I got Gerritt. My house is burning to the ground as we speak no thanks to *him*. I got out. I need you to send a car. I'll ping your phone on the location."

"What the—"

Stephen hung up the phone. He sent a pin to Sikes and stood up. He pulled Gerritt to his feet and drew his gun, pointing it at him.

"You even think about trying anything at all, and I'll shoot you right here and now. You'll get no fair trial."

Gerritt put his hands in the air. "Like I said, I'll cooperate."

"What do you know about my brother?" Stephen snarled.

Gerritt shook his head. "I'll talk when I get to the station. I'll tell you everything I know but not until I know I'm safe."

Stephen growled and turned away, closing his mouth. He just held the gun on Gerritt. But his mind was racing. This had been too easy. The way Gerritt had been stalking Stephen almost seemed like he wanted to get caught. But why?

Stephen refused to give Gerritt the satisfaction of asking. Besides, he knew Gerritt would just lie or say nothing. But Stephen had time to think about something else as he waited for the police to show up.

Stephen had just snapped. He'd used his position of authority, his gun, and his anger to attack a man who was unarmed and willing to surrender. Was all that justifiable considering it was Anthony Gerritt's property where the four women had been held hostage, where Gerritt had attempted to blow up his partner and then set Stephen's house on fire? A sketch artist had clearly drawn Gerritt after Lacy gave her description. With startling clarity, Stephen realized that Gerritt's involvement, and to what degree, still needed to be proven in a court of law. But Stephen had taken Gerritt's impending punishment into his own hands.

Stephen knew all about corrupt law enforcement agents. Was he corrupt now? How had it come to this? Mak's words came back to him.

Man, would I love to see you lose control.

Stephen had lost control alright. It hadn't been pretty. And it might cost him his job. He'd already lost his relationship, his partner—for the time being—and his house. Add to all that the knowledge that his brother was killed for some reason that was unknown to Stephen but known to Anthony Gerritt. The criminal was right, Stephen had no idea where to start looking for answers.

Stephen wasn't sure how much more he had to lose.

58

WILTON

The sun had risen on Stephen's house. It was hard to believe a few short hours ago, Stephen had watched this structure engulfed in flames. All his belongings were still smoldering in ashes. He'd lost so much and yet nothing at the same time. He should feel emotional, but he didn't. Everything was replaceable. He didn't spend enough time there to call it home or mourn this loss.

Stephen pushed the gas pedal of his Tahoe as he drove away from what was left. His phone rang. His eyes flicked to the console on the dash. It was Sikes.

"Hey," Stephen answered.

"Where are you right now?" Sikes asked directly.

"On my way to KC Metro PD to give my statement. Sorry, I'm just now heading that direction. I needed to deal with the insurance company," Stephen was apologetic. Time had slipped away once officers showed up to take Anthony Gerritt away. A tow truck had come to impound Gerritt's car. Then the fire department had come to douse and contain the fire. Stephen realized in the middle of watching helplessly from the sidelines that Gerritt's weapon of choice had been fire. Most serial criminals had methods of destruction they continuously returned to. This was his.

It had taken too long to send pictures of the damage from his phone to a secure portal for the insurance company only to have an agent from the emergency, after-hours line explain that he would have to pay his deductible first and they would send out an agent to assess the damage next week.

"No, it's okay," Sikes said. "Maybe give your statement later. They're letting Anthony Gerritt go."

"What do you mean? Are you saying they're releasing him?" Stephen's voice was just below a shout. He could feel his blood pumping. He opened and clenched his left fist in a quick, almost manic gesture, the right one firmly gripping the steering wheel.

"He's been released. Yes. He's already out. I need you to come in, Wilton," Sikes commanded in a low, authoritative voice. "The DA made a deal with Gerritt."

Stephen wised up in that moment. "What did Gerritt give you?"

"The location of the missing women," Sikes announced.

"And?" Stephen asked.

"Provide us with valuable intel to take down an organization he claims is larger than himself," Sikes stated.

"In exchange for?" Stephen asked.

"Total immunity," Sikes said.

"BS!" Stephen exploded.

"We've got a team on the way to go get the women now. It's a done deal," Sikes' voice was low with a hint of finality in it.

"What?" Stephen exclaimed. "Where are they going? When did they leave?"

"Your emotions have you compromised, Wilton. I'm not putting you back out there." Sikes voice held a warning.

"You have got to be kidding me!" Stephen's voice shot up. "He set my house on fire! I could tell you what the insurance *thought* they would cover to rebuild and fix the damage. It's not enough.

Gerritt sent pictures of me having dinner with the woman who broke it off with me because my job is *too dangerous*. Did I tell you how she took the news when I had to call her and tell her she might be in danger now? It wasn't good, Sikes. Dead silence. All of this only proves that she'd made the right choice to leave me. Gerritt kidnapped four women and hid them underground. And tried to kill my partner. Shouldn't *that* be enough? After all of that, you aren't even going to let me help with the rescue?"

Sikes went silent for half a minute. Stephen said nothing as he waited him out. Finally, Stephen's phone dinged with a text message.

"I sent you the address. You are only there for backup, Wilton," Sikes warned.

"When is the rescue?" Stephen asked.

"Now. They're on the way as we speak. Reroute."

"Wait. That's not an address." Stephen pulled into a parking lot and looked at the text. "Those are road coordinates."

"The women are en route. We've got a road barricade set up. They will be crossing the border into Kansas in the next hour."

"Bold move bringing the women to our backdoor," Stephen muttered.

"Unless they were trying to kill two birds with one stone," Sikes hinted.

"Meaning?" Stephen shot back. Stephen put the coordinates on his phone. He followed the GPS out of the parking lot.

"We think Gerritt and crew were getting ready to transport the women out of state. I think the goal was to take you out first. They immobilized Mak. They wanted to get you out of the picture as well." Sikes let the words fall.

"Good Lord!" Stephen exclaimed.

"Wilton, I need to know I can trust you out there. We're going to talk about what went down last night. No more of this going rogue on the bad guy, right?"

"Yeah. I can do this. Do we have enough cars and officers in place?"

"Yes, we got highway patrol involved. Trust me, I've been working on this for hours," Sikes promised. "Since they took Gerritt into custody."

Stephen grunted an *okay* and hung up the phone. He just hoped he wasn't too late to get in on the rescue. He and Mak had worked too hard not to see a resolution. In a way, he felt like he was doing this for her.

After ten minutes of driving, Stephen pulled up to the road-block just on the outskirts of Kansas City, which looked organized and ready to take down the criminals transporting the women. There were two highway patrol cars parked side-by-side, physically blocking over half the road. The other vehicle was a US Marshal SUV. Four highway patrolmen stood to one side and several US Marshals stood to the other.

Stephen got out of his car, on guard and ready for battle. He immediately scanned the area. Bulletproof vest in place and gun securely in his hip holster, Stephen approached a highway patrolman who appeared to be in charge. Stephen flashed his badge at the patrolman, whose uniform said Sgt. Forestman. He nodded in acknowledgement.

"I'm a little late to this ambush," Stephen admitted sheepishly. "Do we know what kind of car we're looking for?"

The patrolman looked as if he had all day to stand on the street. He hooked his thumbs in his pockets. "A black 2023 Ram ProMaster," Forestman answered.

"A cargo van. Let me guess, it has tinted windows?" Stephen smirked, thinking of Anthony Gerritt's truck.

"In the front—yes. No windows in the back." Forestman scanned Stephen. "You the guy who turned in Anthony Gerritt?"

Stephen stiffened. He looked at Forestman's face, but the

large aviator sunglasses covering his eyes didn't give any emotion away. Finally, Stephen nodded.

"Good job bringing that one in. There's been an APB for him for quite a while." Forestman's voice held approval.

"Is your team briefed on what's happening here?" Stephen felt a touch of concern. "You know Gerritt cut a deal and they turned him loose, right? He's an informant now."

Forestman nodded. "We know and as much as it sucks, we can't touch him if he shows up today."

Stephen hadn't considered that, but of course Gerritt would go about his plans with his crew. Any other actions on his part would lead to suspicion and point to him as an informant.

Stephen's eyes looked over the horizon, but there wasn't a car in sight. "So, you know we're looking for three women who have been held captive for a very long time?"

Forestman grunted in the affirmative. "Yeah, they tend to give us the information we need to do our jobs."

"Right," Stephen said, taking the clue. "Glad you guys are out here."

Forestman saluted.

Stephen looked down the line and found two of his marshal buddies. He went to stand with them. They tilted their heads and fist-bumped Stephen. Stephen's conscience burned and he wondered if they knew about his fit of rage last night.

"You okay, man?" Marshal Jefferies quietly asked Stephen. He was tall and thin. His arms were crossed over his chest.

"Depends. What do you mean?" Stephen mirrored Jefferies, crossing his arms too.

"Heard your house burnt to the ground last night," Jefferies answered.

"Yeah. It was a bad night," Stephen answered.

"Surprised to see you here," Marshal Miller leveled Stephen with his glance. "Kinda making us look bad, Wilton. If my house burns down, I won't be coming to work the next day, I can tell you that."

Jefferies snorted.

Stephen grinned reluctantly. So, they didn't know about Stephen losing control. Stephen would have relaxed, but he didn't have time. The vehicle was heading their way.

They could hear the tires squealing as the cargo van attempted to stop short and whip about, but the vehicle was too big to move quickly. Stephen, like the rest of the officers, pulled his gun and went on defense.

The first shot sounded, followed by a sound like a popped balloon as a highway patrol car sagged on its side.

"They're shooting out the tires!" Stephen heard a yell.

Everyone dove for cover when the single shot became rapid firing from a semi-automatic machine gun. The gunfire was coming from the driver's side, which was angled toward the highway patrolmen. The passenger side window remained up, leading Stephen to believe either there wasn't anyone in the passenger seat or Anthony Gerritt sat there, not retaliating.

Given the focus of the gunman, from where Stephen was huddled, he could see he had clear path to the back of the car.

"Let's go," he commanded Miller and Jefferies. Stephen led the way as his co-workers ran in hunched positions to the back of the cargo van. Stephen fumbled with a folded lock-picking tool on his keychain. He had finished picking the lock on the cargo van when he noticed the gunfire had ceased. He heard the driver's side door open and shut, then quick footsteps shuffled in gravel on the road.

"Take the women and go," Stephen whispered to Miller and Jefferies. Stephen flattened himself to the back of the car. He heard the soft click of the back door open and knew the girls were escaping. He took the opportunity to pop out and surprise the man who was walking toward him.

"Drop it," Stephen commanded in a loud voice. He could see

a few highway patrolmen rushing forward to provide backup, guns trained on the perp.

The man was so surprised, he immediately released the machine gun and let it clatter to the ground.

Stephen recognized the man he faced from Lacy's sketches. If memory served him right, he was Boyd Allister.

"Hands up where I can see them—" Stephen's sentence was cut short.

The loud sound of a gunshot rang out near Stephen's head. A red spot formed on Boyd's shoulder as he stood in front of Stephen. Stephen glanced at the highway patrolmen who looked as shocked as he felt. He whirled around.

Anthony Gerritt stood behind Stephen with a hard look in his black eyes, holding a Glock. Stephen didn't take time to assess what had happened. He immediately shoved Gerritt up against the back of the cargo van. With his forearm pinned against Gerritt's throat, Stephen grabbed the hand Gerritt held a gun in and hit it multiple times against the van.

Sergeant Forestman had reached them. "What happened?"

Gerritt unclenched his fist and dropped the gun. It clattered to the ground. "I'm on your side, marshal!"

"I just watched you kill that man. You're on *your* side. What would he have told us if we got him in custody, huh?" Stephen pushed his arm into Gerritt a little harder.

"I was protecting you," Gerritt managed to get the words out. "He's not dead."

The patrolman who'd stayed with Boyd yelled out a confirmation. "He's alive."

"You can't kill people, or shoot them, when you're informing," Stephen hissed in a low voice. He could feel the presence of Forestman and one of his patrolmen taking in the scene. He turned to Forestman and pulled Gerritt off the truck. He quickly pinned Gerritt's arms behind his back. "Can you search him?"

Forestman immediately started checking for other weapons.

"Maybe you can give me a list of dos and don'ts," Gerritt sneered, taking in a gasp of air now that he could breathe better. "He had a knife in his hand."

Without changing his position, Stephen looked at the patrolman who was with the man Gerritt had shot. The patrolman looked around and nodded upon spotting the knife laying by Boyd's side on the ground.

"He's pretty good with that thing. I've watched him kill more than one person that way," Gerritt said. "You're welcome."

Stephen stepped back once Forestman gave Stephen the okay. "Any more men in the car?"

"Nope, just me and Boyd here," Gerritt admitted.

"Can you guys please search the van?" Stephen asked. He pulled handcuffs out of the back of his bulletproof vest and cuffed Gerritt.

"I'm not considered an enemy anymore," Gerritt protested. "I signed an agreement."

"Oh, after that stunt, you can take a ride back down to the station. They can decide what to do with you from there. The way they did last night." Stephen ground his teeth in disgust.

"Van's all clear," Forestman yelled out.

"Great," Stephen responded. "Can you give this guy a ride to the station? We'll take the women."

"Will do," Forestman said with a nod. He grabbed one of Gerritt's arms and the patrolman grabbed Boyd off the ground.

Stephen walked over to the marshals who had loaded the women in the back seat of the US Marshal SUV. Stephen opened the back door and quickly scanned each woman from head to toe. They were sitting huddled together quietly, but he could see the conflicting emotions of hope and fear in their eyes as they clung to each other. He flashed his badge.

"I'm US Marshal Stephen Wilton. Man, it's good to see you

girls. We've been looking for you. Isa?" Stephen looked from face to face.

One girl nodded at him.

"Lauren?" he asked.

Another woman smiled weakly in his direction.

"Emma?" His eyes fell on the last girl.

Tears clouded her vision and she quietly said, "Yes."

"Let's get you out of here. We'll be taking you back to the US Marshal office. We'll ask you some questions and let you know what our next steps will be. How does that sound?" Stephen asked, well aware they had little energy left to even acknowledge his statement.

Once the doors were shut and locked, Stephen knew that they were all safe. The vehicle had bulletproof windows. He allowed himself a moment of gratitude that they had rescued the remaining women from Anthony Gerritt.

For a moment, as tears welled up, the only person Stephen wanted to talk to was Mak. But Mak was still in the hospital. At least he thought she was. He watched as the SUV pulled out and he followed in his vehicle back to the US Marshal building.

59

WILTON

Stephen stayed with the women until they gave statements. They needed to go to the hospital. But they needed the same discretion Lacy had been afforded—to remain anonymous for now. Once they saw a doctor, they would have a nice hot shower. But right now, the marshals were working on a plan. All of the women had seen the kidnappers. Similar to Lacy, these women would need to be protected.

Granted, Gerritt had maimed one of the other kidnappers today. Gerritt had confirmed the man's identity. The perp was Boyd Allister. Stephen was sure Gerritt had already been released again, though Stephen didn't think Gerritt deserved freedom. Especially after the stunt he'd pulled so soon after becoming an informant.

For now, Stephen chose to focus on the women.

"Do you know how we found you?" Stephen asked.

They each shook their heads.

"Lacy Donovan. She escaped and worked with a sketch artist to find the men who captured you. Since you all can identify the men who kidnapped you, we would like to place you in witness protection. That's where Lacy is right now. We don't normally do this, but since you were all held by the same men, are you opposed to staying with her until we bring them to justice?"

That's when the room exploded in a wave of emotion. Tears ran down their faces. The women all huddled close for a group hug.

Stephen could hear their excited, whispered words.

She did it! She got out safely.

She's alive.

She saved us!

Like she said she would…

Finally, they broke apart.

"Yes," Isa said, seeming to be the spokesperson. "We want to be in protection with Lacy."

"That settles it then," Sikes said as he turned to leave the room to make arrangements. There was a knock at the door and Marshal Miller came in, carrying bags of food, plates, and drinks. He started laying the food out.

One of the girls gasped, and this brought another round of exclamations.

Sikes jerked his head to the side to indicate that Stephen should follow him.

"Are you crying?" Sikes asked when he finally looked at Stephen.

"Yeah," Stephen wiped his eyes. "How are you not?"

Sikes shook his head. "Apparently, I'm dead inside after so many years on this job." He started walking to his office. "Not only are we going to send the girls to Lacy, we'll move Lacy into a more suitable safe house that will accommodate more people. Lacy and the agents will meet the women there."

"Sounds good," Stephen nodded.

"There," Sikes said. "You got your resolution."

"Appreciate it," Stephen said, feeling grateful, even if Anthony Gerritt was now roaming free yet again.

"Shut the door, would you, Wilton?" Sikes tilted his head

sideways. He waited until Stephen did so. Then he plopped in a chair. "I've never seen you lose it like you did last night."

Stephen deflated a little. He surmised what was coming next. He'd been fired before.

"Anthony Gerritt was pretty messed up when they picked him up. Broken nose, bruises all over his face, and a messed-up shoulder. But I look at you and I don't see a mark on you. You can't tell me you were defending yourself. Then there's this."

Sikes pushed a button on his computer screen and Stephen could hear the recorded 911 call from the fire. He'd left his phone on when he hit Gerritt's window. There was a loud, hollow pop sound.

Can I help you? came Gerritt's gravelly voice.

Get out of the truck, now! Stephen had yelled.

Okay, I'm going to open the door now, Gerritt had responded.

No! Keep your hands where I can see them. I'll open the door. Stephen was clearly angry.

I'll cooperate. Gerritt's voice was calm.

Then there was the sound of a shuffle. It was unclear who was doing what in the shuffle. Then Stephen rattled off his address and hung up the phone.

"Did you announce who you were or read Gerritt his Miranda Rights?" Sikes was asking a question he knew the answer to. "We got lucky with the informant deal. We wouldn't have been able to hold Gerritt thanks to your actions. What do you have to say for yourself?"

Stephen sat silently, trying to decide what to do next. "Am I going to need a lawyer?"

Sikes looked disappointed but slowly shook his head. "Not right now. Gerritt isn't pressing charges. In fact, he didn't say a word about you. For all we know, he got beat up before all this went down." Sikes tapped the computer screen where he'd played the recording. "Should I assume that wasn't the case?"

Stephen stared at him, not saying a word. But his mind was

working furiously. Why hadn't Gerritt complained about him? Then he remembered Gerritt's words. Gerritt claimed to have information about his brother. Stephen clenched his jaw. This was how Gerritt pulled people in, Stephen knew. Gerritt found ways to make himself invaluable to people. Stephen wouldn't do it. He wouldn't fall into Gerritt's trap. Stephen got into this business to help people. Not to help himself.

"I did it," Stephen admitted, looking into Sikes' eyes.

Sikes nodded and seemed to let out a breath he'd been holding. "Thanks for your honesty, Wilton. I'm not going to say it's okay. There were lots of questions and concerns when Gerritt came in. But I do understand the stress you've been under with this case. First Mak, then Alyah leaves, then Gerritt burns your house down... It's a lot. Too much. I can't keep working you that way. You need to take a break."

"When you say *break*...?" Stephen's voice trailed in question.

"You need to take care of yourself. You can't help anyone if you can't help yourself. I'm just as much to blame here. We typically have you guys working with a law enforcement counselor. Have you seen anyone since Booker was killed?" Sikes asked.

Stephen's pride stung a little, but he knew where Sikes was going with this. Sikes wasn't wrong to ask. Stephen shook his head.

Sikes wrote down a number on a piece of paper. "I threw you into a new case before you had time to process the last one." Sikes handed Stephen the paper. "Go see this therapist. Get better. While you're at it, go see your partner. Rumor has it she's getting released sometime today and she's a little grumpy since she'll have to be on bedrest."

Stephen stared at the number. He had no place for pride and ego here. His job was at stake. He would make an appointment. This marshal job had been tougher than his detective job had been.

"Will do, sir," Stephen agreed.

He called the therapist to make an appointment as he walked out to the parking lot. As luck would have it, they had a cancellation at noon. Stephen hit a drive thru for coffee and a sandwich. With nowhere else to go, Stephen drove to the office to wait for his appointment. He scrolled through his phone as he ate his sandwich and drank his coffee.

Then he went inside to wait in what turned out to be a very comfortable lobby. He was glad for the cancellation. Starting therapy immediately would show how serious he was about working on himself, which would likely get him back to work sooner.

Stephen smirked as he thought about Mak's new favorite podcast, the *Mind, Body, and Soul Guy*. He supposed this is what she meant by taking care of his mind and soul.

60

WILTON

Stephen stood, hesitating on Mak's doorstep. He'd never been there before. Sure, they had been running together, but he usually met up with her at the park. He definitely didn't want to intrude on family time the first day she was back.

Boundaries, Stephen, he chastised himself as he turned to leave, having talked himself out of visiting Mak on the day she got home from the hospital. Halfway down the walk back to his Tahoe, the door flew open.

"Get in here, Wilton," John's voice sounded behind him.

Stephen turned. "I was just getting something out of the truck," he lied.

"No, you weren't. It's fine. You're welcome to come in. Besides, we're having a *Welcome Home* party. The more the merrier," John held the door wider for Stephen, who had turned around and followed John.

Once the door shut, Stephen lowered his voice. "Did you talk to Sikes?"

"Yes. Sikes told us it was safe to come home," John answered.

Stephen nodded but had to wonder if Sikes was right. Informant or not, Stephen didn't trust Gerrit as far as he could throw him. If Gerrit was out there, no one was safe. Immunity deal or not.

"Do you have information we should be aware of?" John asked, his voice still lowered.

"It's all under control at the moment. Just keep your eyes and ears open," Stephen warned.

A noise that sounded like engines revving blared from down a hallway somewhere in the house.

"Thanks for the advice," John nodded. "I'd advise you to do the same. Keep your eyes open for what comes next."

"What—" Stephen didn't have time to ask.

A bright pink Barbie Lamborghini was speeding its way toward him with three-year-old Harper behind the wheel, followed by Mak, who was moving fast in a... Stephen blinked.

"Is that a motorized wheelchair?" Stephen asked. "Should she be—"

"Look out," Mak yelled. She wore a strong brace around the middle of her body that looked a little like a strait jacket.

Stephen flattened himself against the wall. He could hear Harper giggling hysterically.

"We can't keep her confined to a bed. This is the only way we could get her to promise not to try to walk everywhere." John motioned for Stephen to follow him.

Stephen entered the large kitchen, and his eyes fell on a nice-sized island in the middle. A solid marble countertop held party hats, decorative plates, and noise-makers. "Nice cake," he said.

On top of the island was a kiddie cake with the words *Get Walkin' Soon!* As Stephen listened to Mak and Harper zoom around the house, with peals of laughter in their wake, he missed Anna. His daughter was still in Canada. Where she would stay until he knew it was good and safe for her to come home.

John smiled at Stephen as he cut a few pieces of the cake. "Think we need candles?"

"Of course," Stephen decided to encourage the silliness. "Do you always have parties like this?"

"Actually, yes. Makayla and I live like every day is our last. We celebrate often for big and small reasons. She closes a case. I land a new consulting client. Harper spells her name. You name it, it deserves dinner, a movie, cake, ice cream, tent forts in the living room, etcetera."

Stephen watched as John put three candles on top and lit them. "Three candles?"

"She wants to be back to work in three months." John shrugged.

"Three months? The doctor thought three to six," Stephen gasped. "That's a stretch, even for her, don't you think?"

"Uh-oh," Mak's voice sounded as she drove around the corner. "Those are fighting words. Challenge accepted, sir!"

"Mak," Stephen grinned reluctantly. "How are you feeling?"

"Good enough. Glad to be home." Mak smiled from her lowered place in her mobile chair. "How are *you* feeling?"

"Uh... I feel like that's a leading question," Stephen stalled.

"I know Alyah went home," Mak said with compassion in her eyes.

"Yeah," Stephen agreed. "Do you know why?"

Mak shook her head.

Stephen looked between her and John and wished for the hundredth time he had what they had—a supportive partner who lived in the moment celebrating life.

"She was afraid of my job. She said it was too hard watching me leave, putting myself in danger, wondering if I would make it back," Stephen admitted.

John bobbed his head. "It takes a certain kind of person to be able to handle it." John looked at Mak fondly.

"Handle what, exactly?" Mak narrowed her eyes at her husband in mock defiance.

"You, of course." John came around the island and swooped to kiss his wife.

"What's the certain kind of person I'm looking for?" Stephen asked when the couple stopped making out in front of him.

"A strong one," John answered.

"Come on," Stephen protested. "Wasn't there a moment in all of this that you thought Mak should quit this job?"

"Actually, Mak was concerned after her car caught on fire. And right before she went into surgery. She didn't like the idea of putting us in danger," John admitted as he plated four pieces of cake.

"Yep, for half a second, I thought I could just walk away. Leave this job. Then I wondered, what would happen to the rookie? I knew I had to stay and protect you." Mak crossed her eyes comically.

"Hey!" Stephen swiped at her but missed on purpose. He wasn't quite sure she was solid enough yet for a sucker punch to the shoulder. "You're the one who got yourself blown up!"

"Well, someone had to take one for the team," Mak said, taking the piece of cake John gave her.

"Ha ha." Stephen took a bite out of his own cake.

Harper came running into the room at that moment wearing only underpants. Giggling hysterically, she shook her booty and ran out of the room.

"Go put some clothes on!" John chased after Harper. "We have company!"

"So, you're gonna give yourself time to heal before you come back to work, right?" Stephen asked.

"Depends. Sikes wouldn't talk work details to me when he

visited earlier. But he said we got our guy. The sketch artist was able to pinpoint Gerritt. But what happened with the case? All wrapped up in a bow?" Mak asked.

Stephen shrugged. "Not quite. Wrapped up as much as it could be. In fact, we found the missing women this morning. Had to catch them on the run. They were in transit, but we barricaded a road. We brought them in. They'll go into witness relocation with Lacy Donovan."

Mak's eyes filled with tears. "Best news of the day. How did you know where they were?"

Stephen paused to give her the moment, then continued. "Anthony Gerritt made a deal, agreed to become an informant, and then they released him—"

"Released!" Mak shouted.

"That's what I said, too." Stephen clenched his jaw. "He has information on what he says is a *larger operation* than we know."

"I hear you were the one to take him down," Mak smirked. She waved her phone, indicating that she'd gotten a text from the work rumor mill.

Stephen walked to the doorway to make sure Harper wasn't close by. "Yeah, right after he'd sent me pictures proving he was stalking me, then set my house on fire. I pulled him out of his truck and…"

"What?" Mak gasped. "Don't stop now!"

Stephen mimed holding him down and punching Gerritt.

"No way! He attacked you?" Mak asked.

Stephen shook his head.

"Oh!" Mak's eyes widened as she caught his meaning.

"I just sort of lost control," Stephen admitted.

"As would I have," Mak nodded. "He put you through a lot. Not to mention Alyah leaving and what's going on with your brother…"

Harper ran back in the room wearing pink and purple pajamas. "Let's party!" she yelled. She put her hands in the air and started jumping around.

"Pajamas? It's afternoon, Harpy! You ready for bed?" Mak teased.

"No way! Today is pajama day!" Harper giggled.

Stephen had to smile at her silliness. At the moment, she was reminding him of Anna.

John followed Harper back into the room and picked up a piece of cake as if debating. "I don't know if I should give you any more sugar."

"Sugar!" Harper punched an arm in the air. "Cake, cake, cake!"

"What do you say?" John asked.

"Please? Pretty please with frosting on top?" Harper batted her eyelashes comically.

"Here." John gave her the plate. "Why don't I set you up with a movie, so you have a few hours to chill and come down off the sugar high."

John left the room again.

"Are you gonna be okay, Wilton?" Mak looked concerned.

"Yeah, I just had an appointment with a therapist. If I'm lucky, Sikes will let me keep this job." Stephen held up crossed fingers. "But for now, I'm on leave."

"I've been on leave before. It sucks. I'll do anything to get back to work ASAP."

"What about you? Are you gonna do the work, the physical therapy?" Stephen asked.

"You better believe it!" Mak said.

Stephen's phone buzzed. It was a text.

Sikes: *I'm gonna need you to come back to the office, Wilton. There's been an incident.*

"Speaking of Sikes, I'm being called back in." He held up his phone and jiggled it at Mak.

"Good luck, Wilton." Mak's eyes were compassionate.

John came back in the room. "What'd I miss?"

"Wilton just got called back in to work," Mak said.

"Thanks for the cake. Glad you're better, Mak. See ya around, John." Stephen waved and left.

Here we go, he thought. *Here's the point where I lose my job.*

61

WILTON

Stephen sat in the US Marshal official conference room across from Deputy Director Rob Sikes and Attorney General Alex Kross. Stephen almost stopped short when he saw Kross sitting in the room. He'd met the man once and the fact that Kross was here now was not good news.

"There's been an incident," Sikes began.

Stephen nodded but said nothing. Sikes had said as much when he'd texted.

"Anthony Gerritt is gone," Sikes announced.

The words seemed to linger in the air taking their sweet time to register in Stephen's mind.

"I'm sorry, what?" Stephen shook his head. "Do you mean *gone* as in Gerritt took off again?"

"Dead," Attorney General Kross stated. He had a deep, authoritative voice. He began laying out photos of a gruesome murder. Anthony Gerritt was unrecognizable under all that blood.

"Gunshot to the head and multiple stab wounds," Sikes said.

Both men were staring at Stephen.

"When?" Stephen asked. He knew what they were thinking.

"Called in around 3:20 p.m. The estimated time of death between one and three," Kross stated.

"I have an alibi if that's what you're asking. I went to therapy after I left work. From there, I went to Mak's. I was there until you texted me. She can vouch for me." Stephen knew that's what they needed to hear. He just never thought he'd have to defend himself from a place of false accusation. Something hardened in his heart.

"We'll verify your alibi." Sikes nodded. "In the meantime, after further discussion with Kross, we've decided to put you under a temporary suspension pending the investigation for over-defending yourself against Anthony Gerritt, who came in fully willing to cooperate in our investigation."

"Sir, with all due respect, earlier you told me you needed me to take a break and asked that I schedule time with a counselor. I did. I have another session scheduled. I am happy to take a break. But, an actual long-term *leave?*" Stephen tried to keep his voice firm but felt like his emotions were starting to show. He needed his job. Without it, Stephen didn't know who he was.

"Again, we've decided disciplinary measures are necessary for your actions. We will be in contact pending further investigation. Please don't leave town," Sikes stated.

"Let me be clear," Stephen sat up straighter, looking from Sikes to Kross. "Am I under investigation for the murder of Anthony Gerritt?"

"Not at this time," Sikes said.

"Am I being charged with anything?" Stephen pushed.

"Not at this time," Sikes repeated.

"Why am I not allowed to leave town?" Stephen asked. "I need to clarify this because my daughter is currently in Canada since I needed to protect her from any fallout of this case I was working. And my parents live in Arkansas. As you further might remember, my house burned down last night so I have no home to return to here in this area. So, with all due respect, I will be happy to comply with any investigation. But the minute I leave this meeting, I'm leaving town."

Attorney General Alex Kross steepled his fingers.

Sikes seemed to be pondering Stephen's words.

The silence in the room was palpable.

Finally, Kross leaned back in his chair. "You drive a hard bargain, Wilton." He nodded. "Go. Be with your family. Just make yourself available for any next steps and meetings. I'm sorry about your home."

Stephen nodded and stood.

The two men followed his action.

"Will that be all?" Stephen asked.

"Yes," Sikes said.

Kross nodded and reached out a hand to shake. "You take care of yourself, Wilton."

Stephen grasped his hand and nodded. Wordlessly, Stephen left the building. He got in his vehicle, turned up the music in his car, and hit the highway to Arkansas.

62

WILTON

It was late when he knocked on her door. Beth didn't care. She'd been expecting him. She opened the door wearing a short, silky robe that did nothing to conceal her feminine curves under it. Her shoulder-length black hair was wavy tonight. Her big blue eyes drew him in.

She smiled demurely and grabbed his hand. She pulled him into the house and locked the door behind him, brushing against his body ever so slightly on purpose, he knew.

Beth stood right where she was, inches away from him. She looked at him with those wide, concerned eyes. In a voice that trembled a little when she spoke, she asked. "Are you here to tell me you have news about my sister?"

Stephen shook his head back and forth.

"Nothing?" Beth persisted. "You have no leads whatsoever?"

Stephen hesitated. Telling Beth the truth would put Lacy in danger. But maybe he could tell her something. "We found evidence that suggests she might be alive."

Beth gasped. "What evidence? Where is she?"

Stephen held up a hand. "You know I can't give you details

of an ongoing investigation. Just know for now that all is not lost."

"Thank you!" Tears sprang to Beth's eyes, and she threw herself into Stephen's arms.

Stephen hugged her back, letting her body warm his. He put aside his anger over the marshals launching an investigation into him. They'd had the audacity to assume Stephen's involvement in Anthony Gerritt's murder.

Sure, Stephen had snapped. He was human, after all. But he wasn't a murderer. Stephen felt his back prickle the way he might feel if someone was watching him from across the room. He noticed the blinds were up on Beth's back window. Outside, it was as dark as the emptiness Stephen felt deep inside.

Beth gently turned Stephen's face back to hers, stood on her tip toes, and kissed him. Stephen lost himself in the kiss. In that moment, he forgot his leave, the investigation against him, Alyah leaving him, and the fact that he was currently homeless. He kissed Beth back, feeling a passion he had been holding himself back from.

Maybe a break from work would be good. Stephen could take time to discover who he really was outside of work. He could look into his brother's murder. At that thought, he raised his eyes to the back window again. He felt odd. Exposed, though he was fully clothed. Like there was danger lurking in the long, dark shadows of the night.

Stephen shook it off. Once a cop, always a cop, he supposed. Was he being paranoid? Still... someone had shot and stabbed Anthony Gerritt earlier today. Most likely his larger organization had figured out Gerritt had made an informant deal. Saving the women right out from under them must have looked bad for Gerritt. Not to mention Boyd was alive to snitch about the conversation he'd probably overheard. Stephen didn't feel bad about Gerritt. But he hadn't killed the man either.

Unaware of the eyes that were watching his every move,

Stephen forced his thoughts back to Beth and allowed himself to be pulled deeper into her kiss. Besides, Stephen had noticed the last time he was here that there was a privacy fence in Beth's backyard and a large expanse of open land beyond that. There was nothing to fear. They were safe here.

Here. That's where Stephen planned to stay. Right here, in this moment with Beth. Beth's warm hands worked their way under Stephen's t-shirt. He felt her lift it over his head. In turn, he untied her robe and watched it gently fall to the floor. Her black bra and matching panties were the color of Stephen's dire circumstances.

Don't let your guard down, Stephen's gut screamed at him. He had always had good instincts, but he turned them off.

Beth took half a step back, gave Stephen a scrutinizing look, then closed the blinds and turned off the lights.

THE END

WHY HE LIED

If you like *When She Vanished*, order book 3 in A Mak and Wilton Thriller series—*Why He Lied*.

PROLOGUE
TREVAN

Trevan Collins lay on the ground, face up, staring sightlessly at the ceiling with eyes that had begun to swell and bruise prior to his final exit from this world. His face was evidence that Trevan had put up a fight before he died. A trickle of blood ran from the corner of his mouth and dripped onto the tan carpet where his body lay motionless.

That little drip wasn't what caused the large stain of blood now soaking into the ground under him. The once oozing blood was coagulated in the grisly, open gash on Trevan's neck. It had left him gasping and sputtering until he finally gave up his life a few short hours ago.

Tonight—the last hour of his life—had started with a knock at the door. But that's not when the end began. It wasn't even when Trevan had gotten his hands on that fateful photo. No, that had just pushed the button on the countdown clock to his final days.

The beginning of Trevan's expiration was that fateful night over seventeen years ago. That night, they—Beth Donovan, Davey Stinnert, Greg Wilton, Jacob Greenly, and Trevan Collins —became the Delinquents, and they would never be the same.

They were all in the wrong place at the wrong time. The outcome was a murder that none of them were charged with, yet they all paid the price for. An incident that had cost them their childhood and their innocence. Jacob had ended his own life less than a year later.

As a result, the Delinquents would cling to each other like a lifeline with a closeness no one on the outside would ever understand. They were bound by the toxicity of murder, then drugs. It was no life. It was slavery. Then they grew up. Minus Jacob and Greg, of course. Greg was a different story. He'd taken a bullet for all of them.

It was sheer, stupid luck that Trevan had found the photo. Adult Trevan now knew things teenage Trevan was too naïve to consider. The murder accusation had been just that—an accusation. The Delinquents would never have been charged. It had all been trumped up. The perfect opportunity to manipulate a bunch of high schoolers—popular, well-liked ones at that—into doing the bidding of the Corruptors, as they called them.

Trevan had swiped the photo that proved who killed Greg and had given it to Greg's little brother, a US Marshal. That's what Trevan was thinking about when he'd heard the knock at his door over the loud, rage-rock music he was playing that would serenade him to his death.

It was probably his duplex neighbor, Scott, knocking to ask him to turn down the music. For half a second, Trevan considered ignoring him. Trevan shook his head back and forth as he wiped his hands on a kitchen towel. He pulled chicken out of the oven and turned the heat off.

Can't a guy make dinner without getting interrupted? Trevan muttered, feeling edgy and irritable. He wore those feelings like the clothes he put on his back every day. He couldn't remember a day in the past year when those emotions hadn't dictated his mood.

For years, things had gotten better. Once they all graduated from high school, the Delinquents were off the hook. The Corrupters didn't seem to need them anymore. Until Trevan got the summons. He, Beth Donovan, and Davey Stinnert, the last Delinquents alive, all showed up on trembling legs to a secret, underground meet-up. If they didn't show, they knew what would happen to them. Just like that, the gang was back together.

There were three major players in the room when they arrived. Anthony Gerritt, Mickey Upton, and Boyd Allister had all stood in front of them, eyes dead and glaring, a trifecta of pure evil. That's when Trevan knew. His life was about to get so much worse.

The loud pounding at his door brought Trevan back to the present and he yanked the door open. "What do you want now, Scott?"

Only, the person who stood on the other side of the door wasn't Scott. It was the last person Trevan ever expected in this neighborhood, yet here he stood on his doorstep.

"Get in here," Trevan hissed, pulling the man into his house, looking around outside to check if anyone saw him. "What the hell are you doing here? It's not safe. What have I told you about that?"

The man clenched his jaw, a clear flash of anger. "We need to talk about this." His deep voice was low and deadly calm.

Trevan stared at what the man had clutched in his hand. Trevan wondered how he hadn't seen it when he'd pulled the man into his living room. Trevan froze, the color draining from his face. He didn't have to see it to know exactly what was in the envelope. He quickly weighed his options. *That damn envelope is going to be the death of me, one way or another,* he predicted.

"What did I tell you about coming here—to my home?" Trevan said with a menacing growl of anger. "You're gonna get us both killed."

"Explain this," the man demanded, ignoring Trevan's threats.

"No." Trevan pushed the man. "You're gonna get the hell out of my house and hope that no one saw you come in. You're a stupid man. Suicidal. You know that?"

The man, who was angrier than he let on, pushed Trevan back. His light hair fell across his forehead. Trevan supposed some would find him attractive, but what did he know? The man wore a black hoodie, black jogger pants, thin black gloves, and black tennis shoes. The thought hit Trevan and made his stomach turn, ice flooding through his veins. The man did not plan to be seen. But that wasn't for Trevan's protection.

"Start talking!" the man growled.

Trevan shoved the man so hard the envelope fluttered to the floor. Trevan launched at the man, landing on top of him. He got a punch in before the man rolled Trevan to the side with such force that Trevan hit his head against the wall. For a moment, Trevan saw only black.

Then Trevan shook his head and came to just in time for a large, powerful fist to connect with his mouth. Pain exploded in Trevan's face, and he slid his tongue over his teeth, wondering if it had knocked any of them loose. He could taste the metallic tang of blood.

Rage overcame Trevan and he flew at the man, using his body weight to move him. Both of them hit the opposite wall. Trevan was pretty sure that hit left a mark in the drywall.

"We're on the same team, you piece of shit," Trevan raged as he attempted an uppercut, but the man launched to the side.

"Debatable," the man grunted. "If we were, you would explain how this came to be in your possession."

Trevan was on his feet now, but so was the man, which surprised Trevan. Trevan never would have expected this man to fight him, but he sure was knocking the wind out of Trevan at the moment.

"I don't owe you an explanation," Trevan said as he took a hit to his temple that knocked him off guard. A follow-up hit exploded into Trevan's eye socket. Trevan staggered back two steps into the living room, trying to keep his balance.

What he saw when he opened his good eye made him freeze. This guy was serious. He wielded a knife. It wasn't just any knife, either. It was a butcher knife, and Trevan could see that it was sharp. The man was advancing. Trevan looked around for a weapon. He came up short. He knew the back door was just behind him. If he could back up just a few more steps…

But the man was on him. He tackled Trevan to the ground. The knife was at Trevan's throat.

"Talk," the man commanded.

Trevan could feel the sharp edge stinging as it touched his throat.

"It never sat well with me how it ended. I thought—" Trevan dared not move or even gulp. It was hard enough to talk with a knife pressed against his Adam's apple. "I thought it would give me some good karma, you know? I'm a bad guy. I do shitty things. I needed to set something right."

"Bullshit," the man growled. He pressed the knife into Trevan's throat harder. The sting gave way to pain. "You're bringing on a lot of unnecessary attention and I want to know why."

"Man, I'm just tired," Trevan said, then he blinked a few times, feeling surprised by his own honesty. His life had never been his own. He was tired of playing puppet in someone else's theatre. When he heard about Anthony Gerritt's death, Trevan knew they would stop at nothing. No one was untouchable. Word had gotten around that Gerritt had turned snitch. Trevan didn't believe that. He did believe that Gerritt had made a mistake. That's all it took. One mistake and you're out—in a horizontal box. "I got nothing else to say. If this is it for me, then just do it."

The man didn't need any more coaxing. Trevan felt the sharp slice of the butcher knife blade as it slipped in quick and deep through Trevan's neck. Trevan gasped, trying to take back the air that left his windpipe in a whoosh.

Trevan could see the man watching him with no emotion in his eyes. He could feel the liquid that ran down his throat, slowly at first, then in spurts, until it became a pool of thick, viscous liquid underneath Trevan's now motionless body. Trevan's vision was fading.

Trevan lay gasping in surprise and pain. He actually thought his words would make the man reconsider. But before Trevan bled out on his own living room floor, Trevan wondered one thing.

Why didn't he ask me what he really wanted to know?

ALSO BY ADDISON MICHAEL

A Mynart Mystery Thriller series is ghostly suspense with psychological elements. If you like complex heroines, paranormal twists and turns, and gripping suspense, then you'll love this dark glimpse into the psyche.

Book 1 - *What Comes Before Dawn*

Book 2 - *Dawn That Brings Death*

Book 3 - *Truth That Dawns*

Book 4 - *Dawn That Breaks*

Book 5 - *What Comes After Dawn*

The Other AJ Hartford - A phantom on a train. A mysterious kidnapping long ago. Can she connect the dots before all her futures disappear forever? If you like good-hearted heroines, ghostly phenomena, and nail-biting high stakes, then you'll love this mind-blowing adventure.

A Mak and Wilton Thriller series is a pulse-pounding crime thriller series with a strong female lead, stimulating twists, and relentless suspense.

Book 1 - *When They Disappeared*

Book 2 - *When She Vanished*

Book 3 - *Why He Lied*

Book 4 - *Why She Fled* - Releases July 31st!

REVIEW REQUEST

If you enjoyed this book, I would be extremely grateful if you would leave a brief review on the store site where you purchased your book or on Goodreads. Your review helps fellow readers know what to expect when they read this book.
Thank you in advance!

~ Addison Michael

ABOUT THE AUTHOR

Addison Michael is the oldest of six siblings. She grew up with a golden reputation and a well-hidden dark side. Writing became her outlet. Addison's dark side emerges in the crime and mystery thrillers she writes today. She lives in the Midwest and believes in writing what she knows, so her stories are often set in the Midwest region. From cabins surrounded by acres of desolate woods to rural police departments and eclectic personalities, Addison Michael captures the essence of small-town living.

You'll find the following tropes in Addison Michael thriller books:

- Cabin in the woods
- You can't go home again…
- Unreliable narrator
- Kidnapping/missing person
- Addiction/recovery
- Femme fatale
- Serial killer

Made in United States
Cleveland, OH
20 May 2025

17039218R10175